I0532708

REAP &

REVEAL

BOOK III OF THE REAPER SERIES

LISA MEDLEY

Reap & Reveal:
Book Three of the Reaper Series © 2015 Lisa Medley

ISBN: 978-0-9908856-7-2

Cover and formatting by Sweet 'N Spicy Designs
http://sweetnspicydesigns.com

All rights reserved. This copy is intended for the original purchaser of this book ONLY. No part of this book may be reproduced, scanned, or distributed in any printed or electronic form without prior written permission from the author. Please do not participate in or encourage piracy of copyrighted materials in violation of the author's rights. Purchase only authorized editions.

This book is a work of fiction. While reference might be made to actual historical events or existing locations, the names, characters, places and incidents are either the product of the author's imagination or are used fictitiously, and any resemblance to actual persons, living or dead, business establishments, events, or locales is entirely coincidental.

Published in the United States of America

Lisa Medley

http://www.lisa-medley.com

To all of the great members, past and present, of Ozarks Romance Authors. Thanks for helping me show the world that monsters need love too.

Chapter One

Nate Blackburn whistled for his hellhound, anxious to flash home after a less than fruitful night of demon hunting with the Authority. Of course, his quarry was an angel. The fallen kind.

Bocephus came bounding down the alley, drool dripping in stringy ropes from his floppy jowls. The great black beast heeled and sat at his side, resting his basketball-sized head on Nate's shoulder. Another long night and Nate was still no closer to finding Maeve.

It was near dawn and a chill shimmied up his spine. He told himself it was the December cold. Most of the demons would be looking for holes to crawl into to rest from their incessant debauchery and death mongering. Even they had to recharge.

A practicing witch, Nate had always known there were things that went bump in the night. But before taking up with the reapers, he'd never actually killed any of them. Now, of course, that had changed. Everything had changed.

Nate stroked the hound's head, twisting his fingers into his thick coat, reluctant to call it a night despite his lack of success. Bo had tracked Maeve's scent all through downtown Meridian, Arkansas, without managing to pin her down. She was always one step ahead...or several. What he found instead was her wake of destruction. The newly soulless wanderers and dead bodies were beginning to pile up. Even with eight active members of the Authority plus Nate, it was getting more and more difficult to collect the casualties and carry them to Purgatory. And now, because the disappearances had not gone unnoticed, the city was lousy with out-of-state manpower, too. Hell, the FBI had even made an appearance and implemented a citywide curfew. Not that it was doing any good. The media posted daily headlines urging people to stay inside, but even with the curfew and the added officers, it was impossible to keep businesses closed and people off the streets, especially at night.

It was a dangerous time for everyone in Meridian—supernatural and otherwise.

Few humans could survive a soul extraction, and if they did, they were left as nothing more than a primal shell. The reapers called them wanderers. To Nate's pop-culture mind, they were zombies minus the incessant drive to eat fresh brains. One thing was certain. Even the wanderers were as good as dead.

All the reapers, except for Kylen, who remained dubious, hoped that at some point the humans who had been soul raped might be restored. That would mean their untethered souls would have to be rescued from Hell before they became part of its machine. Then they would have to somehow be reinsouled. It had never been done before, and Nate was far from certain that it could be done. Still, they put in the effort. Hope was one of the few commodities they had left.

A cat's cry caused him to tighten his grip in Bo's scruff, and a growl vibrated through the beast. Sometimes a cat was just a cat. Sometimes it was something else entirely.

Sure enough, an imp rounded the corner of a long, brick building ahead as he continued down the alley. Clinging to the wall, the imp blinked its yellow eyes at him before shimmying up and onto the roof. More followed. The imps were scouts—minions for demons who walked the earth. And that meant one thing: a demon was close.

Looked like Nate was going to earn his pay tonight after all.

Bo whined beside him, but from anticipation rather than fear. The dog liked nothing better than to dispatch demons, a trait Nate admired.

The demon that entered the alley was riding a teenage boy's body. Thank God. Nate didn't think he could stand to take down any more women. If the demons discovered his weakness for that particular flavor of host, he'd be lost. The reapers who were part of the Authority weren't as sensitive as he was. They didn't care what sex the hosts were. Maybe, if he were very lucky, he'd live long enough to become so jaded.

The demon walked toward him with all the confidence of a demon in a fresh host. He twitched and jerked his new body down the alley toward Nate, not yet realizing he was walking toward certain death. Bo lived for this shit.

Nate gave the dog the attack signal and his skin crawled as he watched Bo take the young host down like a bear on a bunny. The act was complete in a matter of seconds. Bo looked back for reassurance of a job well done and further instructions.

"Good boy. Eat."

Bo ate. He could tear and crunch though a body in minutes. Good thing, too. The alternative was even messier. Imps watched, hovering overhead along the edge of the roof. When the black demon left the ruined host body in a stream of shapeless fog, it flew up and over the building and the imps followed it, disappearing from view. Nate watched and waited. No other souls streamed out. He was grateful for that at least. The demons were soul poachers, and these days they didn't even wait until a person was dead. Nate and the Authority reapers were in an all-out war for the souls of Meridian. If they lost Meridian, they lost the world.

The demon wasn't dead, but the host most assuredly was.

Lucky bastard.

Most of the folks in the bar tonight hadn't been so fortunate.

Nate had called in Samkiel and Raguel, the nearest reaper cleanup crew, to take care of the casualties after stumbling upon the scene. One body or even a couple, he and Bo could dispatch. Dozens were a different story.

When the biggest Hell release portal in decades opened in Meridian last May, several demons were freed to wreak havoc on the population. Just when the local reapers nearly had things under control, Camael, a fallen angel and the former Chief of the Order of Powers, had raised the stakes by opening another portal. The dozens became thousands and the whole situation became five billion times worse when Camael inhabited the body of Nate's newly assigned reaper partner, Maeve.

He hadn't seen her since.

And now? The full power of the Authority had been reactivated, after many years, and a new team of ten reapers had been recruited to put down the demon invasion and protect the realms from further infiltration.

Hell on Earth was one thing. Hell in Heaven? Unthinkable.

Nate's long-time friend Deacon Walker was the leader of the Authority. He was sympathetic to Nate's cause, having lost a friend and fellow reaper, Kylen, to demonic possession for more than a century. The problem was that reapers were the perfect hosts for demons and, as it turned out, fallen angels. While demons burned through human hosts in a matter of days, sometimes hours, a reaper could be ridden indefinitely.

Maeve was a reaper.

Nate…was not.

The jury was still out about Nate's particular supernatural persuasion. While he possessed some of the more desirable traits and abilities of the reapers, his powers hadn't manifested enough for him to be fully invested as a reaper. There was no way of knowing if they ever would. The only word that still described him most days was *witch*.

The tattoos along his biceps itched and prickled as he prepared himself to head home. To most people, his markings looked tribal, but they weren't. They were very specific magic sigils. Magical protection. A guy couldn't protect himself from every spell, but it sure seemed like a good idea to try, particularly under the current circumstances.

He grabbed hold of the scruff of the hellhound's neck and felt the familiar pull from the invisible subway reapers used to travel from consecrated ground to consecrated ground—one perk he shared with the reapers. The alley before him shimmered and his vision faltered as he was dragged into the darkness that would bring him home.

***

Six silver-bullet travel trailers circled him end-to-end as he landed in the common area of Ruth Scott's family home. It was all that was left. Only the stone walls and fireplace had remained standing after Camael had burned the place to the ground despite Nate's circle of protection. Construction on the destroyed building wasn't supposed to begin until spring, but work was already under way. They'd salted the earth, reconsecrated the ground and enforced the circle of protection to include each and every member of the Authority as well as the auxiliary members.

Maeve wasn't among them.

Their combined reaper Reiki energy and Nate's spell made the place a fortress against all supernatural beings and the four elements when wielded with magic. Live and learn. Of course, his supernatural protections didn't do shit to keep humans away. That was what shotguns were for.

Deacon had a small arsenal stored in the communal area where they shared meals in the center of the compound. The first reconstruction had begun there—an octagonal domed structure had been erected in spite of the winter weather. They needed a place to regroup and strategize as well as eat and relax—and escape their roommates. There was only so long a guy, or in this case two, could hole up together in a thirty-foot trailer. That was way too much reaper testosterone in way too little space.

The only ones who didn't seem to mind the accommodations were the couples. Deacon and Ruth lived together in one trailer, and Kylen and Olivia shared another. The other reapers lived with their partners.

Nate lived alone.

Though Maeve was officially his partner, he couldn't imagine her agreeing to live with him even if she were here. Upon initiation, each member of the

Authority had been partnered with a reaper who complemented their abilities if not their personalities. Maeve had clearly drawn the short straw when she was paired with Nate. Even now, he wondered why they had been partnered at all when they'd immediately been given separated mandates. Nate was to use Bo to track the demons for the Authority and Maeve was to protect the home front. That had been the plan, anyway.

Still, the compound had become his home. He'd given up his apartment months ago. It wouldn't do to have demons, imps or worse things following him back to endanger his neighbors after a night's work.

Before becoming a member of the Authority, he had been an EMT. Now he wasn't sure what he was other than a glorified babysitter when needed. Since Temperance, a guardian angel, had been sent to watch over Ruth and her unborn, he wasn't even needed for that job anymore. After Maeve's abduction, he'd switched from being lead demon tracker to fallen-angel tracker. Now he spent all of his time in the field with his hellhound doing just that—tracking Maeve.

What he thought he was going to do with his limited powers once he found her, he didn't know, but he was driven to find her. Obsessed, even.

Laughter and the smell of bacon wafted from the kitchen. His heart felt like a stone in his chest as he made his way to his trailer, bypassing the breakfast crowd. Bo had other thoughts and loped toward the sounds of food activity. It wasn't Nate's day to cook and he wasn't up for a debriefing. He needed rest, rejuvenation and…retribution.

Sooner would be better than later.

For them both.

Chapter Two

Maeve was biding her time.

Camael had finally laid her body down to rest for a few hours inside a cold, silent crypt where she doubted she could have slept under normal circumstances. This situation was far from normal. While her physical body needed rest, her mind was busy. She felt her body and Camael's consciousness shut down, but her own mind raced in the quiet expanse.

It was not an easy task for a reaper, accustomed to unrestricted freedom, to be a prisoner inside her own body. Not only had she given up possession of her physical self when she'd invited the fallen angel into her shell, she'd also given up her free will. She had no physical control of her own body. She'd tested the limits endlessly in those first few days. Like a bird trapped inside a house, she'd flung herself toward the plate-glass window that separated her from the outside, from freedom.

Even her thoughts were no longer her own—she had to be careful to keep them buried from Camael. If she worried on any particular reflection for too long, he took notice. She didn't want to risk leading him back to someone she cared about.

He already knew where Ruth's home was located, but the reaper compound was out of his reach. Camael sensed the newly reinforced boundaries, which meant Maeve was also aware of the changes. The one blessing of the situation was that she could examine Camael's thoughts just as easily as he could hers. Since he was so supremely confident she'd never survive his departure, he rarely bothered shielding his thoughts from her at all. In his overconfidence, he'd laid himself open to her mentally.

The constant struggle between them was exhausting. Physically, he'd nearly run her body into the ground the first few weeks before he realized he would lose his primo ride if she were to fall into a reaper coma. While he could bail out of her at any time, leaving her to deteriorate and eventually even die if she wasn't replenished and healed with light energy, she knew he wouldn't. Because then he'd be back to riding humans if he wanted to walk the Earth.

And oh, did he want to walk the Earth.

Camael didn't plan to abandon his host anytime soon. His stripped-bare angel essence was venomous to human hosts. Even more so than demonic energy, as it turned out.

The glee he'd felt about successfully blackmailing her into this possession was eclipsed only by his hubris. He honestly thought he was invincible now that he had such a strong earthly body. As he'd learned, there were only two rules for riding a reaper.

Rule number one: fuel up.

Rule number two: keep your head. Literally.

As long as a reaper kept her energy and her head, she could live indefinitely. Indefinitely was beginning to feel way too long to Maeve. The past three months had been excruciating. How Kylen had survived more than a hundred years of being ridden by a demon, she had no idea. She wasn't sure she would last six months.

Her one consolation and the thing that drove her to survive was the fact that she'd learned enough of Camael's inner workings to know how to defeat him. She simply had to live long enough to do it. But given how firmly he was controlling her, her prospects didn't seem very promising.

You think too much, my dear.

Maeve cringed. How had he snuck up on her like that? She needed to be more cautious.

Only of ways to destroy you, Camael.

No. Not only of that. You dream, as well.

You can't know my dreams. My unconscious mind is closed to you.

Are you so sure?

Yes.

What makes you believe so?

Because if it wasn't, you'd already be dead.

Ah, such brave words. Be careful what you wish for. If I die while inside you, you die, as well.

An outcome I am more and more willing to accept.

Hmm, we shall see.

She refused to dwell on anything even remotely usable by Camael with her conscious mind. She filled her head with eighties' song lyrics and recitations of the Lord's Prayer, which she hoped caused him equal amounts of pain and discomfort.

***

Nate pulled off his boots, stripped down to his boxers and made his way to the tiny trailer bathroom to brush his teeth. A narrow strip of morning light sliced through the edge of the blackout curtain across the bathroom skylight. It hadn't been all that difficult to adjust to working nights and sleeping during the day. Hell, as an EMT, most of his shifts had been nights. Somehow, as exhausting as that job had been, this one was worse.

Traveling through the consecrated subway was taxing on all reapers. Each trip burned hundreds of calories, and if they carried souls or passengers, they burned even more. Deacon's woman, Ruth, had nearly died in a reaper coma during her first week of training. It wasn't unheard of for a reaper to become so depleted that human doctors would pronounce him or her dead.

Nothing good happened from that point onward.

Nate shuddered. The thought of being buried alive until he *did* finally deplete was horrifying. He didn't know how long the actual depletion might take. Hours? Days? Years? Perhaps they could remain dormant indefinitely. He had enough problems to worry about without borrowing trouble. Besides, he wasn't a reaper. Not really, anyway.

His thoughts turned to Maeve. Kylen had survived a century of possession. He knew Maeve was still alive because Bo continued to pick up her trail every time they went back to Meridian. More than that, though, he could *feel* her. They were bound to each other in an inexplicable metaphysical way. Ever since she'd saved his life by sharing her energy with him, he could sense her, like a bright light in the back of his mind.

Since that night at St. Mary's Hospital, he'd felt more alive than ever and, like an addict, he craved another hit of her reaper mojo. He doubted she would have given it to him even if she could. Deacon had later explained that she had feared her energy would kill Nate instead of healing him. The strangest thing about it was that she had not shared it willingly—it had leaped into Nate like lightning to a metal pole...

Nate had lived.

And now? He'd give anything to be able to return the favor.

His connection with Maeve wasn't the only thing that had resulted from that night. Since then, Nate's eyes had been opened to all things reaper. He could see human auras now, though thankfully not his own...at least, not unless he was extremely agitated. Another by-product was that he could see the true forms of the supernatural creatures that walked the planet hidden from mankind. It was enlightening to say the least.

The reapers searched for and were drawn to humans with white auras. White was the aura of death. The other colors held clues to a person's emotions, thoughts and personality, and were helpful in dealing with them, but white was the color that mattered most to a reaper. A white aura meant that a soul would need reaping soon.

And now Nate could see auras and so much more.

He dropped his toothbrush into a cup on the thin ledge of the bathroom sink, then walked to the end of his trailer and crawled into bed. The original white window blinds had been covered by blackout shades all around the trailer. Even now, in the full daylight, his Airstream trailer was cavelike, save for the thin sliver of light from the bathroom skylight. He wished he'd shut the door before lying down. Instead, he pulled a pillow over his face to block it out and let his body sink into the downy mattress, another upgrade he'd splurged on with his new reaper income. Even though he wasn't a reaper, the powers that be in Purgatory compensated him the same as they did the others at Deacon's insistence.

Welcoming the silence and the darkness, he struggled to turn off his worries and the niggling sensation he should—*could*—be doing more to find Maeve. Discovering where she had been wasn't getting the job done. What he needed to know was where she was going to be next. He fell asleep pondering that impossible task.

Maeve was awake. And alone. At least briefly. The smooth concrete floor was hard beneath her stretched-out body and he could barely make out the concrete walls and ceiling of what he recognized as a cemetery crypt. All of this he saw in her mind, not from her eyes. Her body was asleep, but her mind churned on.

Maeve replayed the night's events in her consciousness, horrified by what she'd been forced to do. Nate watched remotely, as silent and helpless as Maeve had been while the events unfolded.

Camael had used Maeve to kill two humans on their way from the cemetery to the bar. He'd snapped their necks and left them dead in the street—a distraction to attract the attention of the human officers of the law who were becoming an increasing nuisance.

He felt her further abhorrence as she realized what Camael intended to do when he walked her into the smoke-filtered lights of a bar. It was a rough clientele, which suited Camael just fine. Weak souls were more malleable, and nothing made a soul weaker than an overabundance of alcohol and hard times. It was like taking candy from a baby. Or in this case, a soul from a drunk.

Camael himself didn't harvest the souls. Even though he was capable of extracting a soul if necessary, there was no need for him to dirty his hands. He had minions for that. As he pushed his way through the crowded dance floor and up onto the small stage, a cadre of his demons flanked the entrance and exit on both sides. No one would leave this bar intact. He'd summoned plenty of demons, nearly a dozen, to make sure of that.

His appearance on the stage, or more Maeve's appearance, stunned the crowd briefly and brought all eyes forward as the band stopped playing. A hush fell over the bar as they waited in anticipation to see what was about to happen. A few whistles sounded from the corners, then hisses and boos as Camael continued to survey the room silently through Maeve's eyes. She felt a slow smile cross her face as Camael spread her arms wide, closed her eyes and tilted her head to the ceiling in expected triumph.

"Yes!"

Then the room fell to chaos. The demons swept through the bar, tearing souls from the patrons' pitifully weak bodies in dark gray torrents, the empty bodies slumping to the floor. The sounds of skulls and bones cracking against the hardwood sickened Maeve.

Some of the humans clamored back to their feet after a few moments, others stayed down. Herding the screaming, still-souled bar customers toward the center of the room, the demons worked their way inward. Panic grew, but since the demons carried no visible weapons and weren't physically assaulting them, the patrons were confused about what the exact threat was. The fallen weren't bleeding or visibly injured, but many were obviously dead, and the others...

The clientele couldn't see the souls of their fellow revelers. What they could see were the vacant eyes of the afflicted staring back from the faces of the still-living victims.

It happened in a matter of minutes. Too quickly even for help to be summoned.

The only sound remaining was the shambling of the survivors as they bumped into tables and chairs, clattering around in mindless forward motion.

Camael laughed, pleased with the progress. Taking no chances, he opened a slight chasm beneath the dance floor. The wood cracked and splintered as the ground tore open to reveal a temporary exit portal to Hell. Steam and sulfur rose from the slim fissure and the demons stepped into the chasm one by one with their bounty: nearly a hundred and fifty souls.

It was all very efficient. Camael smiled before closing the portal behind them.

Maeve screamed silently.

Nate woke, gasping for air as he thrashed about, trying to disengage himself from his covers. His heart galloped painfully in his chest. He panned the room, trying to assure himself he wasn't in the crypt, wasn't still in Maeve's mind.

How the hell had that happened?

Through his connection with Maeve, he now knew that Camael planned to hit every bar downtown, grid by grid, while the pickings were still easy. He could probably have two more nights of success before people stopped going out and stayed home out of fear or by decree. Collecting souls from door to door would be much less efficient, but he had no doubt Camael could make it happen.

Dammit.

Things were about to get a whole lot worse.

This wasn't his first lucid dream. Nate had experienced them before. But it was the first one he'd somehow shared with Maeve, and it was more intense than any of the visions he'd ever experienced before.

While he had seen inside more than a few Meridian crypts during his patrols with the Authority lately, he didn't recognize this particular one. From what he could remember, there was no way to determine her location. The nameplates attached to the various stone urns and boxes hadn't been discernable in the darkness. There were hundreds of cemeteries dotting the Arkansas countryside, twenty-eight in Meridian alone. She could be anywhere.

Nate took some comfort in knowing she was still nearby, relatively speaking, and not in Hell. He'd been to Hell before, and he didn't need a repeat performance. The only thing that could drag him back there was if he had a snowball's chance of bringing Maeve back with him, alive and without Camael. But he knew that fighting Camael on his home turf would be a suicide mission. Camael commanded legions of demons in Hell on behalf of Lucifer and now thousands on Earth.

Here. In Meridian.

With a population just north of half a million, the initial demon impact hadn't been noticed immediately, but now? After an entire bar clientele had been obliterated tonight, the city's finest wouldn't be able to contain the collateral damage any longer.

Nate dragged a hand through his hair, pushing it out of his eyes as his other hand twisted his sheet into a tortured ball. His stomach growled as his sight adjusted to the pitch-black interior of the trailer.

How many meals had he slept through?

Still wired from his dream, he went through the motions of battle prep and was dressed and armed in record time.

When he pushed his trailer door, it met with immediate resistance. A tuft of black fur curled around the edge of the door, and then a fist-sized black nose followed as Bo rose from his guard position in front of Nate's trailer door. A smile curled up the corner of Nate's mouth. He was starting to dig that dog. The dumb beast had better not get himself killed in all this mess. That was, if a hellhound *could* be killed.

Seemed like every other damn thing around here was immortal, or nearly so. Everything except for him. He was plain old vanilla human compared to the rest of this motley crew. Well, vanilla with some sprinkles maybe. A human with benefits. A human deluxe. A human… *Oh, shut the hell up already.*

He stroked Bo's ears and was rewarded for the gesture with a hot, pink tongue snaking around his wrist, leaving a Pacific-banana-slug-sized trail of drool along his arm.

Nice.

Wiping the dog sludge onto his black tactical pants, he made his way to the shared kitchen in the growing darkness. Now that the leaves had fallen from the trees, there was no ground foliage to hinder his view. His eyes followed the landscape behind the house, up the Ozarks Mountains to the horizon and the last vestiges of the setting sun.

Another night of hunting ahead of him.

Another chance to find Maeve.

Chapter Three

Camael had rested his still-new body for long enough and was up and moving again. It took an ungodly expenditure of energy to open a portal to Hell. He was just as spent as this body, or he wouldn't have stopped to rest for the night, particularly not in this dank crypt. He was far too high on his success to want to take a break. Unfortunately, rest had been *very* necessary and a vexing concession of his current condition.

Meridian National Cemetery was the closest place to downtown where he could seek respite after wreaking his beautiful chaos. He could have traveled through the fresh Hell portal he'd opened for the demons, but his lingering angel essence made it agonizing for him. The last time he had tried it after possessing Maeve's body, had led to several days of painful recovery in his suite in Hell. Thankfully Maeve's body was unaffected, but his lingering angel essence had been fried. It had felt like he was being skinned alive.

Recovery was pure torture.

Not a problem for the demons since they were born for this, their essence woven from the very fabric of Hell. They shed their hosts as soon as they arrived and then awaited their next opportunity to arise topside. Camael, on the other hand, didn't have time for another long recovery. He wanted to preserve this body for as long as possible without toasting it, or himself, to oblivion, so he had decided not to take any more one-way trips to Hell than were absolutely necessary. He was so close to his goal. He couldn't afford any more delays.

As a result, Camael had to travel the old-school way, through the consecrated subway, then through the more stable Hell portals formed on freshly desecrated ground like the one Grim and Deacon had destroyed at St. Agnes Catholic Church. Since his fall, he was a mutant combination of light and dark, which he supposed made him at least fifty shades of gray. It was one of the many infuriating limitations he'd encountered after his fall.

Changing teams had not been without its consequences.

The body he now inhabited was one of those consequences. As a punishment for falling, his body had quickly been corrupted. His wings had been the first to go.

While he was in Hell, he could manifest any form he wanted, but above ground he needed to borrow or steal a physical body. His go-to animal form was the leopard, which he could still manifest in Hell. It was the form he spent most of his time inhabiting there, prowling the labyrinth of corridors and levels. He was very comfortable in that skin. Only on occasion did he indulge himself in his old form.

He'd spent a great part of the past twenty-seven years after his fall down below, settling in and feeding his grievances. Lucifer had been more than happy to take him in and add another fallen angel to Team Dark, but he had not pushed. Lucifer had coddled and groomed him instead, letting his need for vengeance fester and build until it demanded an outlet. Only then had he made his offer and tapped Camael for this mission.

He had gotten lucky with this host; she was the only way he could complete his undertaking. Another piece of luck had come his way too: Meridian was ripe for the picking. The city was so spiritually porous that the line between consecrated and desecrated was easily dissolved. Of all the possible locations, the Earth's vital energy flowed through the pathways of Meridian like no other place in the world. The consecrated subway used by reapers was made up of ley lines, the spiritual and mystical channels along which energy surged. And Meridian was full of them, in fact, it was the hub. So what better breeding ground to corrupt those lines, open a permanent portal and unleash Hell's legions?

Geographically isolated by mountains, Meridian, Arkansas was still populous enough that his first few test releases had been all but unnoticed both inside and outside the city. It was the larger second wave of releases that brought down the wrath of Heaven and the reactivation of the Authority. It didn't matter. By the time his full assault was under way, which would be very, very soon, ten reapers and the seraph Grim wouldn't be able to do a damn thing about it.

In fulfilling Lucifer's dream for *his* children—created from the ruined souls of his utmost rival's offspring—to inhabit the Earth, Camael would also find his own revenge. Luckily there was enough wrath to go around. As a matter of fact, it would be the most bounteous resource of the new world order.

Camael dusted the crypt dirt and dust from the fitted, black cargo pants his host body wore. He liked black, but it was notoriously difficult to keep clean.

Every little speck stuck to it and stood out. It was maddening. He sighed, this place was well below the standard of luxury he had come to expect. He much preferred his accommodations in Hell. And what was that smell? Perhaps his host was due for some maintenance. He'd forgotten how much work it was to take care of a body in the long term. It would have to wait, but not for much longer.

His days of discomfort were numbered.

For mankind, however, they were about to begin.

***

Maeve would give anything for a shower. For a toothbrush. For her freedom.

It wasn't like she'd been suicidal or worse—a Hell groupie—when she'd agreed to the current situation. She certainly hadn't sought out this fate. What she had been was in the wrong place at the wrong time. For Ruth and most of the people in St. Mary's Hospital, she'd been in the *right* place at the *right*time. Camael had demanded a new body since his own was visibly failing. He'd planned to make a run for the pregnant reaper, Ruth, and her burn-damaged body, sensing an easy target.

At the time, Maeve had been all that stood between Ruth and the determined fallen angel. Camael had threatened to open a portal and let the entire hospital fall into it if one of them didn't agree to his demand for a reaper body. Knowing there was only one decision that could be made, Maeve had made it.

Camael hadn't opened the portal completely, but the damage had already been done and the hospital began to crumble around them anyway. It was the first of many atrocities she'd been responsible for under her new incarnation. No telling what fresh horrors awaited her this night.

From her unusual and precarious vantage point, she watched and waited for her chance. She didn't have a hundred years to endure. Camael was very close to making his big move and she had to find some way to warn the reapers.

She'd sensed Nate in her dreams, but she had no idea how or why. Damn guy was like a fly that wouldn't leave her alone, buzzing in and out of her thoughts, which of course she had to keep suppressed from Camael. It was wearing her out. She was obsessing. The more she tried to keep thoughts of Nate at bay, the more insistent they became. *He* became.

Ever since their unexpected energy exchange, things had been strange between them. Not that they'd had much of an opportunity to explore any of that.

She'd expected her energy to kill him like it had her brother, but instead it had snapped Nate back from death. He'd come out on the other side staring at her with his big, brown puppy-dog eyes like she was his long, lost owner. And Maeve, who wasn't used to feeling soft, had felt something too. Of course, it didn't hurt that the guy was built like a WWE wrestler, which was fairly okay for a puny human. And he did have some formidable skills. But still…

What. The. Hell.

Her skin crawled involuntarily now even thinking about it, and she snuffed that line of thought before her physical reaction got Camael's attention. This body-snatching gig was insufferable, but she had managed to gather vital recon that none of them would ever have been capable of procuring any other way.

Somehow she was going to have to overcome Camael's hold and break through for long enough to warn the others, or all of this…would be for nothing. And they would all be damned.

Her body's physical activity shook her to awareness. They were on the move and out of the cemetery. She shuddered inwardly as she realized they were heading back downtown for another round.

Well, of course they were.

Camael needed a few more elements for Lucifer's plan—which he now shared—to fall into place. In the meantime, collecting a few thousand more souls would keep the reapers plenty distracted while he worked toward his goal. One soul in particular was the key. Camael was excited to have recently turned and nudged the puzzle piece until it fell into place. The last piece would seem so obvious when the time came because like all good plots for world domination, this one would need that same age-old catalyst.

The sacrifice of a pure soul.

And he had the perfect one in mind. A supernatural soul no less. With it, he could hold open the Hell portal indefinitely and all of Lucifer's children could stream out and claim what was meant for them.

Are you ready, my dear?

Does it matter?

Camael's laughter rang through her head as they made their way downtown.

Chapter Four

The reaper kitchen was part *Animal House*, part Army mess hall, and part *The Waltons*. It was clear to Nate which part the reaper Raguel fell into as he tried to impress the three women of the household by tossing pizza dough into the air.

"You see? Nothing to it. A child could do it." Ragu caught the dough over his arm and let it slide gently to the granite tabletop.

"A child *is* doing it," Samkiel offered, accepting the full wrath of Ragu's playful glare.

"Ah, but you'll be begging for more very soon, my friend. Once you've had Ragu's saucy meat and dough, you won't go back to any other."

A brief moment of stunned silence followed, and then laughter exploded around the room. It had been a long time since most of them had had anything to laugh about. Even Ruth was in the kitchen tonight, although in a wheelchair, visibly pregnant and under the fierce eye of Temperance, her guardian angel. Or more accurately, the unborn child's guardian angel.

Even though Ruth was only four-and-a-half months along, she was advancing quickly. Maybe reaper pregnancies were different. Deacon had been no help in that department. Being born himself was his only source of knowledge on the matter. Besides, the guy was scared to death with worry over her most of the time, so even gentle questioning nearly pushed him into full-blown paranoia. Nate had learned to get his answers elsewhere.

He'd been caring for Ruth as best as he could, getting occasional advice from the OBGYN at Oakland Hospital since St. Mary's Hospital was out of commission. Permanently.

The media has pegged the disaster as an earthquake along the New Madrid fault line. It was the biggest disturbance that had been measured since 1811. The building wasn't even salvageable and demolition had already begun. The place was sorely missed in the community. Being at the city's epicenter, it had also cared for a steady stream of homeless people who were now so far from Oakland's ER, the EMTs and several off-duty docs and nurses had formed a team of their own to offer triage and minor care in an empty warehouse clinic nearby the former hospital's location.

Olivia had been a mitigating force behind the group's formation, and she had even set up a free kitchen that fed the homeless downtown. Kylen had forbidden her to conduct any nighttime visits. Not that Nate could blame him after what had happened the last time she was downtown alone.

Nate sat heavily on a chair, as exhausted as if he hadn't slept at all. Of course, with those dreams of Maeve, it almost felt as though he hadn't.

"'Bout time you turned up in here." Deacon crossed the room and took a seat next to him. "What happened to you last night? We debriefed after everyone got in, but Oreo said he saw you head straight to your trailer. What gives?"

Bo circled, chasing his tail three times around, then settled onto the floor beside him, resting his head on Nate's lap with a sigh.

Nate threaded his hand through the hellhound's fur. "Just didn't feel like recapping a night full of failure."

"It's more than that. We need to keep track of how many demons we see, how many we kill, how many are potentially left. We've made a real dent these past few months. We need to keep the pressure on. Which means every pair of eyes is important. Yours included."

Nate felt every pair of said eyes in the compound settle upon him.

"You know Bo and I weren't looking for demons, Deacon." Nate stared hard at the reaper.

They'd had this conversation several times. Deacon was the leader of the reapers now. The Powers. But he wasn't Nate's boss. Not really, because Nate wasn't a reaper.

The rest of the Authority crew could now enter and travel through the consecrated subway from unconsecrated ground. They could also consume the unhosted demons, destroying them in a permanent manner as a result of their allegiance to the Authority. And a few had other gifts. Like the ability to transport the wanderers to a holding cell in Purgatory.

Those gifts were a little bit special. While Nate had always been able to travel through the consecrated subway from wherever he pleased, he did not share most of their other gifts. The dreams were new, however, and he needed to tell Deacon about it... Still, he couldn't bring himself to lay it bare before the entire group.

"Nate—"

"Don't start with me, Deacon. If it was Ruth out there, your priorities would be elsewhere, as well."

"It's not just that we need you and Bo to track demons for us, Nate. We can't protect you if you're out there doing the Lone Ranger thing."

"Bo is with me. He can protect me. You've seen him shred a demon." Bo gave a little whine in agreement and licked Nate's pant leg.

"I agree that finding Camael is imperative. It's your methods that worry me. What will you do if you do find her without us to back you up? Bo may be enough to protect you from a few demons, but you won't stand a chance against Camael alone. At least stay within sight or sound of one of the teams. Promise me that."

Nate shook his head. "I don't make promises I can't keep."

"Dammit, Nate—"

"Pizza's ready! Dinner...is served." Ragu pulled a steaming pizza out of the former fireplace turned wood-fired oven to cheers of appreciation.

Nate's stomach growled. Deacon gave him one last hard look and retreated back to Ruth, filling a plate with pizza for her as he made his way through the food line. Nudging Bo's twenty-pound head off his lap, Nate joined the back of the line. He was starving.

Ruth's close encounter with a reaper coma had been all he needed to convince him to take care of himself. So far, knock on wood, he hadn't needed to replenish anyone since they'd set up the new compound. Even though the other reapers acted like a bunch of frat boys in their free time, they were dead serious about maintaining their health and their strength.

Each had been chosen for their particular skill set by Grim himself and recruited to the Authority. Except for Maeve, who was fairly new, and Ruth, who was brand-spanking-new, the rest of them had been reapers for well over a hundred years each. Deacon and Kylen were two hundred plus some change. The only active reaper older than them was Grim. Yes, *the* Grim Reaper. Grim had enjoyed the sunset of his career mostly free of demon activity. But now that was in the past.

Thinking of nasty demons brought Nate full circle, back to the puzzle of what to do about Maeve. How was he ever going to be able to anticipate where she would be next? He certainly wasn't going to be able to capture her and exorcise the angel if he couldn't lay physical hands on her. Camael was too smart to walk onto a demon trap even if it could hold him. Besides, Nate had only successfully accomplished that once—with a demon. He'd never trapped an angel. Didn't even know if it was possible.

It had to be possible. After all, for every yin there was a yang, right?

Last in line, he grabbed a slice of pizza and tossed it over to Bo, who snatched it from the air and swallowed it in one gulp.

Damn, that dog can eat.

Nate piled three more face-sized slices onto his own plate, stacking them like pancakes and headed back to his chair. He almost made it, too.

Then his head exploded.

Chapter Five

Maeve made her way down a narrow alley—Camael's puppet—weaving around overfilled Dumpsters toward a neon Pabst sign, swinging from its one remaining hinge in the little torrent of wind that stirred up like a dust devil.

A storm was coming.

She blinked and felt that troubling sensation again in the back of her conscious mind, an itch she couldn't scratch. One she dared not acknowledge. It was the same as when she'd sensed Nate in her mind, watching...waiting. She wanted to close her eyes, to silently warn him off, but her body was at Camael's mercy and his thoughts and her own battled within her.

Of course, she needn't have worried. Camael was oblivious to her current quandary. He was single-minded and determined. This nightclub was much larger than the bar they'd hit last night.

Music pounded through the heavy steel door as he leaned her back against the cold bricks and waited. He sent his senses into the night and called his demons. Once created, the demons could cycle endlessly through host after host. With seven billion plus people on the planet, they would live as parasites in one body after another until every human host was depleted. By then, Lucifer would have perfected a satisfactory form for them to animate indefinitely. He was close even now.

The dark one had a vivid imagination. Camael was confident the new evolution would thrive in place of mankind.

As it was meant to be.

Scanning the alley, she could sense Camael's growing impatience even though it had been mere seconds since he'd sent the call. He still had at least a thousand demons scattered about the city despite the reapers' incessant meddling. They'd had a larger impact on his work than he had anticipated, but after a few more nights, he'd have everything he needed. Everything except the sacrifice, that was, and for that he'd have to wait. Because without it, the portal would never stay open.

Ridiculous how such a small thing could make such a tremendous difference in the success or failure of his plan. Of course, failure wasn't an option. Lucifer didn't have to clarify it for him. Camael had known what he was signing on for from the very beginning. He was going into this eyes-wide-open.

The ember of hatred still smoldering within his now black heart helped him remember what had gotten him here. And exactly who was responsible.

He raised Maeve's face to look up into the night sky and she noticed the faded Sunbeam Bakers advertisement painted on the side of the alley wall. The little blonde girl, hands folded in prayer under the words "Not by bread alone."

Indeed, Camael thought. *Neither bread nor prayer was going to help the souls beyond this door.*

He smiled as the first of the demons walked toward him from the street, his yellow eyes shining.

***

Nate opened his eyes to a sea of faces, all way too close to his own. He was lying on the floor next to the granite bar, his pizza nowhere in sight. Raising his head, he quickly thought better of it and resumed his position, waiting for the Tweety birds to stop flying.

Deacon held him down to the floor with a hand pressed to his shoulder. "You stay where you are a little longer. Get your bearings. Given the way your head cracked on the bar when you went down, I'm pretty sure you have a concussion."

Concussion? Yeah, that seems about right.

He raised his hand to his forehead and felt the goose egg growing there. He didn't have to see it to know it was already purple.

How long had he been out?

One minute he was filling his plate and the next he was in an alley and Maeve—

He attempted to jerk himself upright again. "I know where she is."

Deacon's brows inched toward the center of his forehead. "You know where who is?"

"Maeve! I know where she is right this minute. We have to go. *Now!*"

"You're in no kind of shape to go anywhere…now or later. You're going to stay here and rest."

"She's downtown near Foster and Stearns. There's another bar. A big club. Camael is gathering his demons. Again. This might be our only chance!"

"And you know this how?"

Nate swallowed hard. He was not a fan of the overshare, but if he was going to convince them to get going, it was now or never.

"I saw it. Through her eyes. I've been having dreams...visions."

"For how long?" Deacon asked.

"A few weeks now."

Deacon's brow furrowed more. He was obviously wondering how any information from a man who'd just hit his head hard enough to knock himself unconscious could be trusted. Nate didn't blame him, but he'd recognized the advertisement on the side of the building through Maeve's eyes. He knew he was right.

Nate struggled against Deacon's hold, desperate to be upright and stop the relentless pounding in his head.

"Maybe a shot of juice would make him travel-worthy?" Raguel offered. "His melon is dented pretty good, but it would at least keep him from dying in his sleep."

"Nice, Ragu. Like he needs to worry about that," Ruth chided.

"We don't have time for this. We need to move!" Nate tried to rise to his feet again, then turned his head and yakked into a quickly produced trash can instead.

"Yep, that's a concussion all right. Who's off duty tonight?"

Ouriel made his way to the front of the huddle. "I am, boss. Dare and I got meal detail tonight."

"Try to heal him, Oreo. He didn't care for my energy the last time I tried to help him, and I can't risk being depleted if we're about to face Camael. Dare, you're back on duty."

The reapers backed away, leaving Ouriel plenty of room to work his reaper Reiki magic.

"Careful, Oreo. Don't overdo it. We don't want to short-circuit anything."

Ouriel's hands began to glow with the green light Nate had learned to associate with healing. Placing his palms on either side of Nate's head, Ouriel pushed the warm light into him and for a split second, he could feel it fill his skull like candlelight in a jack-o'-lantern.

Nate chuckled.

"Think that's enough, Oreo. Our boy here seems to be feeling better," Deacon warned.

Ouriel withdrew his hands and retreated into the small crowd of on-looking reapers. Nate scanned the faces and breathed a sigh of relief, happy his eggs weren't scrambled and that the pounding had subsided.

The momentary feeling was quickly replaced with mounting anxiety. They needed to go. Now.

There was one of them he trusted implicitly to be his immediate backup. He looked at Deacon. "You got my back?"

"Absolutely. You heard the man. Foster and Stearns, people. We'll see you there."

Bo nudged his head under Nate's arm and helped him to his feet. Nate's fingers curled into the scruff of his neck and the three of them flashed to the now empty alley.

Nate didn't know which was worse: the screams emanating from the bar or the laughter he heard underneath them.

Maeve's laughter.

Chapter Six

Wait." Deacon grabbed Nate's arm and pulled him away from the steel door.

"You hear that shit? We can't wait." Nate drew his short sword from the vertical scabbard along his back.

"We need a plan. When we walk through that door, we can't just start slicing and dicing this time. The demons are going to look the same as the civilians. We need time to recon the situation." Deacon drew his scythe and held it tight against his leg. "We need a distraction."

Bo growled low and bared his teeth at the door.

Deacon nodded at the dog. "How 'bout we send Bo in first? He can smell demons through the door already. He won't have any trouble picking them out for us."

Nate stroked the beast's head. The last thing he wanted was for the dog to get injured, but he was a *hellhound*, for God's sake. He'd probably outlive them all.

"All right." Bo licked his hand in agreement. "Then what?"

"Then we keep them occupied until our reinforcements arrive. After that…we clean house."

"And Maeve?"

"If we can capture her and somehow render her unconscious, it will buy us some time to figure out how to expel Camael without hurting her in the process."

"Time is wasting. Let's go."

The melee inside the bar reached a crescendo as Deacon opened the door and Bo slunk through, his head and chest low to the ground, though still as high as Nate's upper leg when he followed behind him.

The second Nate spotted Maeve, *the plan* left his brain. He forgot to even worry about Bo. His one, all-consuming thought was to reach Maeve. Without even processing the pleas of the remaining bar clientele, he edged around the main dance floor where the demons had herded them like sheep, then zigzagged through the maze of overturned tables and chairs. His boots peeled from the sticky floor covered in spilled beer, mixed drinks and worse things with each step.

He felt like he was trudging through quicksand in slow motion, almost as if he were still in a dream, but this time, all of his senses were firing. The dank smell of vomit, sweat and booze filled the dark bar. It was the smell of all bars. It was the smell of desperation.

Nate didn't hesitate as he crossed the last few feet to Maeve and when she turned to face him, amusement animated her face as her mouth tipped into a gruesome smile.

Maeve, but not Maeve.

His body began to hum with anticipation. He felt his aura manifest before he saw it—an electric blue cloud of color that turned Maeve's amusement into fear.

Whether it was her reaction or Camael's, he didn't know.

He reached for her.

Maeve turned her gaze to the floor in front of her and he heard the floorboards groan then crack. A portal was opening. The demons abandoned their mission and pushed through the crowd to stand along the thin fissure, riding the hardwood surf as it spread open. Six inches. Twelve.

The smell of sulfur steamed from the fissure.

The still-souled bar patrons coughed and gagged in the stench as they stumbled toward the red exit sign at the back door just as it opened, revealing the rest of the Authority. The team filed in like S.W.A.T., making straight for the demons who were now separated from the rest, courtesy of Bo.

Without thinking, Nate tackled Maeve to the ground and all hell broke loose.

A bright, electric-blue force field encompassed them both and the chaos around them fell away as Maeve's Reiki light latched onto Nate like a lifeline. Maeve fought and struggled beneath him for her weapon. Involuntarily, he continued to draw in her energy in great waves. He watched an internal struggle play out across her face as she fought Camael for control.

Digging deep, he began to recite the one exorcism incantation he knew. The one that had worked on Kylen's demon.

"Ex is vir everto, Camael, solvo is humanus vacuus vulnero physical vel mental, ex is vir nunquam ut reverto ut alius victus res a vomica super vos ut nunquam iterum reperio refugium in terra plagiaries."

An icy chill filled their electric blue bubble and his breath chuffed out in small white clouds as he continued to chant. Maeve flailed and clawed at him, tearing his clothes and skin in her struggle, but she couldn't penetrate the bubble. Nate watched as the Authority fighters dispatched the demons in silent warfare, carefully avoiding the partially opened portal.

After Nate's third recitation of the verse, the light around them blazed, then arced from her heart to his, and an invisible fist closed inside the center of his chest in a brief but sizzling compression, preventing his heart from beating.

He was dying.

Maeve's energy filled him, racing through his body in shafts of fire until he was sure he would burst into flames. Then he saw the first tendrils of oily black smoke ooze from the center of her chest. Her heart chakra.

Camael was abandoning his host.

Fear crawled up Nate's spine as he brought himself up to his knees beside Maeve. Camael wouldn't willingly leave her, not while her body lived.

So she was dying, too.

Camael's essence continued to stream out of Maeve, pierced through the blue energy field and into the partially opened portal, filling it with a smoldering roil of black fog. Maeve lay boneless and unanimated. Seconds later her chest rose several inches from the floor and a smaller gray stream followed in Camael's wake as he slipped into the portal and vanished.

Camael was stripping her soul on his way out.

Nate closed his eyes and reinforced the aura field, actively drawing forth Maeve's energy this time, hoping beyond hope her soul would follow the powerful flow. There was no way in Hell Camael was taking her with him again, not any part of her.

Closing his eyes, he visualized the stream of gray flowing into him and willed her soul to him.

There was no reason for him to believe it would work. He wasn't a reaper.

Pressure built against his chest and when he opened his eyes, he realized her soul was pressed against him. It couldn't seem to break through. He reached for Maeve's body and took her hand in his, sparking another arc of power. Instinctively, he opened his mouth to receive her soul.

The soul streamed into him, drawn inside like he was a vacuum, and pummeled against its new restrictions like a caged beast. Maeve's body remained still as stone beside him and the last of her light extinguished, allowing the sounds of the bar to return to his senses.

But there were no sounds.

The bar was silent as a grave as the Authority reapers stood and gaped at Nate.

***

"Somebody want to explain to me what just happened?" Zachriel asked, toeing his boot at the severed head of the host before him.

"Looks like Nate just found his mojo." Deacon approached him cautiously, hands out in a supplicating, calming gesture.

Bo moved to Nate's side and growled a low, rumbly warning at Deacon.

Nate looked from the unconscious Maeve to the reapers and back again.

What the hell had happened?

He reached for Maeve's neck, feeling for a pulse. It was faint and irregular, but it was there. Thank God.

He pulled her head and shoulders into his lap as Bo edged nearer, snugging up against him, literally guarding his back. Nate glanced around the bar at the remaining carnage. Dozens of beheaded demons and dead humans lay scattered across the floor, but no wanderers or living humans remained in the bar. Samkiel must have already gathered the wanderers and ferried them to the Purgatory holding area. The other reapers would clean up the bodies.

He could only imagine what tomorrow's headlines would be as the survivors' stories made it into the press. There would be no putting the genie back into the bottle now.

He hoped he hadn't been too late for Maeve.

Maeve didn't stir other than the faint breath that passed her parted lips. Nate had a ridiculous urge to kiss those lips, but he resisted. Most of the Authority still gaped at him and the rest of the bar stank of demon.

Wrong time, wrong place was an understatement.

He gathered Maeve into his arms and rose to his feet. She weighed nothing and her body was cold against his. She was practically a wraith. A shudder ran up his spine. Since she was as un-souled as one of the wanderers, that thought was a little too close to home.

"Dare, perhaps you could take Maeve to Purgatory. See Rashnu, no one else. He'll find her an appropriate place to…rest," Deacon said.

Dare stepped forward to relieve Nate's burden, but stopped when Nate felt his chest vibrate with a warning growl of his own.

"Nate?" Deacon asked.

"He's not taking her to Purgatory. She's mine. My partner. My responsibility."

"You reaped her soul, Nate."

"She's not dead."

"She wouldn't want to live this way, Nate." Kylen flanked around Nate's side, but stopped when Bo turned to face him, baring his teeth.

"You of all people, Kylen, should understand why she's not going anywhere," Nate said.

"I never lost my soul, Nate." Kylen took a step closer.

"Neither has she. I'm holding it for her. That's all."

"Dare?" Deacon cut his gaze to Dardariel.

"One holding cell is the same as the next I suppose. But she can't be left alone."

Deacon scrubbed a hand down his face, shaking his head. "This is a terrible idea. Camael may be gone, but he'll find another body, then another. At least he won't be riding a reaper anymore, though, which means we have another chance to shut this shit down."

"Tell us what to do, boss." Leo walked to the edge of the jagged, still-open abyss and looked in.

Nate heard the wail of sirens in the distance heading toward the bar.

"The rest of you...clean up this mess. Nate, take Maeve home. For now. We'll talk more there."

Bo pushed up against Nate, his head pressed through the crook of his arm, resting in Maeve's lap. A bright light filled the bar as Dare and Ragu gathered the decapitated bodies in their reaper glow and dissipated.

It sure beat burning the bodies. Another one of Nate's past duties.

Nate concentrated on his trailer and willed them into the consecrated subway. As exhausted as he was, the room shimmied and wavered much longer than usual before he felt the pull.

What had he done?

Chapter Seven

Nate landed outside his trailer, thankful to have bypassed the commons area again. No way was he ready to explain how he'd come by Maeve, and how he intended to help her to Oreo and the women. Not yet.

Honestly, he didn't have a plan.

It had all happened so fast. Hell, he didn't even really understand any of it.

Maeve's soul flitted inside him, alternately making him euphoric and nauseous, looking for a place to land and clearly uncomfortable in its new environs.

His heart hurt. Both a physical and emotional pain beat against his ribs with each constriction of the treacherous muscle.

What had he done?

He snugged Maeve's body against him tightly, holding her frail form with his left arm as he grabbed the door handle with his right hand, flinging the door wide so he could carry her inside. Shuffling, he side-stepped through the narrow passage to his bed and eased her down onto the still tangled covers. By force of habit, he slid two fingers along her slim throat searching for the reassurance of her still beating heart.

Yes. She lived.

Barely.

The door slammed shut behind him and he heard Bo settle outside it. They were safe.

For now.

Nate pulled off her boots one by one, and then hesitated, staring down at her. He had no right to undress her any further. She wasn't in any immediate medical distress and had only the most minor physical scratches and injuries, but she obviously hadn't bathed in weeks. Her once silky hair lay in tangled, jet-black ropes around her head. Her pale, porcelain skin was translucent and seemed thin and unsubstantial to protect her from the elements, let alone contain the powerful force of her soul, which still fluttered for escape inside *him*.

He traced a finger across her slack cheek, a sputtering trail of turquoise light sparking along its path while his embattled heart pounded inside his chest.

Weariness filled him. It would take time to recover from whatever they had experienced together. His own eyes grew heavy with lassitude.

What he *could* do for her now was make sure she had nutrition, and as soon as the other reapers returned, they could offer her their healing energy, too. The best he could hope to do was to maintain her physical body until he found a way around their unusual dilemma.

Reluctantly, he left the side of the bed and pulled the plastic storage crate from the couch on the other end of the trailer. Finding what he needed, he unwrapped the IV nutrition bag and dragged the hook from beneath the couch. They hadn't needed to use his purloined supplies since the house had burned to the ground.

He walked back to his bed and fastened the hook over the bookcase style headboard, then unraveled the tubes and needle, hanging the bag from the hook. Gently parting her eyelids, he shined his pen flashlight into her eyes to check her pupils. Without her soul, her brilliant green eyes had faded to a light gray color.

She still wore the sleeveless black tank from the end of summer. A human would have died from exposure. While winter in Arkansas wasn't as extreme as other parts of the country, it got below freezing many nights and she hadn't been well maintained. Maeve wouldn't have been oblivious to the temperature or her conditions. Evidence of her physical suffering was clear to him as he examined her.

He tapped the inside crook of her elbow and pressed lightly, searching for a good vein. After several long seconds, he settled on one. Not a good one. She was very dehydrated and her veins were shriveled like dry grass. Uncapping the needle, he turned her arm to face straight up and slid the slim piece of steel home in one quick push. Nate flipped the clip on the tubing and the nutrition solution began to drip into Maeve's arm.

His efforts seemed far from adequate and he wished there was something—anything—else he could do to alleviate her condition. He reached up and brushed her tangled bangs to the side, then released a heavy sigh. It wouldn't be long before Deacon would be at his door, demanding answers Nate didn't have.

He wouldn't let them take her away to languish in a holding cell somewhere with the hordes of soulless wanderers they'd "rescued." Nate hadn't seen the accommodations himself, but he was sure they would not be up to his standards for Maeve.

He would protect and care for her. Whatever it took.

There was one other thing he could do for her here that no one else could. His tattoos grew tetchy beneath his shirt sleeves in anticipation of what he was considering. The sigils that circled his biceps were his magical barometer as well as protection, always monitoring the flow of magic, his own and others'. He'd been given his first one when he was sixteen, after a near fatal first encounter with black magic from a rival in the coven. The boy had been placed on probation by the Coven Board and banned from using magic for a year. Nate had learned a valuable lesson as well. Magic could be deadly.

The kid had never liked him, looked at him as an outsider since Nate hadn't been born into the coven. When they vied for the affections of the same girl, Liam chose to summon dark forces to eliminate his competition and Nate had nearly drowned on dry land alone in his room. Soon after, Nate designed the permanent protection sigil that was tattooed on his bicep. The first of many. If he were the paranoid type, he'd have two full sleeves after everything he'd seen lately. As it was, he was confident he'd covered the most common magical bases with his ink.

Opening the drawer beside his bed, he retrieved his smudge stick and lighter. While they were safe inside the circle of protection he'd cast, its purpose was to keep supernatural outsiders from entering their compound. Now he needed to make sure Maeve didn't unwittingly find her way outside the safety of his trailer unattended. While that seemed impossible in her current state, he didn't know how the nutrition IV and healing energy would affect her if and when they managed to adequately revive her physical body. Without a soul to animate her, she'd be running on sheer survival instinct, which included eating—anything—at the top of the list. At least that's what they'd seen with the humans so far.

He shuddered, imagining the wanderers being fed like animals in a zoo.

The lighter flared to life and he ignited the bundle of herbs, and then blew out the flames to let the packet smolder. Due to the small size of his lodging, the task of cleansing the structure didn't take long. Wafting the smoke into the four corners of the trailer, he recited the cleansing words aloud, the low murmur of his incantations the only sound in the room.

Next, he removed a ball of hemp twine from the same drawer and cut four three-inch strands. A binding spell was serious magic, but without it, Maeve might wander into even more danger. He laid the strings on the bed beside her. Closing his eyes, he summoned the energy of the elements and cast another, very specific circle of protection around his trailer.

He reached over and plucked a single hair from Maeve's head from the root then another from his own and twisted them around one of the strands. Choosing a length of twine, he began to tie the knots as he chanted the spell.

The first knot binds my intention.

The second knot binds any ill-wishing

The third knot binds the one called Maeve to these four walls.

These knots shall hold the spell, until these knots are undone well.

Nate wrapped the knotted length snugly around Maeve's thin wrist and tied the final knot, binding it to her physical body as well.

Unless he unbound the rope bracelet or physically removed her himself, she would remain safely inside the trailer. It was wrong to impose one's magical will upon another. Free will was what made people human, but Maeve's free will had already been compromised. He assuaged his guilty conscience with the justification that it was *for her own good.*

Satisfied, he crossed the trailer to the couch, emptied it of the other storage crates, and then stretched out across it, exhausted. Maybe some rest would grant him a clearer perspective. Maybe not.

What he needed was a miracle. And stronger magic. The kind of magic only his coven could provide.

***

The last thing she saw was Nate coming toward her in the bar like a man on fire, then a blinding light. She'd felt every torturous tendril of her essence as it ripped free from its moorings. She'd fought against him, but as her own toxic energy was drawn forth and stirred with Camael's angel essence, a noxious union resulted.

Camael became infused with her venomous energy, which he'd been unable to access on his own despite his possession of her body. Had he known the potential effects of her poison, no doubt he would have redoubled his efforts to tap into it. One consequence of riding a reaper was that while their bodies were much more durable, their greater gifts, or in Maeve's case—curse, were unavailable to their parasite.

When her energy had been drawn against her will into Nate once more, she'd been helpless to stop it. Somehow, Nate had been able to wrench Camael out. Whether by his own power or the combination of her poison and his enhancing energy, she didn't know, but Camael hadn't been able to maintain his hold inside her. What did any of it mean for her now, though?

As she'd looked down on her body while in transit, she was certain that this was it, the end. The one saving grace was that she'd managed to keep her head. Camael could be defeated. She knew how! But now that her soul had been reaped, how could she ever warn the other reapers?

Soon she'd be sorted and sent to her final resting place, but it would still be too late.

The darkness overcame her and she stopped struggling, letting the weariness engulf her. She would have to accept whatever came next. She knew that, but something inside her could not, would not, stop fighting.

***

While Nate slept, his mind stirred, trying to solve the problem of Maeve's displaced soul.

Her energy had latched onto him like a magnet. He couldn't have stopped it any more than a man could have stopped a hurricane. Regret, guilt and elation all fought for control of his emotions. She was free of Camael, but was he really a better jailer?

His one driving motivation over the past few months was to free her and bring her home. But not like this.

Not like this. Not like this. Not like this.

His mind reeled as the mantra echoed through him and he became aware of Maeve's soul reaching into his consciousness, twining around his own until he wasn't sure where his memories ended and hers began.

Images played across his mental television as he eavesdropped on her memories, feeling like a trespasser in his own body.

He watched the replay of the day Maeve had walked away from her family, her home, and it filled him with grief and despair. Everything had changed after her brother's death, and she could no longer stand the pitying look in the eyes of her parents or the fearful looks of her peers. Her departure would only earn her a short reprieve. It wasn't a long-term solution. Maeve knew she could never escape her past, but she could add some distance to it. Mute it into something she could bear. In a few years, she'd have to return for reaper training because the pull of the dead would become too strong to ignore. By then, if she were very lucky, the reaper community would find someone else to pity. For now, everything was too raw to be revisited and analyzed over and over.

Her brother's death had been deemed an accident, but the powers-that-be wanted to study her. See exactly what made her tick and why she seemed to exude such destructive energy. The last thing Maeve wanted was to become a lab rat or worse—a weapon. She was desperate to control her destiny.

She'd left with a backpack and a knife. Having already managed to make it through a quarter of the reaper training, Maeve was certain she could take care of herself on her own. She'd wait as long as she could before returning. One thing was for sure: this place would never be home again.

As she struggled back toward consciousness, Maeve began to realize she wasn't dead. Not just yet anyway. She was entombed once again, although clearly not in her own body.

Her host's eyes snapped open and for the first time since her escape from Camael, Maeve was afraid. Inexplicably, she was still in her reaper's vessel. Whose? Why? Panic filled her and she reached out.

***

Help me.

The words, not his own, sat Nate upright on the futon, eyes opened wide as he instinctively reached for his weapon, long discarded somewhere in the trailer.

Save me.

Cold sweat broke out across his chest and beaded on his forehead as panic filled him.

How? he asked, unable to believe that he was somehow communicating with Maeve.

Was he still dreaming? Awake?

Please, take me home.

The line blurred into reality as he came to alert consciousness and the dream faded.

Nate raced across the trailer to Maeve's lifeless body. No sign of awareness emanated from her. She laid as still as death and just as silent.

Nate took her hand in his and sat beside her on the bed. She needed another IV. Her body was greedily soaking up the nutrients and eagerly drawing Nate's energy from his own body at their slight contact. He couldn't heal what afflicted her. Not even her body. His own light was still too depleted. The hour or so of fitful sleep he'd just experienced wasn't enough to rejuvenate himself, let alone another.

He'd dreamed of her, whole and beautiful, restored. But the dream had been cluttered and jumbled. He wasn't clear what had been dream and what had been memory.

Her memory.

But of course, that was impossible.

Wasn't it?

Chapter Eight

"Nate!" Deacon pounded on the side of the trailer. "Open up. Bo won't let me in."

Nate sprang to his feet. He'd somehow managed to doze off again, lying beside Maeve on the bed. How long had he been out? The slight lightness inside his trailer suggested he'd been out much longer than he'd anticipated.

His heart raced with the sudden disruption and he ran a hand through his hair, smoothing his clothes as he crossed to the door. He pushed it open with resistance as Bo continued his duties as sentry, but then the great beast rose with a resigned sigh and moved out of the way.

"What?"

"How is she? Any change?"

"No."

"We need to talk."

Nate backed away from the door and let Deacon inside.

Deacon swept his eyes around the trailer and landed on Maeve in all of three seconds. There was no hiding anything in a thirty-foot trailer. He eyed the IV solution.

"Nutrition?"

"Yes."

"You got one of those for yourself?"

"I'm fine."

Deacon's internal struggle was visible on his face as he pondered this next statement, arms crossed over his chest and his head tilted to the side.

"Nate. We'll talk to Rashnu together. Maybe there's a way to store her soul in an external source since her body is still alive. But you can't continue on this way. You'll grow weaker and weaker with her soul inside you. I liked Maeve. A lot. But this situation is untenable."

Nate's anger began to percolate.

"Not going to happen."

"Kylen was right, Nate. About her not wanting to live this way. In a vegetative state? You're the medical guy. You know what that means. The lights are on, but no one is home."

"Her condition could change."

"Yeah, it could get worse. Much worse. And so will yours."

Nate shook his head. Medically, he understood the words, emotionally they didn't compute. He had Maeve's essence inside of him and as long as that was the case, there was hope. She was not lost like the others.

"I won't let her go. Not yet."

"Then at least come to see Rashnu with me."

"I'm not leaving her. Not like this. And I'm not going to risk the possibility that Rashnu will take her from me."

Deacon blew out a sigh and hung his head. "That's what I figured you'd say."

"Can you heal her body? Give her energy at least?"

"Not directly. She wasn't kidding about her light being poison. How you managed to survive it, I have no idea, but her brother died as a direct result of her attempts to heal him. I contacted her family, what's left of it anyway—a cousin—after your incident with her. We were very lucky."

Nate's heart stuttered in his chest. "You know where her family is?"

"He was the only member left in the States. I guess after what happened with her brother, she fell off the planet for a while, then reappeared to finish her training. She hadn't been in contact with any of them in a long time."

Take me home.

"So if she wanted to *go home*, where would she want to go if not there?"

"Has she spoken to you?"

"Not exactly."

Deacon gave him a stern look, obviously interested in hearing more, but Nate refused to fill him in on the details.

"It would seem to me if a reaper wanted to *go home*, he or she most likely wanted to pass over."

"You mean die?" Nate tried to keep the horrified look off his face, but felt he was failing as blood rushed to fill his ears with a sound like the pulsing ocean.

"Yes, Nate."

Refusing to consider that as an option, he reached up to adjust the IV setting.

"The IV solution won't be enough to sustain her, and if she doesn't awaken coherent enough to eat actual food, she'll continue to fail.

"You're the only one who can share Reiki with her, Nate. We can take turns recharging you and you can relay the energy, but…"

"What?"

"You're going to discharge like a leaky battery. We can fill you up, but you'll drain back down almost immediately with her soul inside you. And if you get physically injured or sick? Well…"

"You might not be able to heal me at all."

"Yes."

Nate crossed to the bed and stared down at Maeve. She looked so peaceful, her face relaxed and calm. Nothing like her trademark fierce expression. "It's a chance I'm willing to take."

"Okay, then. We'll take turns with you. Whoever pulls meal duty also pulls Nate recharging duty. Guess I might as well get you started."

Deacon walked over and faced Nate, placing his open palm against his chest. "At least we don't have to worry about frying your circuits now."

"How's that?"

"You reaped your first soul, my friend. I guess you're a reaper after all. Welcome to the club."

A sad smile crossed Deacon's face and his hand began to glow a healing shade of green. He pushed the energy directly into Nate's heart chakra and the warmth filled his body, radiating through him with a slow burn. Maeve's soul agitated inside him, awakened from its repose. For a brief second, Nate feared that Deacon might have double crossed him and was trying to draw Maeve from him against his will.

When he tensed with apprehension, Deacon withdrew his hand.

"You good?" Deacon asked, backing away from him. "Did I hurt you?"

Nate relaxed, Maeve's soul stilling against the intrusion. "I'm fine. Thank you. For everything." He followed him to the door.

"Nothing has been settled here, Nate. We're only delaying the inevitable."

"Thank you anyway."

"Okay, then."

Deacon took one last look at Maeve's body and touched the door. Hesitating, he turned back to look at Nate. He seemed like he was about to say something, but then he shook his head, apparently thinking better of it, and opened the door. Bo bullied his way past Deacon, circling him to lie down at the foot of the bed.

As Nate pulled the door shut behind his friend, Bo let out an exaggerated sigh. After that spare sound, the silence in the trailer was deafening. He was hopeful that he'd have a few hours of reprieve before the rest of the crew came calling.

He wondered how long he'd be able to hold Maeve's soul before it was too late to reinsoul her, or if that point had already arrived and he was just too blind to see it. It didn't feel that way. He had faith that she could still be salvaged.

At least he could do one thing—fill her body with his fresh energy. Then if he stayed here, by her side, he wouldn't have to worry about losing her soul out in the field or wondering what was happening to her back home. Here, they would both be safe.

Gliding his hand along her arm, he marveled at the pull of turquoise light from him. His body was a converter now, taking the energy of others to transform it into a life-sustaining transfusion for Maeve. His heart swelled at the idea that he was the only one who could give this gift to her. Surely that was more than sheer coincidence.

She would have shrugged it off, but he knew better. He could feel in his very soul how *right* their connection was. Maeve's body drew in his light like a sponge did water and her pallor improved drastically. Way too soon, he watched the brilliant turquoise dim to a pale sky blue and he withdrew.

Exhausted by the effort, he lay down beside her once again and waited.

Waited for her body to heal. Waited for some means to return her soul. And waited for a chance to prove to her that home didn't have to mean death.

Chapter Nine

Days passed and Maeve remained in her comatose state with no sign of improvement. Nate scratched at his new growth of beard, already itchy and thick. He'd left the four walls of his trailer once, at Deacon's insistence, to join the others in the compound for dinner. Otherwise, he'd stood constant watch over Maeve.

There had been no sightings of Camael at the compound or in Meridian since his expulsion from Maeve. While the demons continued to keep busy, their master was curiously absent.

Nate couldn't disguise the fact he was weary. Weary from the constant refilling and discharging of energy and the parade of dreams, his as well as Maeve's, that played continuously every time he fell asleep.

He was on the verge of depletion himself and with the incessant stream of well-meaning visitors, he was close to snapping. Everyone was concerned about Maeve, as could be expected, but they'd all started to look at him with the sad expressions of pity he could barely tolerate. They knew what he still refused to admit.

He was on a death watch.

Pouring energy into her was like pouring water through a sieve. Olivia had come in one day to give Maeve a sponge bath, dressing her in one of her own nightgowns, which had somehow visibly diminished her even further. Nate could see Maeve's ribs pushing up against the thin fabric.

Despite his best efforts, she was declining. His own body wasn't faring much better. He'd taken to tucking in his shirt to keep his jeans from sliding down his hips. They were a pitiful pair.

Efforts to contact Maeve's remaining cousin had failed, but Deacon had managed to get word through to her parents. They had long since ascended into the Heavenly realms, though, and were unable to return to Earth. The way things were going, Maeve would soon be joining to them.

True to his word, Deacon had arranged for the reapers to visit Nate and keep him charged, but each replenishment filled him a little bit less, like he was an overused battery. He feared that any day now they would all burst in for a reaper intervention and take her from him...body and soul.

With the lack of restful and restorative sleep, he was beginning to lose touch with reality. He wondered if he had the strength to do what was needed. One person might be able to help him. Give him the answers he required. The question was...would he?

A knock at his door snapped him out of his maudlin reverie.

"Nate? I'm coming in." Deacon pulled open the door and walked in.

Bo lifted his head with mild interest, and then resumed his passive protection at the foot of the bed.

"You look like hell."

Nate didn't bother responding. The bastard was right of course—about everything—but he wasn't going to let him know it. Guy code and all of that bullshit.

"What are we going to do here, Nate? You have to make a decision, or it's going to be made for you. You're dead on your feet. We won't lose you both."

The choice was an impossible one.

For him to continue, he'd have to let her go, but how was he supposed to do that? She was a part of him now. Deacon might as well ask him to amputate his leg.

Kylen had already given him the bullshit speech about *honor amongst reapers*. Well, if that "honor" had been *honored* by Deacon, Kylen's possessed ass would have been dead a long time ago and he wouldn't be spending his off time wrapped around Olivia, rockin' that damned trailer like a pontoon boat in a hurricane.

The longer Deacon stared at him, the more agitated he became.

Maeve's soul brushed through him like a chill, sensing his agitation. If Deacon turned on his power and tried to draw her forth, steel would be the only weapon that could stop him. They both knew it.

Nate didn't want to fight the guy, but if it came to blows or worse, so be it. He would defend what was his.

And Maeve…was his.

Deacon took a step forward and his hands began to glow.

A gasp from the bedroom broke his concentration and demanded their attention. Nate turned to see Maeve's body convulsing on the bed.

"Shit." Nate raced to her side and attempted to restrain her as her body heaved from the bed. As soon as he made contact, her thirsty shell began to pull the weak charge of energy from him, taking what it needed and filling her with light.

The IV ripped from her arm and a stream of blood trickled from the puncture wound.

"I've got her. Take care of her arm." Deacon pressed her writhing body into the mattress, holding her in place.

The second Nate withdrew from her, she stopped fighting and they both watched the light fade from her once more. This time, she stopped breathing.

Nate pressed two fingers against her throat, searching for a pulse. Nothing. Not even a spark flickered between them.

"Start compressions," Nate ordered, sliding his hand under her neck and tilting her head back for rescue breathing.

Deacon complied and began rapid chest compressions as Nate breathed. The trailer rocked with their efforts, but Maeve's body remained still and unanimated. After several long minutes, Deacon stopped and stepped back from the bed.

"What are you doing? You can't stop!"

"It's over, Nate. Her spark is gone."

"No, it's not. Go get the AED! It's worked before. Go!"

"No, Nate."

Nate felt the energy swirl inside him like liquid fire. Maeve's soul fluttered against his walls like a butterfly in a glass jar. Flames of rage kindled inside of him.

This is not happening.

He couldn't breathe.

Nate felt his aura ignite before it manifested. Like a match to kerosene, it engulfed him. He drew in a deep inhale, then bent to Maeve's mouth once more to resume rescue breathing. Exhaling into her, he forced all the energy he had into her, willing it to fill her, restore her, save her.

The burn of his tattoos was the first indication that something beyond him was happening. Something magical. His sigils pulsated and flared, as pictures flashed through his mind—more memories that weren't his. He tried to focus on them, but they rolled by like a cartoon flip reel.

Maeve's soul went supernova, filling him with her light as it raced to the surface. Before he realized what was happening, her soul streamed forth, threading between the two of them, tethering them together briefly.

Maeve's eyes opened wide and radiated with turquoise light, Nate's mouth still firmly fixed on hers as her body tried to empty him of his energy and light

"What the hell?" Deacon bent closer, examining Maeve, but careful not to touch either of them. "Holy shit."

When Nate's breath was completely gone, he broke the hold and abruptly withdrew. Maeve's soul snapped free from him and dissolved into her limp form. Gulping in a great breath, he fell to his knees beside the bed, completely spent. Several seconds later, Maeve took a gasping breath herself and caught his gaze with her bright green eyes, wide and terrified.

His heart pounded and he thought he felt the slightest flutter brush inside his chest, but then it was gone.

"Maeve?"

She blinked rapidly, turning her head toward him, continuing to drag in shuddering breaths. A tear rolled from her eye and down her cheek. Nate reached to brush it away and the turquoise spark flickered weakly between them as she flinched from his touch.

"I'll be damned." Deacon stood and looked down at them both. "You reinsouled her."

Nate passed out.

Chapter Ten

Maeve was afraid.

A quick survey of the tin can-sized bedroom left her with more questions than answers. She didn't recognize her location. There were two men with her in the room, and while she couldn't see the face of the one who was lying on the floor, the other, standing over her, looked vaguely familiar. His name eluded her.

Friend or foe was the next question.

Sweat broke out across her forehead and began to pool in the small of her back as she clutched the sheets and scooted herself up and back against the headboard, searching with her eyes for a weapon in case these two turned out to be enemies.

Her mind was a jumble, as if she'd just awoken from a long, long sleep. A Rip Van Winkle sleep. Mentally, she searched her mind and body for traces of the intruder Camael, who had held her hostage. That memory was the freshest. Seconds later, fragmented pieces, shattered memories, photo flashes flooded through her in such a random and chaotic manner she had no context as to sequence or importance.

It was like watching hundreds of movie trailers haphazardly sliced and diced together. The reel made no sense.

The man in front of her was speaking in earnest, but she couldn't process his words. He might as well have been speaking Yiddish from far, far away. She didn't know Yiddish.

Pretty sure.

Her eyes blinked rapidly as she tried to physically stay above the deluge. The tide of thoughts filled her like tsunami waves and she squeezed her eyes shut despite the potential threat before her. If she couldn't gain control of her mind, her body would be of no use to her.

Her head twitched and she tried to shake things into place. So not helpful.

Maeve clasped her hands onto either side of her head and screamed.

***

"Maeve! Maeve! Look at me." Deacon tried to engage her as he moved around the bed to tend to Nate, but she looked dazed.

Shock, he thought as he bent to look at Nate.

Hell, the guy had just recovered from a concussion and now it looked as if he'd hit his head again on the way down. Blood trickled across his face from the fresh wound, just to the left of his previously healed head wound. The man was a hazard to himself.

Deacon pushed a jolt of green energy into him in an effort to revive him.

He kept his eyes on Maeve as he tried to process what he'd just witnessed.

Nate actually managed to reinsoul Maeve.

To his knowledge, it was a feat that had never been successfully accomplished before. The implications were staggering. It seemed that Nate had developed, practically overnight, into the single most powerful person in their circle. Maybe in the realm.

Even Grim, who was a seraph now, couldn't reinsoul.

He'd certainly never seen or heard any proof of it anyway. Not even a rumor around the reaper water cooler in Purgatory. The power was like the unicorn, elusive and fictional.

Nate moaned before opening his eyes and immediately slapped a hand to his forehead, which Deacon was sure he'd regret.

"Again?"

"Yeah, we need to get you a helmet."

Deacon helped him to his feet and watched as Nate's gaze shifted to Maeve. He lunged toward her, but Deacon took hold of his elbow.

"You might wanna give her a minute...or sixty. I think she's a little scrambled."

***

Nate eased down to sit at the side of the bed, watching Maeve's bright green eyes, which flashed from terrified to ferocious, then to confused. Without her soul rattling around inside him, continually testing the boundaries of his mind, he felt suddenly vacant. She had filled a void in him that he hadn't realized existed.

The slightest caress still brushed against his consciousness, even now, but it was nothing like the full force her soul had been. It was more of a remnant. Maeve's essence was indeed a force to be reckoned with. He reached out to her, unsure.

"Maeve?" he called.

She darted her eyes between him and Deacon like a wounded animal. Her silence was unnerving. He needed some reassurance that she was well and whole.

"Hmm, I don't think she's gotten her sea legs. Maybe more familiar faces would help. I'll get Olivia. Ruth can't make it up the trailer steps, but Olivia can." Deacon made his way to the door, and then looked back at Nate. "And maybe Kylen, too. I think you two have a few things to talk about."

Deacon pushed past Bo, leaving the two of them alone.

"Maeve, please say something. You're at Ruth's place. In my trailer. What can I do for you? What do you need?" He brushed his hand against hers, wanting to hold it, but desperate not to frighten her. Her savage gaze spooked him more than any of the demons they'd faced.

Maeve looked down at his hand and her eyes grew round and large as turquoise blue energy sparked between them. She clasped hold of his hand and the sharp jolt made him jerk free of her grasp.

"Sorry. Still not used to that." Nate reached for her again, but she retreated, the moment gone. "Do you know me? Do you remember what happened to you?"

She stared at him, her face unanimated now, giving away nothing for the longest time before she whispered, "Camael."

"Yes, Camael. He's gone."

"Destroyed?"

"Detoured. We have no idea how to destroy him. He'll be back. But you can be damned sure he won't be back in you."

Maeve recoiled into the bed once again. He couldn't blame her, but he wanted her to know she was safe here.

"Please let me help you, Maeve. How can I help you?"

Her eyes filled with tears as she visibly struggled for her words.

"Who are you?"

Chapter Eleven

Olivia spent an hour with Maeve while Nate sat on the couch at the opposite end of trailer like a nervous parent, memorizing the lines on his hands. Deacon sat beside him while the other reapers milled around outside waiting for a report. While she seemed more sedate now that Olivia was around, Maeve still hadn't said another word since their initial conversation. She seemed to understand their communications, answering their questions with a nod or shake of the head, but it was clear that not all of her cylinders were firing. Nate prayed it wasn't a permanent condition. Seeing her like this, scared and helpless, was torture. The fire still burned inside her—he could see it in her eyes—but she was not the reaper he'd seen in action before the possession.

Take me home.

Did she even know her family was gone? Hell, this was her home now. He could be her home. Of course, she had no idea who the hell he was anymore....

Whatever it took, he would make sure she had everything she needed to make a full recovery. Then she would have to decide on her own whether she wanted to stay or go.

Screw Camael and the demons. Deacon and the rest of the Authority had that shit covered. Besides, he had no doubt there would be plenty of reaper drama to go around when Maeve was ready for action again.

A knock came on the trailer door, and when Deacon went to answer it, Kylen pushed his head inside.

"Let's go for a walk, Nate," Kylen said.

A walk was the last thing Nate wanted. What he wanted was to sit vigil until Maeve snapped out of it and was back on track.

When he didn't respond, Deacon nudged him. "Go. She's in good hands. I'll get you if anything changes."

Reluctantly, Nate grabbed his jacket and stepped out of the trailer, shoving his hands in his coat pockets in defense against the cold. With her soul safely reinstalled, he no longer feared Maeve might be taken away from him. Now he worried she'd leave on her own, driven by fear and uncertainty. He could still lose her if he wasn't careful. Still, he followed Kylen without complaint as his friend led him to the trailer he and Olivia shared.

"Come on in."

Nate followed Kylen into the trailer. The setup, if not the décor, was a mirror image of his own home.

Kylen pointed to the small banquet table and opened the fridge to pull out two beers. "Sit."

Nate sat. Kylen opened a bottle and pushed it to him. "Drink."

Nate rolled his head from side to side, contemplating the medical prudence of drinking after cracking his skull. Again.

Screw it.

He sucked down a long pull, and then another, downing two-thirds of the bottle as Kylen waited, watching him from across the table.

"So. Big day for you. What with the whole reinsouling and all."

"Yeah."

"Deacon asked me to have a word with you. As a former demon host myself, he thought maybe I could impart some wisdom to you or some shit. I don't know about that. But I can tell you a few things about how it feels to be possessed. Before and after. There aren't very many of us who have lived to tell the tale."

Nate took another pull and killed his beer, then stared at his hands. "What can I do for her, Kylen?"

"First off, give her time. Maeve had the added bonus of losing her soul in this mess. And now, it seems, getting it back. That should put a whole new fucked-up spin to things. I never lost my soul, so I don't know what that might do to her. But I can tell you one thing—she's going to feel like hell for a few days. I had a lot of really bad memories to sort through, some mine, some my demon's. Most of them were things the bastard had done while riding me. I wasn't in control, but that didn't mean there wasn't any guilty for what my body had done. I had a front row seat to every goddamn crime the demon committed. Every person who was killed. Every soul that was stolen. And that was the easy stuff."

Kylen rolled his beer bottle between his hands, picking at the label. "You got a taste of it when you went to Hell. And everything you witnessed was from the cheap seats. Be glad you weren't a VIP. My demon was high in command, which meant he had full access, but his power was nowhere near Camael's. Maeve is a tough girl, but the stuff she's likely seen? Done? That's the shit that breaks a person."

"You survived it."

"I didn't want to. I wanted to die. You bastards just wouldn't let me. First that bullshit about saving Deacon. Then Olivia? If you want Maeve to make it, you're going to have to be a pit bull of patience and persistence just like you all were with me. And when she's ready to talk, I'll be here. For her and for you."

Deacon pulled open the door without knocking. "Getting dark. We need to go out. Those demons aren't going to slay themselves."

"I'm staying," Nate said.

"No. You're going. Olivia can tend to Maeve. She's not in any danger, and she needs time to work out her shit. Nothing you can do moping around here, pressuring her for answers she's not ready to give. We'll grill her plenty, don't worry, but it can wait a few more hours. Maybe it'll help her get her head back together."

"Thanks, Dr. Phil. You're a real sage," Kylen said.

"Whatever. We need Nate downtown. Now that you're unencumbered, Zak can juice you up before we go. Besides, you need to get out of here for a while. And with this latest development, well…you'll be all the more valuable out in the field."

Nate was conflicted. He knew Maeve needed time. After a brief physical exam, he was confident she wasn't in any immediate physical danger. It was her psyche he feared for now. What he hated most was that Deacon was right—he wasn't needed in the trailer, but the desire to stay put was overwhelming. He had the binding spell in place. She couldn't leave the trailer and that should be more than enough to keep her from running if she were so inclined. He should probably tell Olivia about it, although he doubted Maeve was in any condition yet to test her newest boundaries.

Of course, she'd surprised him before.

Debating the pros and cons, a plan began to form in his mind.

"I want to go to Purgatory. I need to talk with Rashnu."

"I'd say Rashnu will be expecting you," Deacon said.

"Will you take me?"

"You don't need me. You're welcome just like the rest of us. Especially now. But it can wait until we've cleared a few more demons. "

Nate nodded. He knew he could travel there himself. He was just trying to follow protocol. Rashnu probably had the answers he needed. The problem would be getting them out of the asshole.

"Go get your weapons, Nate. Let's roll some demons," Kylen said.

***

Maeve wanted sleep more than anything else in the world. To close her eyes and be alone, truly alone, would be a miracle. But these people? At this rate, she didn't think she'd ever be alone again. She could sense their sincerity, but the intense way the one called Nate kept looking at her was unnerving. The woman, Olivia, was human, but all the others she'd seen were reapers. Still, she couldn't figure out for the life of her why they were all living here together. This was not the reaper training compound. At least, not the one where she'd grown up.

She remembered everything right up to the night she'd first set foot in Meridian as a temporary replacement reaper. Then there was the night in St. Mary's Hospital when Camael had blackmailed her into accepting his possession. Two interesting problems remained. For one, all of her memories before the possession were in a completely random order. The sequence evaded her, like her deck had been shuffled.

Names, faces, events, reapings...all blurred into a *This Is Your Life* episode set on jumble.

Secondly, everything during and after the possession was like a dream, not quite remembered, but buried somewhere in the back of the brain. The harder she tried to pull those memories to the surface, the farther they slipped from her mental grasp. It was infuriating. Worse, it was painful. Her head ached from the effort. Whatever had happened to her during those few lost months under Camael's spell was important to remember. Imperative even. She just couldn't reach it.

Olivia had put names to the faces of the two men hovering nearby—Nate and Deacon—but she couldn't call up any memories to go with them. Olivia assured her there *were* memories of them, which was unsettling, and the girl did look vaguely familiar with her stark white hair. Still, nothing gelled in Maeve's consciousness, no matter how hard she reached for her past.

She needed time and maybe more familiar surroundings to try and put things into place. Panic built inside her, spreading through her chest like the burn of hard liquor. Time was running out. She didn't know what it meant, but she knew that much.

After a while, the two reapers left and Olivia went to prepare some food for her, promising a quick return. The short reprieve was a relief. Maeve stretched out her limbs, testing them for strength and durability. She was thinner. That much she knew.

Right now, her most pressing desire, other than recovering her memories, was to be clean. Besides sleep, a shower was about to become her next big adventure. Sliding her legs out from under the covers, she lowered them to the floor and rotated herself upright. After several seconds of inner debate as to whether or not hurling was on the agenda, her swimmy head and stomach settled and she reached for the wall to steady herself.

Vertical. It was a thing now.

At least her motor skills hadn't taken a complete vacation. She'd reaped enough brain-injured victims through the years to know it didn't take much to upset the mental applecart. Maeve was pretty sure all her pieces were present and accounted for. She just needed to rework the puzzle.

She eased around the edge of the wall to the bathroom door. Bathroom was a generous word to describe the tiny enclosure. It was definitely a one-person proposition. As thin as she was, she wondered if her body would even fit inside the minuscule shower enclosure. By God, she was going to try.

She shimmied out of the nightgown, trying not to think too hard about *who* had dressed her in it. Pulling the door shut behind her, she pulled the shower curtain shut and turned on the water, letting the hot steam fill the room.

Standing naked outside the shower door, she fingered the thin rope bracelet around her wrist and puzzled at it.

Where the hell had that come from?

One thing she was sure of: she didn't wear jewelry, and if she did, it wouldn't be hippy, hemp friendship bands. Briefly she picked at one of the knots. When it didn't give, she abandoned the effort. She'd cut it off later.

Avoiding the very small mirror over the equally miniature vanity was easy enough since it had already fogged over. She was glad she couldn't see her reflection. At this point, she had no desire to obsess on the *before*…all she was interested in was the *after*.

She stepped inside the shower. The hot water flowing over her elicited unexpected tears as relief coursed through her, releasing some of the stress that filled her like venom. But it was impossible to let go of the impending doom lurking just below the surface of her conscious mind. The tears at least rounded off the edges.

What was it! Something so important.

She grabbed the bar of soap and went to work, rubbing and scrubbing until her skin was raw and red from the effort. Would she ever be clean again? She pushed her shaking hands flat against the acrylic shower enclosure, letting the water course over her back, steadying herself as she pinned images to the bulletin board of her mind long enough for a cursory examination before they flitted away again.

No, none of them were the right ones.

And some of them—she was positive—weren't hers at all.

Death. So much death.

She was a reaper, after all, and death was her business and calling. That much she knew. She was a collector of souls and her job was to ferry the souls to their final destination, but not hasten their detachment prematurely. The images that flashed before her now were scenes in which she'd done exactly that.

Murder.

Frustrated, she leaned her head back into the stream, willing the water to wash away the assault of images, and worked Nate's woodsy scented shampoo and conditioner into her hair. She worked through the long and tangled strands, pulling handful after handful of snarls free from her head in the process. At this rate, she'd be bald when she got out.

Satisfied, Maeve shut off the water, immediately missing its soothing warmth. Wringing the water from her hair with her hands, she stepped from the shower only to realize she hadn't thought ahead to retrieve a towel. With a sigh, she searched through the one small bathroom cabinet, but found nothing except deodorant, mouthwash and bottles of hair product, which amused her. Wasn't this Nate's trailer? Did he have a roommate? If not, he was the highest hair maintenance male she'd ever encountered.

Or so she thought. Her mental file cabinet was disheveled after all.

Revived, Maeve turned the knob and pushed the door open, stepping out of the small bathroom.

Nate stood, mouth agape, in front of her.

Chapter Twelve

Nate's eyes blinked in time with his heartbeat. Rapidly. Paralyzed while his brain tried to process the sight of the wet and glistening body before him, he did the one thing any red-blooded male would do. He looked.

Holy shit.

Her green eyes flared and he broke out of his stupor, finally putting two and two together.

"Towel?" he asked.

An icy glare was his answer, which almost excited him more than seeing her in all her naked glory. That glare meant she was on her way back.

To him.

Good God, obviously an overload of naked female had short-circuited his brain. She wasn't his. She was his partner. Nothing more.

A fact he wasn't even sure she knew.

With effort, he averted his eyes as she made a slow puddle on his floor, water dripping from the ends of her hair and her elbows. Shuffling through the cabinet outside the door, he handed her a towel, willing himself to walk away from her.

"Thank you."

Her voice startled him and he spun around to catch her tuck the corner of the wrapped towel between her breasts. Breasts he'd seen bare mere seconds ago. His brain was going all kinds of junior high.

Nate cleared his throat. "You're welcome."

They locked gazes for several seconds before she raised her eyebrows at him quizzically.

"Sorry." Flustered, he looked behind her at the pile of discarded clothes. "I just need to get my weapons. We're heading into Meridian."

He searched her face for recognition, trying to tease out answers to unasked questions.

"You need to stay here. *In the trailer.* I'll have Olivia bring some clean clothes for you. She has a feast coming your way, too." He smiled at her, hoping it came off more sincere than the goofball grin he feared was spreading across his maw. "We'll talk when I get back."

Retrieving his short sword and blades, he snuck an awkward glance at her as she remained rooted in place, watching him.

"You're safe here." The sigils on his arms flared as he walked out the door, reassuring him that she couldn't wander too far.

***

Ruth was dying to get out to that trailer. Olivia had filled her in on Maeve's current state and while she was relieved Maeve was back home, it was clear she wouldn't be out in the field again any time soon.

Temperance, the guardian angel sent to watch over Ruth's unborn child, scowled at her from across the room. Some days, Ruth could swear the angel could read her mind! She'd been confined to bed rest for all but the first six weeks of her pregnancy, and it was wearing on her in ways no one else in the compound could understand. The worst part was she still had four and a half months to go.

Ironically, Ruth had spent most of her life in self-imposed isolation, living in fear of her gift: the ability to see auras. When she met her first reaper, Deacon, her life had tumbled right past the land of Weird and settled firmly into the land of What The Hell. She'd enjoyed gainful employment in her newly discovered profession as a reaper for all of few months before everything went screwy. Choosing to exile herself was one thing. Being exiled was something altogether different. If Maeve was feeling even an ounce of that frustration, Ruth had sympathy.

She was only allowed occasional visits to the commons area. After she nearly lost the baby early on in the pregnancy, the entire Authority had conspired to keep her in her place. While she knew it was for her own good—and the baby's—it was growing more and more intolerable.

If not for the fast satellite internet installation Nate had orchestrated on her behalf, she would have been stark-raving mad by now. Deacon was so busy with all of his new duties that it seemed like she only saw him for a few minutes each day. Olivia, bless her heart, spent hours entertaining her and catering to her every whim. Temperance, on the other hand, was about as entertaining as a Roman statue.

She only came to life when Ruth wiggled toward the edge of the bed. It seemed like all Ruth needed to do was even think about moving to set her angel into action. Temperance's short, red hair stood at attention in all directions around her head. Ruth would have called it a pixie cut except she was pretty sure the angel had hacked it off with scissors or a blade herself. "Cut" was a little too lavish a description. "Shredded" was more apt.

The arches of the angel's neatly folded wings peeked above her shoulders. Deacon had told her that when completely relaxed, an angel's wings could be fully retracted, visible only as a feathered shadow beneath her skin, like a tattoo but smooth to the touch.

Temperance was never relaxed.

The bad news was that her wings had stood at attention from day one. The good news was that Ruth had yet to see them fully extended, a sign of either force or dominance. Since Nate had reinforced the compound with magic, their boundaries hadn't even been tested and God knew Ruth hadn't stepped foot outside the commons area, let alone the grounds.

She clicked her mouse button extra loudly for the sole purpose of annoying Temperance as she searched yet another genealogy website on her laptop. Since she was a prisoner, she had decided to use her time doing what she'd been trained for. With a PhD in Information Technology, she was a research maven, but the one piece of information she wanted the most still eluded her.

Ruth had spent the past several months searching for her birth parents. The traits required to become a reaper were genetic and at least one parent needed to carry the genes in order for them to develop in a useful way in the child. Ruth had no idea from whom she might have inherited the gift until she stumbled across a clue just before her house and the binder full of answers was torched.

She'd read the file. Once. But at least the name was etched into her memory.

Elaina Carter, birth mother.

That was her one lead. She'd exhausted hundreds of ancestry sites from her prison bed and made dozens of unfruitful inquiries, even a few international calls.

There were many, many Elaina Carters in the world, but none had intrigued her enough to send Deacon on a visit to scope things out. There was a soccer mom in Rhode Island, a massage therapist in Detroit, a chiropractor from Amarillo and seventeen others in the US who had died within her lifetime. Each, by all accounts, was completely unremarkable as far as potential reaper attributes went. Deacon *had* been able to determine none of the deceased were eligible candidates. Thanks to his promotion to Powers he could travel freely between the realms at will. None of the sorted souls had been reapers.

Unfortunately, most of his time had to be spent tracking down demons and a fallen angel instead of Ruth's potential birth mothers. Still, she had whittled down the list of eligible candidates. There were several hundred left for her to sort through.

The idea that the name on the paperwork could have been false was not one she allowed herself to consider. Her adoptive father had died when she was very young and her adoptive mother within the past year. Deacon had actually reaped her mother's soul, which was what had begun the chain of events leading to her current state of affairs.

While her mother was alive, Ruth hadn't wanted to add stress to their estranged relationship by searching for her biological mom. At this point, she was questioning the merit of that decision. Even with her superb research skills, tenacious work ethic and copious amounts of time, she didn't feel very hopeful for a breakthrough.

With the baby on the way, however, it seemed all the more important for her to pin down her lineage. If there was an Elaina Carter out there with her DNA coursing through her body, Ruth was determined to find her.

Temperance cocked her head to alert status and cut her eyes to the door moments before Olivia walked in unannounced. She was like an angel ADT that girl.

"Hey, the guys are gone. Wanna break out?" Olivia asked.

Ruth grinned, scooted her computer off her lap and started to swing her legs off the bed, but Temperance was on her like white on rice.

"Temperance, I haven't been out of bed except to pee all day. Hell, you can carry me if it will make you feel better." Ruth hated being carried unless it was to bed and by Deacon. Still, if it helped her to achieve her goal, what was a little humiliation between friends?

Motionless, the angel actually seemed to consider it for a moment. Maybe she was wearing down just as much as Ruth. God knew misery loved company. Instead, Temperance shook her head no.

"Can Maeve come here?"

"Not yet, she's butt naked. She managed to shower and clean up." Olivia held out the armload of clothes she carried. "I'm taking over a few things. I'll see how she is. She was pretty out of it earlier. Maybe the shower helped her feel human again."

Ruth giggled. "Not sure that would be an improvement for her. Being a reaper and all."

"True enough. I'll be back. Hopefully, with Maeve in tow." Olivia spared Temperance a glare before she walked off.

The angel was making no friends with her silent but deadly act. So much for girl power. Solidarity. There was no give to that girl at all.

Ruth watched Olivia leave and then threw her head back against the pile of pillows that was propping her up.

Four and a half more months.

Something had to give.

Chapter Thirteen

Nate was on a roll. After Zak's refueling, he felt amazing. Despite his distracted mind, he helped track and terminate a dozen demons himself. Camael, as expected, was on hiatus. He hoped the bastard was so distraught over having lost Maeve that he'd crawl back into his hellhole and die.

The odds were not in his favor.

Bo lapped at a pool of blood oozing from one of the hosts, sniffing excitedly in hopes of picking some bones clean.

"Not yet, buddy. I called in reinforcements."

He'd damaged the hosts enough to render them immobile, but he didn't want the demons bailing before they could be properly contained. All of the members of the Authority, except Nate, of course, could vacuum the bastards up and dispose of them permanently.

Inappropriate as the moment was, all he could think about was Maeve's naked body. She was fantastic. Even broken and bruised, he was ashamed to admit, he was more than attracted to her. He wanted her. All of her.

He scrubbed his hand down his face, trying to erase any evidence of his deviant thoughts. What he didn't need was a reaper intervention, good or bad, on his behalf. He'd work his shit out himself, but not until Maeve's feet were firmly planted in reality again and she was well.

God, how long was that going to take? His cock twitched.

Betraying piece of shit.

He was an honorable guy. Practically a damned Boy Scout, but it had been more than eleven months since he'd been with a woman. His virgin card had probably been reset.

After the epic blow up of his last relationship, he'd sworn off anything serious. It was hard enough dating on his erratic EMT schedule, so when he hooked up with Sarah, another EMT, it seemed like a match made in Heaven. She wasn't bothered by his hours, but it wasn't long before she wanted to settle down, move in and take over.

Of course, she hadn't known about his Wiccan connections. It wasn't something he advertised and it had never come up in conversation. Like it would. This was the freakin' Bible belt. They didn't suffer witches. Meth heads, sure, but not witches.

Like his politics, he kept his religion to himself. Of course, Wicca was more than a religion. It was a lifestyle and a way of being with the natural world. To Nate, religion and Wicca were a combo deal. Mostly he considered himself a Christian witch and nothing made jaws drop around a work lunch table faster than a mention of that. The next thing that happened was that eyes glazed over and folks suddenly had somewhere else to be.

Whatever. He'd made that mistake once. A long time ago. And he'd learned to keep his personal shit to himself. Being involved with the reapers both confirmed his beliefs and filled him with a whole host of new questions.

As soon as these demons were processed, he'd finally be able to ask some of them....

"Nice work." Samkiel walked toward him, a Cheshire grin across his face.

"Somebody had to pick up your slack."

"Touchy for a guy who just got his girl back."

"She's not my girl. She's my partner. Speaking of which, where's yours? Ragu out getting his beauty sleep somewhere?"

Samkiel clasped his hands together and let the energy build in preparation to vacuum the demons and souls as he counted the number of bodies thrashing on the floor of the warehouse.

"Twelve. Not bad. One more and you would have had a baker's dozen. Ragu had fifteen."

Nate didn't bother to reply. You just couldn't out smartass Samkiel.

"Ready?" He drew his short sword and went to work separating heads from bodies.

The demons streamed out in dark gray plumes.

An orange glow emanated from Samkiel and engulfed the bodies, drawing forth first the demons, and then the poached souls the bastards had stolen. Samkiel absorbed them into his body and immediately began to fade, bringing the motley bunch to Purgatory.

Samkiel nodded as he dissipated. "See ya on the other side."

Bloody hell, did everyone know his business now?

Nate concentrated on his destination. It was a bit after 4:00 a.m. He prayed that by sunrise, he would have at least some answers for and about Maeve.

He felt the tug of the consecrated subway as he flashed to Purgatory.

***

Maeve maneuvered around the tiny bathroom and pulled the jeans and T-shirt over the underwear Olivia had brought for her. Even buttoned, the size-six waistband gaped on her. Olivia had assured her they were in fact her own clothes, retrieved from her sparse apartment by Nate and stored after her abduction. They didn't even look familiar. Regardless, she was thankful for them, especially if she was going have to share quarters with Nate, who was apparently rendered mute by nudity.

She'd spent most of the day curled in a ball on the bed, drifting in and out of sleep. Her dreams had been filled with nonsense, but at least a few gears had clicked into place. The food had helped a lot. She had eaten everything Olivia brought her, which had seemed to be a never-ending supply.

It wasn't enough. While she felt stronger, she was far from herself and her head was killing her.

So many of her memories still evaded her, but at least she no longer feared for her sanity. The best part was she was completely alone inside her head and body. A luxury she'd never fully appreciated until today. Fear still smoldered in her heart and a knowledge that she couldn't explain or qualify seethed inside her.

Something terrible was about to happen.

Olivia, who wanted her to go to Ruth's trailer for some girl time, was waiting outside the bathroom door. Maeve was restless to get out of the trailer, but she didn't feel up to the third degree.

Maeve was confused about a lot of things, but she was rock-solid sure that she never had nor ever would have "girl time" of her own volition. Maybe she could feign a renewed bout of weakness and avoid the whole thing. Of course, then they'd tell the rest of the reapers when they got back and, worse yet, Nate seemed like a mother hen. She'd never have a moment's peace. She longed for the good old days when all the reapers she knew...reaped. The rules had been simple then. No one got possessed and everyone got exactly what they deserved. Rashnu, the Purgatory sorting angel, saw to that.

This demon chasing business was bullshit.

She hung her head in defeat.

Like a bandage. Rip it off.

Maeve knew she was screwed when she walked out of the bathroom and Olivia's face twisted into a smile. That girl was not going to take no for an answer.

"You look great!" Olivia gathered up Maeve's dirty clothes.

Maeve nodded.

"Ready to get out of here for a while? Maybe it will help jog your memory." Olivia pushed open the door and walked down the steps.

Maeve followed reluctantly, but came to an abrupt stop at the doorway when she struck into an invisible wall. Her wrist itched beneath the hemp bracelet and she watched in horror as it came to life, writhing around her arm.

"Come on, it won't be that bad, honest."

Maeve tried another tentative step through the door with the same result. First confusion, then anger began to percolate inside her. No fucking way was she going to be trapped in this trailer. She had just been freed and was not about to accept captivity again, not in any form. She looked down at the bracelet.

Magic.

Resisting the urge to tear the trailer apart, she turned and headed for the closet from which Nate had retrieved his weapons earlier. An impressive array of blades lined the shelves. Any would do for the task at hand. She clutched hold of a six-inch dagger and slid it between the bracelet and her skin, then drew it back against the rope to cut it off.

When it didn't slice through as expected, she got a better angle and tried again. Nothing. She withdrew the blade and grabbed hold of the rope pull attached to the window blinds. Stretching it taut, she drew the blade through it, slicing it in half like hot butter.

The blade was not defective.

Olivia climbed back up the steps and into the trailer. "What's wrong, Maeve? What are you doing with that thing?"

Fear filled Olivia's blue-gray eyes. Maeve couldn't blame her. If she were facing an unstable, pissed off reaper, she'd be scared, too. She flipped the blade around in her hand and presented the dagger to Olivia.

"Take it."

Olivia reached out, unsure and gripped the handle of the dagger.

Maeve held out her wrist. "Cut this string off me."

Curious, Olivia stepped forward, studying the band. "Is it special? Maybe we could just untie it."

"No. Cut it off."

Slipping her fingers around one of the knots, Olivia pulled the band as far away from Maeve's skin as possible. Sliding the blade into the gap, she attempted to slice through the cord. Unsuccessful, her jaw set and she went at it with a renewed vigor, sawing between the knots. Not even a hair of it frazzled off.

"Huh. That's some tough twine."

"Not really. It's been imbued with some sort of magic."

"What?"

"Some sort of spell. I can't leave the trailer."

"Oh, no."

"What do you mean, 'oh, no'? Do you know who did this to me?"

"Well, Nate is a witch, so if it's magic, then...."

Rage filled her anew like white-hot flames. A freakin' witch? Really?

Angels and demons and witches?

This day just kept getting better and better.

If she couldn't physically walk out of the trailer, maybe she could bypass this stupid security system by flashing. She could sense the consecration. Closing her eyes, she summoned what little energy she had left and tried. Nothing major. She knew she wouldn't have the energy to go very far. Hell, getting outside of this tin can would be a start.

Olivia's eyes opened wide in surprise.

Maeve was getting nowhere fast, but she was manifesting a nice mustard-color aura, which quickly developed into a skull-crunching headache. Nausea followed, and then white stars began to burst behind her eyes.

Falling to her knees, she clutched the sides of her head. Olivia's lips were moving, but nothing was processing. Maeve's eyes closed and she checked out.

Chapter Fourteen

Nate landed in the reaper rendezvous lounge in Purgatory. The angel Rashnu had arranged for the Authority to have twenty-four hour access to this opulent chamber to reconnoiter if things got too dicey up top or they needed to rejuvenate in complete safety.

It was the first time Nate had come here of his own free will. He was less than impressed with the help, or more the lack of help, that Team Light had contributed thus far. Ten reapers against thousands of demons was less than a fair fight. It seemed like much more should and could be done to help them even the odds. Deacon and the other reapers didn't seem to be bothered by it, but sometimes Nate wondered if they were all just pawns being moved around a board for entertainment.

The tattooed sigils around Nate's arm burned, alerting him to the fact that Maeve was trying to leave the trailer. He should have warned her. The old Maeve wouldn't take kindly to being restrained, even if it was for her own good. But there was no way to know how she might react now, after the possession, let alone the reinsouling. Jesus, this was all new territory. The last thing he wanted was for her to flash somewhere and end up in even more danger.

A familiar flutter moved through him like a whisper as he reconsidered his options. He wanted to chock it up to guilt over what he'd done, but the flutter was something more than that, an echo of something lost. Of Maeve's presence inside him.

No. He'd made the right decision for her. Until he unbound the knots or escorted her, she would have to stay put. She was in no shape to go wandering off on her own yet. Even at full strength, he worried about the possible repercussions of the reinsouling. Would she recover her personality completely? Her memories? He'd seen a spark of her old self, or what he knew of her anyway. The question remained: Would that spark be enough to reignite her passion to live?

There might be hell to pay when he got back. He secretly hoped so. Seeing her angry was so much better than seeing her helpless and afraid. Whatever the price, it was worth it for his peace of mind.

Nate wasn't even sure how to find Rashnu or Grim. He'd never been outside of this room. Deacon and the other reapers had described the reaper way station to him in extravagant detail, so he had a well-formed picture in his head, but he still had no idea how to get there from here. Luckily, he didn't have to go exploring.

Light spilled in from the hallway as the tremendous wooden door swung open and Rashnu stepped inside.

"I wondered how long it would be before you showed up here." Rashnu all but floated across the room toward the bar.

The dude gave Nate the creeps. His long, wavy black hair and green eyes framed his too perfect face. Rasnhu was like the Barbie version of Angel Ken.

Nate had last been here just before Maeve's possession, for the reactivation of the Authority. The angel hadn't offered Nate any help other than the hellhound Bo and some less than stellar directions to "track" the demons. Why Nate thought this time would be any different, he didn't know, but the angel seemed to be the last resort, hail Mary pass for all of them. Deacon, Ruth and Kylen had each sought his counsel if not solutions to their impossible dilemmas.

Faith was a fragile thing.

Nate wasn't sure how much faith he needed to be worthy of one of Rashnu's favors, but he was ready to lay it all on the table and find out.

"I hear you've finally done something interesting. Reinsouled Maeve?" Rashnu poured himself a drink, brought it to his lips and tilted it back.

"How was I able to do that?"

"One of the many wonders of the world, my friend."

"No. It's more than that, and I think you know that. What am I?"

"Reinsouling has—in the past—been a gift associated with various nephilim. Are you familiar with the nephilim?"

"Biblical cautionary tales of angels having intercourse with human women? Nephilim were their supposed offspring. Mythical sons of renown and power."

"Yes, but sons *and* daughters, and it happened long before the Bible was written." He took another long pull on his drink. "And long after."

"You mean, there are still nephilim?"

"As surely as angels still fall, there are still nephilim among us. Closer than you'd think."

"What does any of that have to do with Maeve? Or me? And more importantly, is this a blessing or a curse?

If reinsouling her only leaves her broken, then why have the ability at all?"

Rashnu poured liquid into two more tumblers, one with a glittering blue substance, the other a pulsating red. He pushed them toward Nate. "Whether it is a blessing or a curse depends on you, Nate. Your free will decides the outcome. You have light and dark in you, as do we all. But yours is particularly turbulent. Now that you've actuated, you'll have to choose a path. With a power like yours, riding the middle will render you impotent to help your friends. But remember, by choosing one side, you'll forfeit the other. While that choice may seem easy on its face, when you dig deeper it might be much more difficult than you ever imagined."

He pushed the red drink toward Nate. "These drinks will show you two possible paths to guide you in your choice. To know the full picture, you'll need to sample them both. Then when you have chosen, drink the remaining contents from your glass of choice. After you drink, the wheels will be set into motion. If you wait too long to choose, you will lose it all."

"Drinking these will give me the answers I've asked for?"

"They will give you answers. What you choose to do with that information will determine your future. As always, it comes down to free will. Ain't that a bitch?" Rashnu drained the remaining liquid in his own glass and slammed it down on the bar. "Be well. And good luck."

Then he disappeared, leaving Nate alone to face his future. His mind roiled. What if he chose wrong? Maybe knowing the future or possible future was a wrong choice in itself. Self-doubt consumed him, but he was ultimately too tempted by the answers that were literally waiting at his fingertips.

He lifted the glass of blue liquid to his nose and sniffed it. It smelled salty and clean, like the ocean and sunshine. Pressing the glass to his lips, he said a silent prayer for strength and poured some of the contents into his mouth. Setting the glass back down on the bar, he held the liquid in his mouth for a second, and then let it slid down his throat.

The room exploded into a kaleidoscope of images and he fell to his knees. Leaning forward, he pressed his face to the cool stone floor, desperate to ground himself. Faces and images pulsed forward before dissipating back into the carousel that raced past him.

The graveyard he landed in the first time he flashed at age five.

The gravestone he leaned against. A name was carved into it, but he was too disoriented to make it out.

A woman with dark hair curling around her face and sad eyes standing with a large group of people around a bonfire.

Camael.

Ruth.

A sacrifice.

The world—his world—in chaos.

Death and destruction.

Grasping for the golden bar foot rail, he tried to steady himself as the new images mingled with his memories and spun farther and farther from his sight. His head bobbed on his shoulders with exhaustion and he wondered how he'd ever survive a look-see behind door number two.

Hoisting himself to his feet, he staggered to lean against the bar, pressing his forearms firmly against the marble ledge. He couldn't stop his damn head from spinning and his stomach was working up a protest, as well. The thought of drinking one more drop of anything made bile rise up into his throat and burn.

If you wait too long to choose, you will lose it all.

Damned angels and their mind games. Why couldn't they just tell you straight out what you needed to know? What you were supposed to do? How could you possibly understand what all the consequences were?

Nate wrapped his hand around the second glass and dragged it across the bar. His knees were weak and unsteady beneath him. Black and white spots formed and popped behind his eyes like soap bubbles.

Bloody hell.

He grasped the second glass until his knuckles turned white and took a pull.

Second verse, same as the first.

Only this time, the images he saw made even less sense.

A great chasm ripping the city in two.

The world on fire.

Maeve's head rolling to his feet.

A battalion of angels descending upon the demon hoard.

Camael leading an army of the undead, human and otherwise.

He placed both palms flat against the bar while he tried to talk his stomach out of the free fall it was intent on completing.

Those were his choices? Bad and worse?

Well one thing was for damn sure, he wasn't going to opt for a future in which Maeve's head ended up detached. So if a choice had to be made, he'd make it. He grabbed the glass of blue liquid and downed it, throwing the empty glass against the stone wall behind the bar, where it shattered into sand.

He had gotten no answers here. Only more bullshit. Just as he'd expected, really.

Toying with the idea of going rock star and destroying the place, his hands clenched in and out of fists at his side as anger built inside him. He wouldn't ask for help again. At least not from this asshole.

There was one place he could count on, one family who would help him unconditionally and without any bullshit: the coven. He'd take Maeve there and let the rest of the Authority sort this nonsense out.

He flashed out of Purgatory.

***

And into the Hell that was his trailer. Maeve came at him, weapon drawn.

Before he could so much as process what was happening, she drew a blade across his raised forearm. The woman was like a banshee, her coal black hair flying, her green eyes aflame.

Looked like he didn't need to worry about her spark returning. What he did need to worry about was her stabbing him in the liver with that pig sticker.

Olivia screamed from the doorway for Maeve to stop, but it was Bo who brought things under control. The dog crashed through the screen door and pressed his great body against the back of her knees. Maeve buckled to the floor and the blade went skittering under the couch. Bo stretched out over her and despite her efforts to roll out from under him, he pressed her to the floor, helpless and spread out, arms and legs akimbo.

Eventually the lack of air, pressed out of her body from the beast's great weight, took the fight out of her. Her eyes rolled back in her head and she stopped struggling.

"Enough, Bo. Heel."

Bo huffed and rose to his feet, then lumbered to Nate's side.

Maeve sucked in a deep gulp of air and snapped back to attention, her eyes scanning for the weapons. She wasn't done fighting.

Nate kicked the closest knife well out of her reach. "Olivia, I think Maeve and I need some time alone."

"Are you sure? She's a little…um…scary."

"Any idea what set her off?"

"Oh, yeah. It was the bracelet. She can't leave the trailer."

Nate pinched the bridge of his nose, wary of Maeve's ongoing appraisal of any possible weapons.

"Leave us, please."

"Okay. I'll send out Temperance. Just in case."

"No need."

Olivia hesitated in the doorway. She'd try to send the angel anyway, he could tell. Whether or not she would come would be another thing. Temperance didn't take orders from reapers or their girlfriends. Right now another damn angel was the last thing Nate needed.

The outer door shut with a snick and Nate eased onto the couch. He held his empty hands forward, indicating surrender.

"I'm sorry about the spell. I should have warned you."

Maeve held out her wrist. "Remove it."

"No. It's a binding spell. I bound you to myself and this trailer to protect you. It's for your own good. Clearly you have some…issues to resolve."

She watched him like a predator, her eyes taking in his every miniscule twitch. She retained the jerky movements of the possessed, still not comfortable back in her own skin.

"I'm not your prisoner."

"No. You're my partner."

Her eyes crinkled at the edges, trying to process what he'd said. "No."

"Yes. Of course, we weren't partners for very long before you were taken, but still...we are partners." Nate studied her. "What's the last thing you remember?"

Maeve eased over to the wall behind her, pushing up off the floor and squatting on her haunches like she was preparing to launch herself at him. He wouldn't hurt her, but he would defend himself, even render her unconscious if need be. She looked feral and unpredictable.

Blood dripped from his arm onto the floor. Bo whined beside him. He needed to dress the wound; in fact, it would likely need stitches. Slowly, he reached beneath the couch and retrieved the blade.

"I can't help you if you won't talk to me, Maeve."

She stared at his arm and he thought he saw the slightest glimmer of remorse cross her face, but it vanished as she lifted her chin in defiance. Well, he could wait. Two could play the silent game. Of course, he couldn't spend his days here in this trailer alone with her waiting for her to kill him in his sleep.

It was a slim chance she'd go for the plan he had hatched, but if she didn't cooperate, he had other ways of bending her to his will. Ways she would not like one bit better than his binding spell.

"Maeve, I have a proposition for you."

Chapter Fifteen

They landed just outside the coven's circle of protection. Nate had purposely asked to be excluded from the boundary after he'd joined up with the reapers in his semi-official capacity. This was the last place he wanted to lead danger to, but under the circumstances, he felt like it was his only option.

He'd left Olivia and Ruth to explain to Deacon and the reapers why and where he'd taken Maeve. Well, at least the why. They had no idea where the coven was and he planned to keep it that way. He had even left his reaper-issued cell phone in the trailer in case Deacon decided to use the GPS to track him. Much to his unease, he'd left Bo, too. The dog had proven invaluable, but there was no way he could bring it to the coven without every single one of them recognizing exactly what the beast was. He wasn't ready to play all of his cards just yet.

Nate led Maeve through the tall grass of the small meadow and onto the trail. Their steps crunched across the frosty ground. The hum of magic filled the air and his sigils twitched along his arms. The sigil of his family crest grew warm and tight across his right shoulder. Everyone in his immediate family had the same marking.

Despite the circumstances, it was good to be home.

Maeve's anxiety was palpable behind him. Convincing her to come willingly hadn't been easy, and for that reason alone, he'd neglected to elaborate on the fact the healer he was taking her to see was also his mother. He didn't need any more potential obstacles. As it was, he was well aware that she'd only agreed to get out of the trailer because she planned to escape at the first opportunity. Once he got her inside the circle of protection, however, she wouldn't get that chance until all of her ducks were back in a row, however long that took.

Six more feet and he was home free.

He felt the metaphysical door open and was glad he'd called ahead. Nate reached back for Maeve's hand. She lifted her chin and walked ahead of him without a word, keeping well out of his reach. No matter. When she crossed the threshold, he breathed a sigh of relief.

Now he had all the time in the world.

***

Maeve could feel the magic surrounding her, but as long as she was bound to Nate, she knew the only way to escape him was to kill him. A solution that was becoming more and more acceptable to her as time went on.

His arm still bled where she'd sliced him open, eliciting a slight twinge of guilt somewhere deep inside of her. She'd been out of her mind with rage when he flashed into that damned trailer all superior and...Nate. She'd lashed out without even thinking.

Survival mode.

Once she'd settled down, Nate had talked for what felt like hours, wearing her down until she'd finally consented to his ridiculous plan. At that point, she would have agreed to anything to shut him up and get out of that trailer. She knew she was still several patties short of a Big Mac, but her will to survive, no matter what the cost, was strong.

Some things were ingrained in you. Some things you felt down to your soul.

Unfortunately, Maeve's most pressing problem was that her soul was splintered. What Nate had pushed back inside her was by far the lion's share, but somewhere inside the man who walked before her was her missing piece. Even now her body recognized it, pulled to him like a moon in orbit.

How the hell was she going to get it back?

Because there was no doubt about it. That piece was the key to rearranging her mental furniture.

Too bad it was still in the wrong storage unit.

Acquiescence went against her grain, but he'd *sworn* to her that his coven's magical healing guru could help her. Until she could figure out how to get that damned bracelet off, it seemed she was at his mercy, barring the whole killing him in his sleep thing.

It was good to have options.

***

Having his back to Maeve was an exercise in trust she hadn't yet earned, but he was making every effort to prove to her that he was acting in her best interest. He watched as his mother approached from across the compound.

They were still in Arkansas, but deep within the forests and protected by a natural magic as ancient as creation itself. First came nature, and then came man. Nate's adopted people and the people before them and the people before them, all the way back to the *first* people had manipulated the elements and nature to their benefit, but it was a skill that had to be honed and maintained for continued success. A skill that had eventually been replaced with science for most people.

Ironic since science itself depended on magical elements. Funny how quickly the non-practicing lost that knowledge.

His mother's eyes swept over Maeve and her smile faltered a little but recovered. He wondered if Maeve had seen it, too. She was combustible at best. He prayed she wouldn't go medieval on his mother and bring down the wrath of the coven before they even got started.

"Nate. I'm so happy to see you." His mother drew him into an embrace and he relaxed into her hold, soaking in her amazing scent and energy.

"Mother, this is Maeve." He stepped aside, staying close enough to the two women that he could intervene in case Maeve went violent again. "Maeve, this is my mother, Rosemary."

Maeve's jaw dropped open, then she cast a withering glance at Nate.

He was busted, but it was too late for her to renege now that she was inside the coven boundaries. Defiant, Maeve crossed her arms over her chest and tried to maintain her cool distance.

Undeterred, Rosemary swept past Nate and wrapped her arms around a stunned Maeve. The whites of her eyes the size of half dollar coins, Maeve endured the embrace without incident, and Nate released an audible sigh of relief as his mother retreated, a slight frown on her otherwise unlined face.

Physically his mother was in her early sixties, but she looked a good twenty years younger. She had lotions and potions Estee Lauder would kill for.

Rosemary touched his injured arm and her lips tightened into a thin white line. "Let's take care of you two. Come."

She wrapped her arm around Nate's damaged arm and pulled him into the compound. Maeve followed behind, tethered by his magical binding leash, fighting him for sport the entire way.

While the basic compound's structure was the same as what he'd helped set up at the reaper compound, a wheel formation with a central community center at its hub, here eight streets radiated from the hub and each street was named after a Wiccan high holy day. They walked down Beltane Street to his parent's two-story home, which also housed the coven's healing center.

Flurries swirled through the air around them, a perfect accompaniment to the elaborate preparations for the upcoming Yule festival. Yule came days before the Christian Christmas, which really wasn't much of a coincidence at all. Early Christians had tried to commandeer the holiday in an effort to eradicate millennia of pagan celebrations. Mostly, it had worked in the western world, but even here there were still pockets of believers who continued the old ways.

Yule was a time of rebirth and celebration. Families would fill this compound in the coming days and plan for the new year. It would be difficult to stay under the radar, but that was exactly what Nate intended to do. The less he had to explain to the coven about Maeve, the better. Many of the more sensitive coven members would recognize immediately that Maeve wasn't human. While the coven was filled with tolerant, like-minded folks—a reaper was an entity that none of the living members, to his knowledge, had seen.

They needed to tread lightly.

Rosemary smiled up at him, her long salt and pepper hair whipping around in the wind behind her, her hazel eyes sparkling with mischief. Sometimes he felt like she could practically read his mind. He'd never been able to hide anything from her, so he hadn't even tried until recently. This was his first visit in months, which would have been enough to spark her curiosity on its own, but he could tell she knew something big was brewing. Though he'd told his parents about moving, explaining that he'd taken a new job with a strict security clearance and wouldn't be able to visit for a while, he'd wanted to distance his family and the coven from the current reaper troubles. Perhaps it was finally time to come clean.

"Let's get that arm looked after." She led him through the arched door on the side of the storefront of her healing center, heading directly into her workshop at the back of the building where the public was not allowed. Maeve followed silently behind, a scowl still fixed on her face.

The scent of a miscellany of herbs, spices and oils filled his nose and memories flooded through him. It smelled like home.

"Take off that jacket and let's get a good look at your wound."

Nate shrugged out of the jacket and Rosemary gasped. "What is that?"

Confused, Nate looked down at his arm, wondering if the wound was worse than it felt…which is when he realized she was staring in horror at his short sword, scabbarded across his back.

"You carry weapons? Here? And like that?" Rosemary's eyebrows rose in concern. She reassessed Maeve, clearly looking for signs of concealed weaponry in her clothing as well.

"A lot has changed, Mother."

Shaking her head, she walked behind a long center island to a small sink against the wall, returning with a basin and washcloth. His wound, which was indeed longer and deeper than he'd expected, hurt like a bitch now that he had time to concentrate on it. Maeve stood against the far wall and watched. For once, he was happy she wasn't chatty. He needed to work up to the impending conversation with Rosemary.

"Ow!" Nate jerked his arm out of her grasp. "That stings."

"You'll get an infection if I don't make sure it's clean. You know that." Rosemary returned to the natural pharmacy, which filled the back wall from floor to ceiling, and chose two vials of liquid stoppered with rubber corks, then snipped off a stem of aloe vera.

"Lavender for healing. Tea tree oil for scarring and disinfecting." She tore open a sterile pre-packaged needle and thread and his heart rate kicked up. "And stitches. Just for fun."

"Anesthetic?"

"I might have some clove oil over there somewhere." She left to rummage through her alphabetically arranged stash, returning with a small brown bottle. "Lucky boy."

Rosemary dropped a trail of oil beads along both sides of the wound, letting them soak into his skin before she sewed his incision closed with quick, expert stitches as he ground his teeth to dust.

Anesthetic my ass.

He'd take modern medicine over clove oil any day.

Maeve appeared unaffected by the whole scene she had orchestrated. Rosemary trimmed the excess thread and smeared the wound with aloe vera before wrapping it with a clean gauze bandage.

"Good as new."

He had to admit the cut felt better already. Once his mother had finished with all the needle sticking, that was.

Rosemary cut her eyes to Maeve. "Now, tell me why you are really here. And *what* is the lovely Maeve?"

"You might want a drink for this."

"Let's all have one. Shall we?" Rosemary put on a teapot of water to heat. She filled three tea balls with loose-leaf tea, creating a blend from several canisters and dropped the balls into three mugs before leading the way to a cozy sitting area by the fireplace.

Nate took notice of how close Maeve snugged up to the fire, sitting on the generous stone hearth, as close as she could get without singeing herself. Those long nights out in the elements were behind her and he could see her appreciation of the warmth. Still, she had walled herself off from him, from everyone, and it showed.

Hell, at least she wasn't a raving maniac here…with his mother.

Nate took the corner of the brown leather couch, sinking into it with a welcome comfort only home could provide, while Rosemary eased into a cane rocker across from him, pulling a fleece blanket across her shoulders like a shawl.

Everything in the workroom was as he remembered it. The warm yellow and red colors of the pine and cedar furniture, the milk chocolate and almond painted walls, the back wall filled with apothecary jars and vials, various other waist-high bookcases filled with ancient books. The sitting area turned storefront, from which she sold potions and curatives, was accessible through an open-arched doorway to his right. Every piece of furniture and fixture was thoughtfully placed so as not to block the flow of chi. It felt as if he'd just moved out instead of more than seven years ago.

Skylights provided most of the daytime light, which made the shop soothing and cheerful. There were several hundred people in the coven who lived in this compound full-time, and his mother was their primary healer. Sure, if things went south and more urgent medical care was needed, they'd seek out western medicine, but Rosemary was their first stop.

She was an amazing healer. Even without magic, Rosemary had a total mastery of herbs and natural medicine. Her skills had been his motivation for pursuing medicine himself. Nate had assisted her for years in the shop and on house calls when necessary. Rosemary treated everything from birthing to easing the pain of the dying. Her gifts exceeded the natural realm in ways he couldn't explain and was only now beginning to truly appreciate.

There was nothing magical in her care of his arm or the tea she brewed on the stove, but when push came to shove, Rosemary could crank up the amp-age and bring Mother Nature to her bitchy knees. He'd seen it.

Well, if anyone was in need of Rosemary's skills it was Maeve. Now all he had to do was convince them both. Screwing up his courage, he leaned forward, smoothing his wet palms over his pant legs.

"Mom…" The whistle of the teapot interrupted him and he leaned back into the couch. Maeve had only the slightest notion of what he intended to ask Rosemary to do and he had no idea how she'd react. After all, Maeve had never been on the receiving end of the sort of magic Rosemary could conjure. From what he could deduce, he was only the second person Maeve had ever shared her energy with after her transition into a reaper.

"Here you go." Rosemary handed him a steaming mug of tea. "And you, dear."

Maeve wrapped her hands around the oversized cup and brought it to her nose, drawing in a deep breath, her eyes closed as she absorbed its healing gifts. He watched as her shoulders relaxed and dropped in relief. Amazing how comforting a simple mug of tea could be.

"Chamomile?" Nate asked.

"Of course, and a few other things. A personal blend." She smiled slyly. "Now. Spill it, Nathaniel. Start with the sword."

Nate spent the next hour getting his mother up to speed, glossing over some of the dicier bits. She didn't even blink when he told her that he was actually currently living with the Authority and his new job was as their demon tracker. Then her eyebrows only rose ever so slightly when he told her about his visits to Hell and Purgatory. It wasn't the reaction he'd been expecting. Maeve remained silent during his confession, much of it new to her as well, he was certain.

He was still curious about how much she remembered, but in any case, he knew she wasn't savvy to his personal goings on the past few months and certainly not his trip to Hell.

"Well, that's quite a story. Demons? In Meridian? We'll need to fortify the protection around the compound and become more vigilant than usual. There will be a lot of visitors over the next few days and the circle will be breached regularly. Do you think anything would have followed you here? Anything…supernatural?"

"No, Mother. We came straight from the compound. Nothing has breached or even attempted to breach it since I recast the circle with all of the members of the Authority. A skill *you* taught me, by the way."

"Yes, and you were always a good student, Nate." Rosemary cast a quick look at Maeve, then back to him. "I knew you were special the first time I met you, Nate." She reached for his hand and took it in hers. "You were our gift. As soon as I read your file, the troubles you'd experienced...Well, I knew you were different. And here, we embrace that difference. Your light has always shone brighter than anyone else's. And now? Nate, your aura is beautiful. You are doing *exactly* what you were meant to do."

Nate shifted on the couch, uncomfortable with receiving her compliments in front of Maeve.

He had never before seen his mother's aura, and he noticed now how amazing and beautiful it was, filled with pinks and greens. Hers was the first pink aura he'd encountered since the change. Pink was a rare color, which represented a perfect balance between spiritual awareness and material existence. Green, of course, represented a natural healing ability.

He was proud of his mother and didn't want to do anything to disappoint her.

"Mother, before you cast a bronze statue in my honor, I need to tell you the rest of it. Maeve was possessed. Not by a demon, but by a fallen angel. I somehow managed to drive him out, but he tore her soul loose on his way out. I retrieved it and later...reinsouled her. But now..."

"Now a piece of her remains inside you."

"Yes!" Maeve spoke for the first time, startling them both.

"I knew it the second I touched you, dear Maeve. You are soulmates in the most literal sense of the word now. I'm afraid there's no undoing that. But what we can do, Maeve, if you are willing, is work on healing the damage done to you while that monster held you captive."

Maeve gave Nate a withering look.

"There's one more thing," Nate offered, rubbing the back of his neck and concentrating on the fire to avoid Rosemary's eyes and the inevitable disappointment he expected to see there. "I bound Maeve to myself with magic."

"You used black magic on her? After all she's been through?"

"It was for her own good. I was afraid she'd flash, and I wouldn't be able to protect her."

The women exchanged knowing looks and Rosemary clicked her tongue at him. "You know better than that. Are you sure it wasn't for your own protection?"

"You got that right," Maeve chimed in.

Jesus, now she decided to go all Chatty Cathy? He felt the tide turning against him, but he wouldn't unbind her, not until he was sure she was of sound mind. The only reason he'd mentioned it at all was because sooner or later his mother would see the bracelet and know what he'd done. Hell hath no fury like a mother lied to.

Especially his mother.

"Maeve, will you let me help you?"

Maybe relaxed by the tea or empowered by his mother's confident presence, Maeve nodded in surprising submission. "Yes."

"Good. Nate, go help your father. He's in the center compound working on the Yule altar. And for gods' sakes, leave that weapon here. You'll start a riot if you walk down Beltrane with that thing strapped to your back, let alone if you try to wield it. Go!"

Nate jumped up. Rosemary didn't make requests more than once. She expected to be obeyed the first time. He found himself wanting to offer words of comfort to Maeve, but was too afraid of being skinned alive in front of his mother. Maeve's look alone could peel paint off the walls.

He was so screwed.

Chapter Sixteen

Maeve sat in the bath Rosemary had run for her, the hot steamy water lapping around her throat as she sank down and breathed in the luxurious vapors of the myriad of oils and bath salts Rosemary had sprinkled into the tub. Eucalyptus, peppermint and something hot and spicy wafted up through the steam. Rosemary had said it was a cleansing bath, but more for the aura and spirit than for the body.

Either way, Maeve was onboard. It was Heavenly.

Her anger had receded to a simmer from a full boil and she felt slightly less murderous. A stab of guilt settled into her heart about cutting Nate open earlier. He did seem intent on helping her, but why was it that men always insisted on smothering you with their "help"?

So far, she'd made it just fine on her own, thank you very much. Right up until she was possessed, and that hadn't even been her fault. What reaper wouldn't have made the same call? Every one of them would have done the same and that was a freakin' fact.

The oils and salts were obviously doing their job because Maeve was so relaxed she was about three seconds from sliding beneath the surface and taking a nap. She tilted her neck from side to side until she heard the familiar cracks and pops. A deep sigh escaped her. Hell, she might even be able to get a full night's sleep…actually at night for a change.

And here, cocooned within the hum of a magic even stronger than she'd experienced at the Authority compound...she felt safe. A warning sounded deep in her subconscious, reminding her she could never be truly safe.

She'd planned to fight Nate tooth and nail until he relented and released her from his childish magical leash, but Rosemary had thrown a kink into that plan. Maeve liked the woman. A lot. If the healer could somehow help her unscramble her eggs, she was willing to at least give her the chance. Nate hadn't warned Rosemary about her poisoned energy, but Maeve would tell her before things progressed. The last thing she wanted to do was kill Nate's mom.

Although the value of Nate's life was still negotiable.

"I think you've had enough, dear. You look like you're about ready to fall asleep."

"Yes, ma'am."

Rosemary held up a fluffy white robe the likes of which Maeve had never encountered. Her first reaction was *Hell No*, but on reconsideration, it looked warm and soft. She toweled off and slid into the robe.

Good God, it feels wonderful.

Warm and soft and homey. She was so going to get her one of these to bring home with her. Then she remembered where she was supposedly living, a thirty-foot camping trailer with Nate, and the appeal evaporated. No sense getting spoiled by too much luxury. Of course, after spending most of her nights the past few months in Hell or used crypts, everything was a luxury.

As she tied the robe around her snuggly, she realized that she didn't have a headache for the first time since regaining consciousness.

That had to be a good sign, right?

Less murderous *and* no headache? Hell, she was practically cured already.

"Come along, dear."

"Maeve. You can call me Maeve."

"Thank you, dear."

Stubborn, just like her son.

Rosemary led her to a large padded table she'd set up in the workroom. Although she'd never had one before, Maeve recognized it as a portable massage table. Flipping a sheet over the table, Rosemary covered it with a fluffy fleece blanket. After adding a pillow, she indicated that Maeve should lie down.

Still feeling unsure, she climbed up onto the table and smoothed out her robe to make sure it still covered her. She'd never been comfortable with putting herself at another's mercy. Even though she was naked beneath the fluffy, girly robe, something about Rosemary inspired her trust. The warmth of the crackling fireplace, the light of its flames flickering across the walls in hypnotic patterns, and the lingering scent of the oils in her hair were all enough to draw her heavy eyelids closed as the older woman fussed around her.

"Maeve, before you fall asleep, I need to ask you a few questions. How are your memories?"

Maeve's eyes flew open and she turned to look at the woman. "Messed up. Like things are out of order. Most of my memories from the past few months, especially during the possession, are…missing. I have a few random memories of that time, but the most important things are gone. Something terrible is going to happen, but I don't know what."

"That's typical with a trauma, but I think yours is more than that. I think your chi is blocked and one or more of your chakras was damaged in the possession and subsequent exorcism."

"Have you repaired something like that before?"

"Not in cases as extensive as yours. But I'm confident it can be done."

"Will it restore my memories?"

"I would hope so, eventually."

Maeve struggled against her overwhelming fatigue. "Would we exchange energy during this process?"

"No. Not really. I'll use a crystal chakra wand to clear each of your energy gates. Why do you ask?"

"My energy is poisonous."

"Do you know this as a result of your possession?"

"No…before. I killed my brother by trying to heal him. The only other person who I've ever had an exchange with is—"

"Nate."

"Yes. How do you know that?"

"Because you and Nate are connected now. Your energies mark you like fingerprints. I knew the second I touched you both that you were bound and not just by magic. You have a bond beyond the magical or physical. Something spiritual. Yin and yang. Your very souls are entwined."

Maeve shuddered. She'd felt it, too, but refused to accept it. To be bound to a man was as good as being a prisoner.

"Can you break it? The bond?"

"I can clear your chakras, but a bond like yours can only be broken by death, however, you two are so connected now that the death of one will mean the death of the other. You, my dear, only have a partial soul remaining. I suggest you guard it well. While it cannot be fully restored, we can seat what remains more firmly into place. But I'm afraid, love it or hate it, you'll always be drawn to the missing piece." Rosemary lit candles around the room, adding to the pleasant blend of aromas, and returned with a beautiful crystal wand.

"To Nate?"

"Yes." Rosemary presented the wand before her across her open hand. "What shall it be, Maeve? Shall we restore you to fight another day?"

"Yes."

Rosemary smiled down at her, looking almost angelic with the firelight framing her hair. "Relax, my dear."

Maeve settled into the table, trying to prepare herself for whatever was to come. The crystal wand was just enough of a distraction to hold her interest. The ten-inch wand of solid crystal was bejeweled with sixteen polished stones and wrapped in copper wire. It was a work of art, crafted with care and skill, and it gleamed in the glowing light. Maeve had never seen anything like it.

"This is a powerful tool. It will amplify your energy, clear your chakras and remove any negative trace energy from your experience. The negative energy will travel through the wand and out into the universe to be absorbed. Once it's out of your body, you should begin to feel better."

Fear crept along the edges of Maeve's mind. What if her energy somehow did injure Rosemary? She wouldn't be able to live with herself.

"We'll start at your root chakra and work our way up." Rosemary held the wand horizontally above Maeve's toes and slowly passed over her legs, drawing the wand up her body to hover just across her hips. She repeated the motion six times. "Open your robe so that I may touch your skin with the wand."

Hesitantly, Maeve obeyed, unwrapping the sash and letting the fabric fall open, exposing her body in the firelight. She wasn't embarrassed in front of Rosemary, but the vulnerability was disconcerting. Like exposing your soft belly to the world.

Rosemary returned the wand to her toes and drew it back to her hips a final time, touching the end of the wand to her skin an inch below her belly button. A flood of warmth gathered, growing in intensity until it became a slow burn that coursed through her to the point of contact before dissipating. The relief was physical and immediate.

"I felt that," Maeve said, amazed that an inanimate object could elicit such a response.

"Of course, you did. But it's only the beginning." She repeated the entire process three more times. Each time she pressed the golden stone against Maeve's skin, drawing energy through her and out, the feeling was less intense, but still noticeable.

"What is that stone?"

"Citrine. It combats negative energy, breaking it up so that it can be absorbed by the universe."

"And the others?"

"Jaspar, amber, mookite, Tibetan quartz, aragonite, yellow calcite and sulphur. The copper wire conducts the energy where I direct it with the wand. It's very powerful for healing energy work. I've been saving it for a special occasion." Rosemary smiled down at her.

"How did you know it would work on me if you've never used it before?"

"Have a little faith."

Faith was something Maeve was fresh out of these days. She had faith in only what she could see and feel, but right now, she could definitely feel something happening.

Rosemary rested the wand horizontally over her hips, right at her belly button and drew the wand up slightly toward her lower rib cage. At the end of the seventh pass, she placed the golden citrine against her skin and the negative energy fled her body.

"The sacral chakra is clear."

Next she moved a hands width above Maeve's belly button and began again. This time her breathing became more difficult, escaping her in quick, short pants.

"Breath slowly. Concentrate on your air coming in and going out, or you'll hyperventilate." Maeve tried to follow her directions, though it was difficult to fend off her panic.

"The solar plexus chakra is clear."

Moving through the chakras, Rosemary repeated the process over and over, working her way across Maeve's exposed body, inch by inch, explaining as she went: heart chakra, throat chakra, brow chakra. Each chakra elicited its own uncomfortable sensation before giving her relief, until only one remained.

"The last is your crown chakra, the largest. First I'm going to stimulate it with massage, then we'll clear it." Rosemary stood behind Maeve and placed her hands on her head. Working her fingers through her hair, she gently massaged her scalp and Maeve resisted the urge to purr.

How could such a simple thing feel so good?

Several minutes later, Rosemary stopped and left Maeve's scalp a quivering and tingling mess. Her vision blurred and for a moment she worried she might pass out. Rosemary walked to the end of the massage table and held the wand above her feet once again.

"I'll do several complete passes, ending at the crown chakra to ensure we've cleared all your negative energy. A clear crown chakra should allow your thoughts and memories to reorganize over time. Don't expect it to be immediate. You'll have to be patient. It *will* take time."

"Something tells me we don't have much time, Doc, but let's get on with it."

Rosemary drew the wand horizontally across her body, gathering the last residual negative energy toward the top of Maeve's head. The purge was an internal stretch and contraction as the energy wrenched upward in a long, slow burn, leaving a tingly residue in its wake.

As Rosemary passed the last cleared chakra with the wand, Maeve watched her. The wand started to shake so much that the healer was forced to grasp it with both hands. Pressure built throughout Maeve's body and she began to shake as well. The wand ignited with a brilliant violet light and she could hear the hum of growing power. Maeve's body tensed, her skin suddenly shrunken and tight. Pain sliced through her head with an intensity that threatened to blow her scalp off. Gripping the edges of the table, Maeve held on and willed the pain to subside as she pulled her legs up as close to her chest as she could against the agony, trying not to scream. The table shook beneath her and she watched as bottles danced their way toward the edge of their shelves against the back wall.

"Almost there!" Rosemary spread her legs for balance and held onto the wand for dear life as she muscled it the final three inches behind Maeve's head. An incantation accompanied Rosemary's efforts, but it was in a language Maeve didn't understand. As her recitation increased, so did the pressure building inside Maeve's body. Certain her insides were about to be torn from her body, she wrenched her neck around like a puppet on a string, helpless to look away from Rosemary's efforts.

The wand shattered in Rosemary's hands and the quartz fragmented to powder, the stones clinking to the floor then rolling away. Maeve lay panting on the table as Rosemary collapsed to the floor.

Chapter Seventeen

Nate stacked logs onto the Yule bonfire in preparation for the upcoming ceremony. As he walked back for yet another bundle of wood from one of the nine pickup trucks parked in a line along Samhain Street, the tattoos encircling his biceps flamed to life. All of them. A powerful magic had been unleashed within the coven, and he had a pretty good idea who was responsible for it.

"Dad—"

"Go. I'm right behind you."

He dropped the wood and they raced down Beltrane to the healing center. Certain that they wouldn't be the only ones to sense the echoes of the magical release, Nate needed to make sure Maeve was out of sight before the lookey-lous arrived. Magic strong enough to leave a wake required pre-approval by the Coven Board, which, of course, Rosemary hadn't requested.

Lucky for them that Garrett, Nate's father, was a board member.

Nate burst through the arched doorway first, immediately catching sight of Maeve splayed across a massage table, semi-naked once again. She moaned softly, clutching at her head.

"Shit," Nate cursed.

Rosemary lay on the floor unconscious beneath the table, covered in a fine white dust. He pulled Maeve's robe closed over her, tied the sash in a hasty knot, then bent to exam his mother.

Alive.

Thank God.

"Rosemary!" Garrett rushed to Rosemary's side and scooped his wife into his arms. He looked at Nate. "Go. I'll help your mother. Get the girl out of sight before the others arrive with their questions."

Nate lifted Maeve from the table and clutched her to his chest. Her eyes were closed, but she was breathing, her face twisted in a tight grimace of pain. Without resistance, he carried her to the staircase and down into the basement to his old room. Tapping the light on with his elbow, he made his way down and into his past.

Nothing had changed down here. Rosemary had left it just as he had...a teenage nightmare. Posters of Megadeath, Ozzy Osbourne, Metallica, Judas Priest and more adorned every square inch of one wall, while his charcoal pencil drawings lined another.

Damn, he'd been in a dark place back then. Looking at his drawings now, Nate marveled that his mother hadn't at least taken them down and stuck them in the bottom of a drawer somewhere. Of course, she was most likely the only one who ever came down here anymore. The one intrusion was the treadmill she used when the weather was too bad to walk outside.

Nate eased Maeve down onto the bed, her eyes still closed. Her expression was no longer pained, but she laid still as the dead. He clicked on the small bedside lamp and flicked off the harsh overhead bulb, casting the room in a warm glow. Arranging her on the full-sized bed, he brushed her damp hair off her face and a turquoise trickle of energy arced between them. He disengaged quickly, fearful of drawing further attention to them from upstairs. He pulled her robe over her long pale legs.

He sat stroking her hair, wondering who he would find when she opened her eyes once more. Upstairs, he heard the first raised voices. Passionate inquiries sounded through his ceiling as the hum of power finally dissipated from the building.

The sound of his mother's voice reassured him, and after nearly an hour of heated discussion, the energy shifted and he knew his parents were alone in the living quarters upstairs.

A soft knock on the door brought him to his feet.

"Nate?" Garrett opened the door and peeked down the stairs.

"Dad. Is Mother okay?"

"She'll be fine. She's resting. Probably will be for the rest of the night. She wanted me to tell you to keep Maeve hydrated and stay with her. She'll talk to both of you more in the morning."

"Dad...I'm sorry."

"Nonsense. She didn't do anything she didn't want to do. We'll deal with the Coven Board. Take care of your girl. Good night."

"Good night."

Nate didn't bother correcting his father that Maeve was his partner, not his girl.

Definitely not his girl.

They'd missed dinner. Food would help revive them both and she did need to stay hydrated, but a few hours of sleep at this point seemed like the best course of action. Besides, Rosemary would be up and cooking before sunrise. He was sure of it.

The basement was colder than he'd remembered. He rummaged through the top of his closet, pulling down a fleece and a wool blanket. Maeve had pulled her body into a tight little ball against the cold and rolled against the wall, leaving just enough room for him to lie beside her. Debating the merits of sharing a bed with her again, his exhaustion overtook his honor. He reached for his scabbard and slid it under his bed, well out of her reach, just in case she woke before him. If she wanted the weapon, she'd have to retrieve it over his live body. A task, even in her misguided fury, he didn't think she was up to just yet.

Lying on top of the wool blanket, he pulled the fleece over both of them and struggled to find a comfortable position next to her without actually touching her on his small sliver of mattress space.

Impossible.

Relenting, he slid his right arm into the C-shaped bow of Maeve's curved body and pulled her back and hips against him. She fit against him like a puzzle piece even with the wool barrier between them. He rested his face against the back of her head and inhaled her delicious aroma.

She smelled so good. Like clean earthy spices.

He left the lamp on, worrying that if she awoke in the dark she might think she was in a crypt again. His heart gunned in his chest as he tried to calm his emotions. With rest, he could share energy with her tomorrow and perhaps aid in her recovery.

Tomorrow.

Tomorrow was December 21—Yule. It was crazy that he was here, back with the Coven during this time of renewal and resolutions. He had more than a few resolutions he'd be offering. Yule was the longest night of the year, and during this darkest time of year, there was a chance to start over.

If anyone deserved a do-over, it was Maeve.

He sent up a silent prayer to whoever might be listening and pressed a kiss against the back of her head, drawing her in tighter. Damn she felt good curled up against him, even if she was currently unconscious.

He knew it wouldn't last.

As soon as she awoke, she'd be back to wanting to Ginsu his ass, no doubt. How long would they need to stay here? Would this one session be enough to set Maeve firmly on the road to recovery? He knew Deacon would be going bat-shit crazy after the way he'd disappeared with Maeve. But, hell. If he'd discussed his plan with him beforehand, he would have found a million reasons why it wouldn't work. Why he needed Nate now more than ever.

Dude had been relying on him to be his wingman for way too long. Besides, Maeve needed him more than Deacon did right now. Even if she didn't want him.

His heart skipped a beat.

This was all such bullshit. He hadn't asked for any of this. Didn't *want* any of this. Well, most of this. And he sure as hell didn't ask to be special in any way.

Vanilla human was looking better and better.

But that ship had sailed and sank. Years ago, if he was being honest with himself.

Being honest with himself typically ended with him wanting to rip the head off something. The imps guarding the gates of Hell sprang to mind. Very satisfying to dismember he was sure. What he wouldn't give to take out some frustration on one of the little bastards right now.

Shit. Maybe Deacon was right. Maybe he did need to be back out there hunting demons. If he could have tracked down even one of Maeve's family members, maybe he would have left her with them.

He was starting to understand why Kylen got off so hard on the demon hunting bit. If dealing with these damn women was going to continue to be this frustrating and gut-wrenching, something had to give or he was going to implode.

Maeve shifted, mumbling in her sleep.

Burying his face into her hair, he pressed his lips against her ear and whispered, "I've got you, Maeve."

He prayed it was true.

Chapter Eighteen

Ruth was about to go insane with Deacon's incessant pacing. She and Olivia had explained to him over and over again what Nate had said when he left with Maeve, and still Deacon wasn't listening. While there was no doubt he was hearing the words, they were not the words he *wanted* to hear.

She knew that the situation in Meridian was dire, but Nate hadn't taken the reaper oath. Deacon wasn't really his boss. The man had free will and had exercised it for God's sake. And for the benefit of another reaper, no less.

If Deacon didn't get some sleep, he'd be in no shape to go out again tonight. Even with his enhanced powers, the man hadn't transitioned into an angel yet. He was still a reaper. Mostly. Without at least occasional refueling and sleep, he'd wear down. Sure, it would take much longer than it would with the other reapers, but it *could* happen.

Ruth was determined to make sure that it didn't.

Nate hadn't even been gone twenty-four hours and one would have thought he'd died by the way Deacon was going on. She was worried for Nate, as well. Her stomach did a little flip every time she thought about any of them going outside of the reaper compound. Here, she knew they were safe. On the outside? Anything was possible.

What Deacon was failing to see was that Nate obviously had feelings for Maeve that went beyond their partnership. Men were so obtuse sometimes, refusing to see what was in front of their eyes.

Forest for the trees.

Bo was even more pathetic. He was lying at the foot of her bed, his watermelon-sized head resting on his plate-sized paws. If that dog sighed forlornly one more time, she was going to go postal. She was wound as tight as a fishing reel.

"Why didn't he at least take his damn phone?" Deacon paced at the end of the bed, holding the offending device in his hand.

"Probably because he knew you'd use it to track him. He doesn't want to be found, Deacon. He's doing the right thing. They'll be back as soon as they can."

"We need everyone on this mission before Camael has time to recoup and, God forbid, find another reaper."

"Nate will be useless until Maeve is safe. What if all of that had happened to me? What would you have done?"

"That's different."

"It's the same, Deacon. Open your eyes. Open your heart. You've been so focused on the demons that you're missing what's happening right here. Life goes on whether the world is falling to hell or not. Love finds a way."

"Woman, what the hell are you talking about?"

"Nate is in love with Maeve."

"He's just worried about his partner."

"Men are so dense. Think about it, Deacon. He's acting out of something much stronger than concern for her as a partner."

Deacon stopped pacing and stared at her, letting the pieces click into place one by one. The *aha* look on his face was comical.

"Finally." Ruth laughed. "You hear something I'm saying."

"This is bad."

"No. This is good. What's the point of all of this fighting without hope, without love? You're fighting to protect who and what you love, and helping mankind do the same. Even if they have no idea what's going on. Nate's not doing anything different."

Deacon sat on the edge of their bed and snuggled up next to her, raising her gown to rest his face against her rounded belly. She ran her fingers through his unkempt hair.

"The reapers around here are dropping like flies for women."

Ruth laughed. "Three out of ten? Four if Maeve complies. Of course, Nate's not officially a reaper."

"He will be. Rashnu approved it. I was going to tell him when I got back, but…"

"What if he doesn't want to be a reaper, Deacon? What if he just wants to live his life and be done with all of this?"

"Until the demons are put down, that's not a choice that's available to any of us."

"Isn't it? Isn't it all about choices?"

"Woman, you are wearing me out. Is there another girl inside here who'll bust my chops?" Deacon caressed his hand across her abdomen.

"God never gives us more than we can handle, right?"

Deacon looked at her and shook his head with a slight smile. "You've been brushing up on the Good Book?"

"All I have is time on my hands, Deacon. I figured I'd read the rule book so you didn't have to."

"How did you get to be so smart?"

"Good genes maybe? Of course, I'll never know if you don't help me follow up on some more of the leads I've found for Elaina Carter. Did you even hear me when I told you I dug up a local lead?"

"How local?"

"Very local. One mention of an estate sale in the Bolton, Arkansas newspaper twenty-seven years ago. Bolton's only thirty minutes away, Deacon."

"Don't they usually have an estate sale after someone dies?"

"Often, but there's no corresponding death record in the State."

"Birth record?"

"Who knows? I have no idea which Elaina Carter she might have been. But the time frame—"

"Do you have an address for the estate that was sold?"

"Yes. 337 Birch Street, Bolton, AR."

"I'll check it out for you on my way home tomorrow. I promise."

Deacon pulled her in close and she melted against him. His hands began to wander and he buried his face in against her neck, burrowing into her hair and kissing his way down her chest. Shooting a glance to the corner of the room where Temperance stood guard, she tightened and pushed him away.

"What?"

She nodded to the corner.

Deacon smiled. The angel was like furniture to him. Another example of his lack of attention on the home front these days. "Temperance, a little privacy here, please. You can fulfill your duty from the other side of the door."

With the angel equivalent of a huff, Temperance faded and disappeared. Ruth heard her settle against the outside of the thin accordion folding door that separated their bedroom from the rest of the trailer.

"Thank you." She gave Deacon an appreciative kiss.

"You're welcome. How thankful are you?"

"Very."

Chapter Nineteen

When Nate awoke, he was entangled with Maeve, both of them wrapped in the wool blanket and most of the fleece one as well. Radiating body heat, her face was nestled against his chest, the top of her head just under his chin.

She fit against him like the yin to his yang.

Before he could settle his inner debate about whether he should slip away undetected or face the music, Maeve's green eyes opened and bore into him. He tried to read the emotion behind them and predict which Maeve would appear this morning, but it was a game his heart couldn't bear.

Her features gentled and he couldn't stop his hand from cupping her face. When she didn't strike out at him, he smoothed his thumb back and forth across her cheekbone. Emboldened, he pulled her in even closer, wrapping his arms around her, trying to physically project what was in his heart.

"Rosemary?" Maeve asked, her voice meek and unsure.

"She's fine. Nothing to worry about."

Her shoulders shuddered and he felt a ripple move through her, followed by a heavy sigh. Her relief was palpable. Maeve pushed back from his hold and unraveled herself from the bedding, sitting up and pulling her robe tight across her chest. She curled her legs underneath her and leaned against the wall, keeping her gaze on him until he began to feel squirmy beneath her scrutiny.

Was she sizing him up for her next attempt at an escape or worse? She didn't seem up to terroristic endeavors just yet, but then again…the element of surprise wasn't a half bad battle strategy.

She leaned forward and Nate braced himself for her attack. Her palms flattened across his chest and she lowered her face to his, searing his soul with her penetrative gaze. Two more inches and their lips would be touching. He banished the thought, but then her lips parted and she slid her tongue across them, making them slick and glossy.

"Thank you, Nate."

He swallowed hard as she held him there, capturing his undivided attention.

So many possible responses came to mind, but he was confident that nothing forming in his head was even remotely appropriate. Or wanted.

"You're welcome."

She rolled her body over his and landed on her feet on the other side of the bed. Her clean black hair fell down her back in a sleep-ruffled pane. When he remembered to breathe, he stretched his own legs over the side and sat on the edge of the bed, watching her take in the sight of his teenage bedroom.

When she turned back to look at him, finished with her circumspect examination, a smile curled across her face. "Someone had a hard on for eighties' metal bands."

He coughed and then laughed. "*Had* is the operative word. I was an angry kid. Lots of angst."

She walked over to the wall papered in his drawing collection, touching one particularly disturbing work—a drawing of an angel consumed in fire.

"Prescient much?"

"They don't mean anything."

Maeve studied them more closely, pulling several from the wall then rearranging them. She pushed the tack into the last one and stepped back to survey her work.

"And now?"

Nate walked up behind her and stared at the wall. He'd drawn most of these ten, fifteen years ago. A chill built behind his ribs and filled his body. At least half of the drawings depicted roughly the last six months of his life, and the rest? He didn't want to dwell on what the rest could mean. His visit to Rashnu flashed through his mind, both paths still crystal clear in his memory. Hell, they were all here. On his wall. He'd just never seen it until now.

Nate moved the drawings again, tacking them so that they laid out the two separate paths Rashnu had revealed to him.

His mouth went dry. "Shit."

"Yeah."

She turned to him. "You don't look so hot."

"I'm fine." Her robe distracted him from the drawings. It was disturbing how easily he could lose his mind around her. "You need some clothes."

"That would be nice, yes."

Her apparent calm threw him. He was pretty sure his current conversation was with Dr. Jekyll, but he wondered how far away Ms. Hyde might be.

"I left my backpack upstairs. Olivia gave me some stuff for you. I'll go up and get it, and make sure everything is okay, then I'll be back. Stay here until I come for you. Please."

She nodded. Nate turned to leave, then remembered his scabbard under the bed. Keeping his eyes on Maeve, he reached underneath and pulled it free. He strapped it on before slipping his jacket over it.

"Planning on being attacked on the way upstairs?" she asked, her eyes filled with mischief.

His lips thinned, unsure how to respond. He opened his mouth and then shut it again. He shook his head in frustration.

He walked back up the stairs, shutting the door behind him and eyeing the bolt at the top of it. He could lock her in. Rosemary had insisted that Garrett add the bolt because she was worried about kids, visiting the shop with their parents, falling down the stairs. It seemed like a particularly good idea at the moment, but he'd already abused Maeve's trust with his binding spell.

No need to add fuel to the fire.

***

Maeve let out a sigh of relief.

God, the tension was going to kill her before Rosemary's voodoo at this rate. That man felt like a ticking time bomb. She was grateful to have a few minutes alone to get herself together. Amazed, she realized she felt good. Really good.

Maybe seventy-five percent good.

Hell, the fact she hadn't snuffed Nate's mom was bonus number two.

Whatever mojo Rosemary had used on her had left her feeling lighter and stronger. Her pre-possession memories seemed to have realigned to an acceptable level. Deacon, Ruth and the reaper compound...*Nate*. She remembered all of it. It was the post-possession memories that were still a black hole. Nothing that she could decipher from what was left of those mangled memories seemed even remotely usable in its current configuration.

Three missing months.

Arguably, the three most important months if the gnawing in her gut was any indication.

She was still plenty hot about the binding spell, but she had to admit that Nate seemed to be on a mission to help her. Maybe it was a good thing she hadn't actually hurt him. Even she knew her efforts so far had been half-hearted.

The damned truth was that he was beginning to feel like family.

God help him.

She studied the drawings again, leaning in for a better look at the closest one. The image, which she'd missed earlier, nearly took her to her knees.

It couldn't be.

Combing through the other pages, she searched for a repeat of the figure, but she only saw it once.

It was a drawing of a woman surrounded by fire, her head sitting askew at her feet. The black and white image was drawn in charcoal pencil, but the woman looked disturbingly like her.

***

Nate followed his nose to the kitchen. The intensity of Rosemary and Garrett's conversation at the table in the kitchen stopped him in his tracks just out of sight of his parents.

"You need to tell him," Garrett implored

"No. He's not ready."

"You're the one who's not ready, Rosemary. We should have told him years ago. Before he moved out."

"I was hoping…"

"You were hoping it wouldn't manifest. Clearly, it has…and more. And the girl…"

"Her name is Maeve, Garrett."

"She's down there now. You don't think *she'll* figure it out? Who do you want him to hear it from? His mother or a stranger?"

"Blessed be, I wish he could hear it from his mother."

"You know it has to be done before he leaves. I'll keep the Coven Board at bay, but for the gods' sakes and his, don't wait any longer. You made a promise. Now, pass the bacon, please."

Nate backed down the hallway and found his backpack in the main living area. After picking it up, he hesitated. Of course, he wanted to know exactly what they were talking about, but a part of him knew that as soon as the answers he wanted were revealed, there would be no going back. For the first time in months he'd managed to sleep a full eight hours. He felt safe here at home and newly confident in his ability to keep Maeve from harm. Even if it was only for one more day or a few more hours, he was going to accept that comfort. Then he'd demand to know what they were keeping from him before he dove back into the battle.

Tonight he'd take Maeve to the Yule festival, and then he'd get his answers from her, as well. One thing was for certain. When he left this compound, nothing would be the same.

Chapter Twenty

Nate led Maeve down Beltane Street, away from the Yule festivities and toward the edge of the community. Preparations were still under way and the main event wouldn't begin until well after dark. He hoped he had enough daylight left to show Maeve around before the festival kicked into full gear. Darkness would be a blessing. The fewer people who noticed Maeve and asked questions, the better, and since most of them had already gathered at the hub of the compound for the pre-ritual feast, the streets were deserted.

The icy wind cut through his too light jacket. At least walking warmed him enough to stave off most of the physical discomfort, and the bonfire tonight would chase even that away.

Maeve had seemed much better today. Downright agreeable even. She'd spent the majority of the day sleeping on and off in front of the fire at his parents' house. She hadn't talked much, answering direct questions and little else. Still, he could sense a change in her. She was coming back together. Whatever Rosemary had done to her had worked—at least partially.

"Aren't we heading the wrong way for the party?"

"I wanted to show you around first."

"A tour? And meeting your parents? I had no idea you were so...old-fashioned."

Nate shook his head. Of course, her sarcasm would be the first thing to fully return. "Do you want to go or not?"

"Don't get your boxers in a wad. I'm still walking, aren't I?"

Stuffing his hands into his jacket pockets, he led her past a variety of now closed shops: the Witch Way Café, his mother's aptly named Hands of Healing Center, the Ritual Majik supply store, Dell's Grocery & Convenience Center, a small library and an auto repair shop. Beltane was the commercial spoke of their community wheel.

"How many people live here?"

"Around four hundred full-time. During festivals like tonight, it swells to more than a thousand."

"Seems pretty self-sufficient."

"It is. There's a school along Lammas Street and even a worship pavilion at the end of Ostara Street."

"A church?"

"A place to be close to nature in a worshipful way. No one here would call it a church. Everyone who lives here practices Wiccan in some form or another. Most full-time residents are here so that they can be immersed in the practice and lifestyle. They enjoy being surrounded by like-minded people."

"And you? Why did you leave?"

Nate held back a secret smile, pleased that Maeve seemed interested in his history and home.

"I was adopted. Garrett and Rosemary brought me into the coven when I was five. Even here I was different. When I found an opportunity to leave, I did. It's been a while since I came back."

"Bad memories?"

"No. Not really. The coven was great to me for the most part. I just wanted…"

"To find your own place in the world."

Nate stopped walking and turned to her. The wind picked up the tips of her hair and whipped it across her face. He wanted to brush it aside, but didn't.

"Yes."

"Hmm." Maeve walked ahead of him toward the permanent Beltane altar at the end of the street.

"Speaking of bad memories. How are yours? How do you feel?"

"Witch, you are full of surprises. Now you want to talk about feelings? Are you sure you're not gay?"

"Hardly."

A wary smile etched its way across her face and she looked away first.

"I think my deck has reshuffled. Everything before Camael's reaper reign seems solid in my mind now."

"And after?"

She picked up a phallic shaped candle and raised her eyebrows at him in question.

"What can I say? Beltane is a fertility festival. Some witches have a sense of humor."

Maeve laughed and carefully placed the candle back on the wooden altar. "You have some strange parties, witch."

"Wait until you see the rest of the altars. Our community is laid out like the Wheel of the Year. At the end of each spoke, or in this case street, on the rim is a permanent altar in honor of each Sabbat of Wicca. This is of course Beltane."

"So how many more are there?

"Seven. Litha, Lammas, Mabon, Samhain, Yule, Imbolc, Ostara. We'd better hurry. It's a little over a mile around the outside of the compound. It will take a good half hour to see them all."

He waited for her to catch up. "Are you cold?"

"A little."

Nate took off his jacket, even though he was freezing his ass off, and spread it over her shoulders. He was glad he'd left his scabbard and sword at home. Having visible weapons at the festival would not have gone over well with the Coven Board. The blades hidden under his jeans and strapped along his calves would have to suffice, although the thought of demon trouble in this well-fortified magical fortress was unconscionable.

She slid her arms into the jacket and zipped it up. "This doesn't mean we're going steady or anything. Right, Richie?"

"Richie?"

"You know, *Happy Days*? Don't you get cable out here?"

"How do you have time for television?"

"You never heard of a DVR? Besides, you make time for the Retro Television Network. Gotta have something to look forward to."

"Isn't that a little too...wholesome for you?"

"What's that supposed to mean? I'm practically drowning in wholesome." She plunged her hands into the jacket pockets and hunched her shoulders against the cold.

"Uh huh."

"I think you have the wrong idea about me."

"I hope not."

"Hoping for some corruption were you? I have a code, too, Mr. Squeaky Clean."

"What? I think you have the wrong impression of *me*. "

"Touche."

They walked to Litha Street without talking. This was not going as he'd planned. Talking to Maeve was harder than talking to Kylen. At least she was better looking. A *lot* better looking.

Good God, he felt thirteen around her.

Maeve picked up a tiger's eye gemstone from the Litha altar. "Pretty."

"An offering to the gods and goddesses for a bountiful summer harvest. And it represents how thankful we are for our many blessings."

"Do you feel blessed, Nate?" Studying the gem that was nestled in her palm, she ran her thumb back and forth over it.

"I'm thankful that you seem to be on the road to recovery."

"Then maybe I owe *you* an offering since you're the one who saved me."

Nate held his breath. He'd never known what to expect from Maeve before the possession, and now she was a complete wildcard. She had reset to the Maeve he'd known, though briefly, before the possession. He was hesitant to scare this new Maeve away...and equally desperate to hold on to her.

She closed the distance between them and looked up. Hesitant, he waited to see what she would do next. Without making him wait, she slid her hands behind his neck and pulled his face down to hers. When she pressed her lips to his, his arms wrapped around her in response, drawing her against his body.

A pulse of energy coursed through him like a spark of static electricity, but he didn't stop. He couldn't. Nate threaded his hands through Maeve's hair and deepened the kiss, desperate to secure the connection he could no longer deny.

Maeve moaned against his mouth, her cold hands sliding under his shirt and up his back, her nails digging into him as she clutched him to her body. Their energies combined, surging through them, binding them beyond Reiki or magic. With a gasp, Maeve pulled away, her eyes wide, round and glowing with turquoise light.

"What are you doing to me?" she whispered, backing away from him. "I saw…"

"What? Did you remember something?"

"Something terrible is going to happen, Nate."

"What? When?"

"I don't know. I just see pieces. Memories—or maybe thoughts—from Camael. I don't know which. Maybe it's already happened. But when we kissed, the pieces began to realign in my head. Now they're gone again."

Nate stared at her, confident he was about to be slapped for his next action. He pulled her to him and crushed his mouth to hers, letting her body draw energy from him. When she leaned back into him, it was his turn to falter.

Shared images filled his mind, a tumble of Maeve's and his own. It was impossible to determine which belonged to whom. Many of them were familiar, but others were not.

The flutter he'd sensed inside him earlier returned, drawn out by Maeve's life force, by her very soul, and demanded the connection be made. Energy built between them as they fed on each other's light, the exchange fueling their mental slideshow.

Maeve pulled away first. Nate held her shoulders, steadying her face as she recovered.

"That was some kiss." She shrugged away from his hands and stared out toward the woods, now completely dark under the canopy. "Who is the girl? Consumed by fire? You know, the one in the drawing in your room."

"I don't know."

"Is it me?"

"How could it be you? I drew it fifteen years ago."

"How can any of this be happening? You should be dead after that little episode. You know that my light is poison."

"Maybe what happened to your brother was a fluke. Maybe he had a defect that went undetected or it was some strange combination of circumstances that could never happen again?"

"I don't think so. He was strong. I'm the one with the defect."

He stepped closer to her, taking her elbow and turning her to face him. "You're not defective. In any way. Maybe you're damaged from your time with Camael, but you've never been defective, never will be either."

"That's what my parents said." Maeve picked at a dried sunflower head on the Litha altar, avoiding his eyes. "But it still didn't bring back my brother."

"What happened with your family, Maeve? After your brother died, I mean."

"Nothing was the same. They forgave me and told me it was an accident of some sort, but they were afraid for me. I couldn't stand their pity. I ran away for a while and tried the normal human things. Even went to college for a semester. It didn't work out. Death was everywhere and once you've actuated to reaper, you can't deny the pull. At least I couldn't."

"You went back?"

"Yes. My parents had passed while I was gone. I didn't even know until I returned. I finished training and threw myself into the work. I was careful, but no one wanted to be around me. Not after my brother...after Jacob died. Work is all I have."

"Not anymore."

Maeve frowned. "Don't we have some more altars to visit?"

Chapter Twenty-One

The hub was packed with witches and it hummed with the cumulative magic of a gathering of so many. There were more than a thousand witches and family members along the outside rim of the hub. It was the largest turnout Nate had ever seen.

He led Maeve back to stand near the Beltane Street entrance. They'd visited all eight altars, taking just enough time for the tour that they could blend in with the Yule crowd in the darkness. He led her to a vantage point where she could still see, but they could still make a quick escape back home when the ceremony was over. Of course, some participants would stay until sunrise. Nate wasn't feeling all that committed to the cause this year.

Harland West, the coven's High Priest, ascended the podium. The P.A. system, a modern concession to their coven's growth, crackled with static and feedback.

"Is this thing on?"

The crowd laughed and Harland continued.

"Welcome, on this longest night of the year. We gather to celebrate Yule, the festival rejoicing our lives, families and blessings. Having you all here is visual evidence of those many blessings. Tonight we'll cleanse ourselves of the old, the negative and the impure, and embrace this as an opportunity for renewal, regeneration and hope. Let us cast our circle, including all who are present in its hold. Then we'll light the Bonfire of the Sacred Woods and send our thanks to the gods and goddesses. Join hands."

Nate chuckled at the sheer dynamics of more than a thousand people holding hands in the tight space, but he took Maeve's in his and they added themselves to the developing chain. Her skin was cold against his. He smiled when she tucked both of their hands into the pocket of his jacket, which she still wore. Somehow he'd forgotten about the cold, finding it difficult to concentrate on anything other than Maeve's immediate presence and his memory of kissing her.

Despite the bizarre complications of those kisses, he found himself wanting more. This party couldn't be over quick enough to please him.

Harland tapped the mike again, sending more waves of feedback rippling through the crowd. The man was ancient, well into his eighties, and it was clear technology wasn't his strong point. But he was also a fount of Wiccan knowledge and had led the coven for the last decade, an admirable feat.

"Let us cast." Harland held up a candle and lit it, giving it to a young boy, who would carry to its ceremonial location. "Guardians of the East, I call upon you to watch over the rites of this Eternal Light Coven…"

Nate felt a shift in the air as the circle was cast and it became a visible presence. He wondered if anyone else could see or if it was a result of his own transformation.

The circle surrounded the hub, sliding along a permanent indention in the ground that had come from years of casting this spell in the same location.

The circle complete, Harland chose a log from the small pile beside him.

"Tonight we burn the nine sacred woods in this first ritual fire of the new year. Birch, for rebirth and regeneration." He tossed the log onto the eight-foot high pile, and then picked up another log from his stash. "Rowan for personal power and success. Ash for divination. Alder for spiritual decisions. Willow for protection. Hawthorn for cleansing. Oak for strength and good fortune. Holly for good luck and safety for your family. Hazel for wisdom." He tossed the last log onto the bonfire.

"Nine woods in the fire be. All once were of living tree. Burn them quick or burn them slow. To each here may blessings go."

Four chosen pyromancers ignited torches and placed them at the base as the stack. When it caught fire, the first tendrils of smoke rose into the clear night sky. The group watched in silent meditation for nearly an hour before attendants returned to the fire and tossed in a small packet. Purple flames danced up out of the fire and floated into the air, flickering into the night. A few minutes later, another was tossed in and the flames turned turquoise.

Maeve squeezed his hand. "It's beautiful."

"Yes."

A few people began to wander about, greeting friends, but the crowd remained thick, most of the guests opting to stay within the circle. Nate pulled Maeve toward the fire. As the most supernatural beings present, chances were good that they were the only two who couldn't physically leave the circle until it was broken.

"What are we doing?" Maeve asked.

Nate pulled a folded bandana from the back pocket of his jeans. "If we collect ashes from the edge and you sleep with them under your pillow, you'll receive dreams of guidance for the coming year."

"God knows I could use that."

"We both could."

They made their way to the fire and Nate picked up a shovel from the edge of the podium. Once Harland gave a nod of approval, he scooped a shovel full of ashes from the edge of the burned down pile. After gathering a half-dollar sized amount from the shovel with his hand, he carefully folded the ashes into the bandana and laid the shovel on the ground. A line had formed behind him of others who apparently intended to do the same thing. Tucking the bandana into his front pocket, Nate reached for Maeve's hand and led her back to Beltane Street.

Harland's voice sounded one last time over the speaker system as he cleared the cast circle. Nate and Maeve stepped past the perimeter and headed home. He kept her hand in his while they made their way back to the Hands of Healing Center and his basement bedroom.

Maeve yawned.

"It was a long day for you." Nate kept his eyes trained forward, trying not to stare at her even though that's all he wanted to do.

"Not a bad one, though. It's been nice to relax. I'd say I can't remember the last time I got to relax, but that might not be the best excuse."

"My mother's treatment was very thorough. Being cleansed of that much negative energy takes its toll. A larger one than can be overcome by a few good hours of sleep. Maybe I should share some more energy with you."

The corner of Maeve's mouth curved up into a sly smile. "Are you propositioning me, Nate Blackburn?"

"I guess that depends on your answer." Nate could feel the blush creep up his neck and across his face. He hoped she didn't notice.

"I wouldn't hate it."

***

Maeve was nervous. Which was just wrong. Nate turned her all squishy and soft inside. *Dangerous.* What was she playing at with him anyway? The guy had to be confused—she was attacking him one moment and teasing him sexually the next. Maybe she was brain damaged after all. How long could she keep using that excuse?

Her mind—what was left of it—told her to leave it alone.

But her body was saying, "Hell, yeah."

Her experience with men so far had been limited to 100 percent humans. All of three of them. She figured there was zero chance that humans could draw energy from her unexpectedly. Based on what she'd gathered through observation, reapers were another matter—they had a way of inadvertently tapping into you and mainlining on your mojo.

After her brother's death, she'd proceeded with the utmost caution. Even thought about dropping off the map completely, but the call of her destiny had been undeniable. Besides, it was the one job where she didn't have to worry about killing anyone. Her clientele was already dead.

Following Nate into the house, her heart kicked up its pace and her hand grew sweaty in his. Every fiber of her being told her to stop. If she followed him down to that basement, things were going to happen. Things that couldn't be undone.

She went anyway.

Her body betrayed her old inhibitions. Life was short and uncertain, even for a reaper, as had been evidenced by the past few months. She liked Nate. A lot. Moreover, her body responded to him in a way she couldn't explain. The energy between them was beyond anything she'd ever experienced. The mere fact that he was still alive after their numerous exchanges, both the casual and intense sharing, and seemed to even crave her light was enough to convince her to take what she wanted.

The house was quiet, the only sound was the crackling of the dying fire in the fireplace as they walked past. Garrett and Rosemary were still at the bonfire. She hadn't had sex as a teenager, but she imagined this was how it would have felt like to sneak into her boyfriend's room past his parents.

Maybe that was part of the allure of Nate. His whole family values vibe was something she hadn't experienced in a long, long time. Her extended family had scattered to the ends of the earth after the death of her brother. Her own parents had retired, passing on soon after the incident, while she was still away from home, trying to forget about what had happened. Reaper families tended to dissolve quickly even under the best circumstances. That was one of the reasons the Authority compound setup had seemed so odd to her. They'd made their own family there. Maybe a family of your own choosing was better anyway.

She was thinking too much. If she kept this up, she'd bail out. Maybe she was trying to talk herself out of it.

Hell.

Nate flipped the light on at the top of the stairs and pulled her in after him.

Out of the frying pan and into the fire.

Chapter Twenty-Two

Nate couldn't believe Maeve was still agreeing to this. He wanted her.

Bad.

Their kisses today had only fueled his desire for her. The more he touched her, the more he craved her, but he also feared at any moment she would change her mind.

His mind was a jumble of emotions. On the one hand he was sure he should go slow with her, but on the other, there was no telling how many tomorrows there might be. He wasn't going to waste another day with indecision.

Nate turned on the bedside lamp and switched off the overhead lights. He sat on the edge of his bed and stared at her.

"Come here."

Maeve crossed the short distance and stood before him. He wrapped his hands around her hips and pulled her to him, burying his head against her stomach. Her hands combed through his hair and he marveled at what a difference thirty-six hours could make.

Pulling his hair, she tilted his face upward. Her eyes searched his, full of questions that weren't going to be answered tonight. Leaning into him, she pressed her lips to his. He tugged her down onto the bed and rolled her against the wall, pressing her into the mattress with his body as he took her mouth with his.

When their energy began to build, he tamped his down with effort, not wanting it to release a new reel of images through them. Not now. All he wanted to experience in this moment was Maeve, pure and simple.

Her hands slid under his shirt and across his back before returning to grasp at the hem. Withdrawing from her mouth, he let her tug his shirt up and over his head.

Slow, his head reminded him.

Faster, his heart rebutted.

When he pulled her shirt off, she moved to unclasp her bra.

"No. Let me undress you." He undid the clasp and watched in awe as her perfect, pert breasts sprang free. Sliding his hands beneath them, he spanned her ribs with his spread hands until they both rested perfectly in his palms. He brushed his thumbs across her nipples and then bent to taste her, taking her breast in his mouth.

Maeve arched beneath him and moaned, so he drew his tongue under the perfect curve of her breast and down her stomach, trailing his palms over every available inch of her exposed skin.

Still, it wasn't enough.

He fumbled at the button of her jeans before relenting and allowing her to undo them. Tugging them down, she shimmied out of them, scissoring her legs to help him along. Her pale, porcelain skin was glorious in the warm light of the lamp. Soft and warm, he closed his mouth against her hipbone and felt goosebumps spring up across her thighs in response.

"Are you cold?"

"No. Don't stop."

"I don't think I could."

Slipping his hands beneath her, he cupped her globed ass in his palms and squeezed, raising her hips off the bed and presenting her exquisite sex level with his mouth. A whimper escaped her as he seized her, plunging his tongue inside her entrance.

Maeve bucked on the bed, pressing into him as he continued to pleasure her. Nipping and licking along her labia, he circled her hard nub with his tongue, flicking it again and again, following with a long, slow lick through her opening. Tasting her sweet essence was the undoing of his control.

Slow was no longer an option.

Unleashed, Nate devoured her, relentlessly sucking and pulling at her swollen sex as she endured his shameless torment. Her hands twisted in his hair and she surged her hips against him, begging with her body for penetration.

"Nate."

Ignoring her pleas, he continued, increasing his assault until she trembled beneath him, on the brink. A ripple of energy leaked from him and coursed into her, driving her over the edge. Maeve's hands clutched the bedding and her body twitched and shook beneath him. Nate rested his check against her thigh and exhaled against her mound, the sensation eliciting a round of soft curses from her.

He crawled up the bed to lie beside her and pulled her spent body against his. Flushed and hot, her skin was as toasty as a campfire in the chilly room. He pressed his hardness against her naked bottom and she reached back between them to grip him through his jeans, forcing out a moan of his own.

"Fuck."

"About time." Maeve turned in his arms and reached to unbutton his jeans.

Happy to comply, he rolled over and off the bed to shuck his remaining clothing. Maeve rolled over to the edge and grasped the back of his thighs, pulling him close to the edge of the mattress.

Tilting her head to the side coyly, she nodded appreciatively at his nakedness. "Well, you *are* a nice surprise, Nate."

Without touching him, she blew her hot breath along his shaft, then licked her lips and slid her tongue under his length from base to tip and back again. When she closed her lips around his tip, he threw his head back and pushed into her mouth. Maeve set the pace, gripping his ass hard, pushing and pulling him to and from her.

Knowing he'd never last against her agonizing assault, he backed away from her.

"Problem?" she asked, full of fake, doe-eyed innocence.

"Not if you stop now."

"Payback is a bitch, isn't it?"

"We'll see."

Pushing her back, he slid his hands beneath her knees and pushed them up roughly, opening her sex to him.

"Do we need to...?"

"No. I don't even cycle."

"But Ruth—"

"Was barely a reaper when she conceived. Trust me. It's not going to happen."

Nate conceded, trusting Maeve to know her body and its limitations,

He let her knees fall back to the bed and leaned down to kiss her. Brushing his lips against hers, he nipped at her lip, pressing his forehead to hers. She softened under him and he parted her legs with his knee, slowly pushing against her entrance with his shaft.

The tip slid in, and his arms trembled as he tried to hold his weight off her. When she wrapped her legs around his back and raised her hips off the bed to meet him, he broke. Sliding his hands under her head, he wrapped them around the back of her neck, holding her in place as he thrust into her in one long motion, filling her core completely.

He held still for a moment, savoring the feel of her slick heat around him. When he pulled back, Maeve gasped and he plunged in again, stroke after stroke. He buried his head against her neck as he pumped into her, whispering appreciations into her ear.

Maeve's nails bit into his ass and her core clenched around him on his back stroke, initiating the most mind-blowing orgasm of his life as he spilled into her with a strained grunt. His neck muscles tightened, threatening to snap as he rode wave after wave of aftershock tremors, the pleasure so exquisite it bordered on pain.

"Easy there, cowboy. You're going throw an aneurysm if you aren't careful."

"You say the most romantic things."

"I'm a romantic type of girl. Or hadn't you noticed?"

Nate rolled off her, fumbling for his discarded T-shirt and offering it to her so she could clean up. The blankets had somehow made it to the floor as well, and he tugged them over them both. Pulling her against the length of his body, he luxuriated in the sensation of her bare skin against his, which was so much better than being separated by wool and fleece.

"I've noticed everything about you."

She traced her finger along the edges of his bandaged arm. "Does this hurt?"

"No, I think it's already healed. All this energy exchange. See, sex is good for us."

"I'm sorry about hurting you."

"Shhh."

Maeve wrapped herself around him, burrowing her head against his chest. She was silent for a while before he realized she'd fallen asleep. Careful not to wake her, he reached to turn off the lamp. His jeans caught his eye on the floor and he remembered the ashes. He rolled out of bed as quietly as he could and retrieved them from his pocket, still wrapped tight in the bandana. Since they were sharing a pillow, he slid the packet underneath, figuring they could both use some advice for their future together.

Assuming they had one.

Pain fisted around Nate's heart. So many things could go wrong. What if she had regrets in the morning? Could he go back to being nothing more than partners with her? Hell, they hadn't even really established a relationship as partners before her possession. Being assigned to someone didn't automatically inspire trust and warm fuzzies. Still, he'd known she was the one for him since the first moment he looked at her after their energy exchange in the hospital.

Somehow, he'd have to make sure she knew it, too.

Chapter Twenty-Three

Camael stood on the balcony of his palatial home in Hell, looking down at the Sea of the Dead. Tonight he inhabited his own familiar pre-fall angel form. Minus the wings, of course. He sometimes found private comfort in it. His leopard form was metaphysically easier to maintain than any other form, and the resident demons, imps and such found his animal shell especially intimidating, which gave him some small joy, but tonight, he needed to drink and to take his comfort where he could.

It had been so long since he'd donned this visage. None of the beings of Hell had witnessed his true form. Only Lucifer, who had known him before the fall, would recognize it. The transformation sent a barrage of memories and emotions through him that would be better off buried. It didn't take long for him to remember why he'd chosen not to wear it for so long.

The demons had brought him several host bodies in offering, each one weaker than the last, but he'd refused them all. After spending time in the reaper's body, he mourned the loss of her strength and resilience.

How the witch had managed to drive him out was still a mystery, one of the many surprises he'd encountered during his extended time in Meridian. Killing Maeve was currently at the top of his *To-Do* list, even higher than opening the final portal. There was no telling what she'd gleaned from her time with him, and it was vital for him to ensure that she didn't pass along any details to her fellow reapers.

He was fairly confident that he had effectively scrambled her faculties upon his exit, but he wanted to be sure. Without her soul, there was no way she would be lucid enough to communicate with the others, but he'd been surprised one too many times to take that chance.

Camael wandered inside and poured a glass full of red wine and tipped it to his lips, letting the warm fluid fill his mouth, savoring its sweetness and sharp bite. Catching his reflection in the mirror, the slightest twinge pinched at his cold heart, reminding him that he did indeed still have one—a heart—however twisted and ruined.

After shaking his head at the image, he walked into his bedroom and removed an iron safe from beneath his bed. He worked the tumbler until the door clicked open, and then removed a clear glass urn from its hiding place inside the padded silk cell. The urn was shaped like an hourglass and constructed of one solid piece of glass. Bluish-gray smoke undulated inside, stretching through the thin neck and filling the top globe before sliding through it again to fill the bottom. He watched it float through the glass, mesmerized by its elegant drift.

The smoke gathered near his hand where he held the urn and pulsated where his skin touched the glass, drawn to his heat and energy. Even now, there was a connection. He rarely brought out the urn after all these years, but tonight he found himself feeling oddly sentimental. He longed, still, for the one thing he could never have—the one thing that had driven him to forsake his very identity and eternal life in Heaven, because without her, his eternal life was far worse than torture.

Swirling, the soul began to glow with iridescence as he held it in his hand. If he were to set it beside his bed, it would light up the room like a lava lamp by morning. Her soul was that pure. Even in Hell, it had remained untarnished, but without the body to put it into, it was nothing more than a sad memento of his short life on Earth.

Why did he torment himself? Especially now? Misery bred misery.

Unbidden, her face filled his mind. Her curly, black hair lifting in the wind and spreading out behind her like the mane of a proud racehorse. He stroked his thumb across the upper globe and her soul followed its path.

Elaina.

He should dash the urn against the wall and quit punishing himself and her. What was done was done. Choices had been made and consequences paid. Instead, he placed the urn on the nightstand beside his bed with care. Ashamed, he realized he needed the light. It was the only thing to keep the crushing darkness from filling him.

What was done couldn't be undone.

Broken, he willed himself into his leopard form and stalked out his door…into the depths of Hell.

***

Maeve woke screaming.

Sitting up abruptly, she tried to get her bearings in the dark room. Where was she? What day was it?

Nothing made sense. Nate was already up and out of bed, searching the room for an assailant he wasn't going to find.

He returned to bed and took her into his arms as her heart pounded in her chest and blood rushed in the same hard tempo in her ears. She tried to slow her breathing and make sense of what she'd dreamed, wondering if she'd ever be whole again. Nate kissed the top of her head and held her close, their night coming back to her in sharp, vivid color.

She felt a blush creep over her face and was thankful for the spare light in the room. The window allowed only a soft glow of the morning sun to peek through.

"Shhh, you're okay."

He rubbed her back in slow circles, and she was embarrassed to admit it was comforting. Nate made her forget to be hard. He was a wonderful surprise. He'd taken her with such abandon last night and God help her, but she'd let him. Never had she let herself go so completely with a man…a reaper…whatever the hell Nate was. He was amazing.

Lying back down, she stretched and slid her hand under the pillow. Feeling something there, she grasped hold of it and pulled it out, trying to figure out what it was in the dim light.

"Ashes?" Maeve asked.

"Yes. Did you dream of guidance?"

"If there was any truth to my nightmare, we're screwed."

"Why were you screaming?"

"It was a memory from my time with Camael— ripped out souls, a sea of dead bodies, same old nonsense."

"Nothing else?"

Maeve hesitated. "Yes. It was probably because of your drawings. My imagination just got carried away."

"You dreamed about my drawings? Which one?"

"All of them. They battled out in my head like the deleted scenes on a DVD."

"And which drawing was the last?"

"You woke me before it was over. I guess I get to experience another year of surprising chaos."

Nate grinned beside her. "That sounds perfect."

"You say that now. And what about you? Any insights into the year ahead?" Maeve asked.

"Only dreams involving food and you. Not necessarily in that order." Nate smiled.

She narrowed her eyes at him, clearly skeptical. "Hmm."

Breakfast smells made their way through the air ducts and Maeve's stomach growled.

"You need to fuel up."

"I'll be okay."

"No. You won't. I don't have the medical means to attend to a reaper coma here. You need food...and energy."

"I don't know, Nate—about taking your energy, not the food. I'm down with breakfast, no problem."

"After last night, I think sharing my energy is the least of your worries."

She shivered. "What do you mean?"

"I mean, I might have to fill you with more than just my blue mojo." Nate slid his hand down her still naked thigh and slung it over the top of his own, slipping his thigh between her legs and against her slick sex.

"Shit. If you start that, we'll never get to eat."

"Then maybe I'll give you an appetizer." Nate kissed Maeve until her toes curled, letting the energy build between them unhindered. Turquoise sparks traveled across her skin as he trailed his hand down her stomach, placing his palm flat against her mound. She squirmed, urging him to slide those oh-so-close fingers into her. Instead he pushed his Reiki light into her mouth.

Maeve felt her throat chakra fill with his light, which then radiated through the rest of her body. As her crown chakra filled, her head started to throb. Her vision blurred with fuzzy black and white spots, and she felt the shift before she realized what was happening.

Her reel was back on track.

Her memories snapped into place and began to roll past her in reverse order, beginning with last night with Nate all the way back to Camael in St. Mary's Hospital chapel.

It was all there.

And she knew how to defeat Camael.

If only she could hold onto it.

Chapter Twenty-Four

Nate broke the kiss and watched Maeve collect herself. He stroked her cheek, waiting for a sign that she was back with him. No images had appeared to him this time. It was at once a relief and a disappointment. He could feel her dependency on him lessening already.

How long before she didn't need him at all?

Pushing the thought away, he waited. After several long moments, she opened her eyes, still radiant with their combined turquoise light. He could see the new confidence in her expression.

"I know how to defeat Camael."

"What?"

"Whatever you did just then…rewrote my scrambled code. I don't know how or why it happened, but you helped me remember. Everything."

Nate stroked his hand along her arm. "Tell me."

"He can be killed—permanently—if he's beheaded in his true form, which he can only manifest in Hell, or if his soul is captured on Earth while it's unhosted."

"How do you know this?"

"Camael had no intention of me surviving our time together. He didn't shield from me at all. Three months is a long time to spend in someone's head. We need to get back and put a stop to his plans."

Nate recognized the implications of her revelation.

"Yes." He palmed the side of her face and traced his thumb across her cheekbone. "You are amazing."

Her lips thinned and a crease formed between her eyebrows. "These drawings, Nate. They're of what's to come, aren't they?"

Nate studied the wall where they hung. "No. Not all of them."

"How do you know that? I think they show us how this disaster ends. We just have to get them in the right order."

"I know the order…well, if Rashnu can be trusted."

"He told you?"

"More like he showed me." Nate pointed to the divided rows of drawings he'd rearranged. "There are two possible paths."

"And this one?" Maeve pointed to the drawing of the headless woman who resembled her.

"Not going to happen."

***

When Nate and Maeve walked into the kitchen, Rosemary was already stacking pancakes onto a plate while Garrett sat at the table reading the Meridian newspaper. The headline above the fold caught his eye: Demons Devastate Downtown Drinking Hole.

He didn't even need to read the story to recognize the photo of the bar where he'd saved Maeve. This wasn't the *National Enquirer* Garrett was reading. It was the *Meridian Messenger*. It was a miracle that the invasion had taken this long to make the papers. The bold headline would turn most serious news patrons off, but still…even the most sensational stories often held nuggets of truth. He wondered how much the public would parse. If news stories like this didn't give the good folks of Meridian nightmares, nothing would.

Speaking of nightmares, though he hadn't admitted as much, Nate had been plagued by nightmares similar to Maeve's. Rashnu's two paths seemed more inescapable than ever. He didn't believe in a predestined future—not as long as free will was in play—but he also couldn't explain how he'd foreseen the images that were now haunting him nearly a decade later. The more he denied his fate, the stronger it seemed to persist. He prayed he was on the correct path.

With Yule behind him, he wondered if they'd all now make it through Christmas, let alone the coming year. The soot dreams only reinforced what Rashnu had already shown him. Time was short, and urgency beat at him. If refueling weren't absolutely necessary, they would have already flashed.

"Good morning, you two." Garrett gave Nate a knowing look, and Nate couldn't help but give him a foolish smile in return.

"Maeve, you look so much better. You're practically glowing." Rosemary set a plate of pancakes in front of her, a full stack of six, and Maeve's eyes grew large. "Don't worry, I'll make more if you want them."

Maeve laughed and reached for the syrup, pouring it over the cakes until it threatened to overflow the high lip of the curved plate.

"We don't have much time, Mom. We need to get back."

"Already?" Rosemary asked.

Nate's stack was equally impressive and for a few moments he could almost imagine he was a regular guy, bringing his girl home to meet the parents. Did he even want that anymore? To be normal?

He'd spent his entire life as an outsider, but his unusual gifts had finally paid off. Maeve was alive and at his side precisely because he was not normal. Had he been 100 percent human, she would be dead and her soul would have been sorted, just like Kylen's Kara. Then where would he be?

Lost.

He squeezed her free hand in clear sight of his parents. He wasn't going to waste any more time pretending to be something he wasn't. Despite everything that awaited them outside the coven's circle of protection, what he was at this very moment was…happy.

Sometimes a few minutes of happiness were all a guy could hope for.

Rosemary sat at the table as the rest of them enjoyed their breakfasts. She smoothed her hands back and forth across the empty place setting in front of her and cleared her throat. Something about the sound told Nate that his world was about to fall apart.

"Nate, there's something we need to tell you before you go." Rosemary cast an apologetic smile toward Maeve.

Her words hung in the air and Nate steeled himself for the blow. Whatever Rosemary and Garrett were talking about the other night was about to come to light. Dread crept through him and a sheen of sweat slid across his body, almost as if he already knew the words that were coming.

Maybe part of him had always known the words that were coming.

"It's about your mother. Your *biological* mother, Nate. She's still alive."

Nate stopped breathing. Was it possible? He'd never looked for her. Of course, he'd always wondered, but something inside him had whispered that he wouldn't like what he would find.

"Where is she?"

Maeve stopped eating and placed her fork on the plate, half of her pancakes already gone.

"She's here. On the coven grounds. We've been caring for her and protecting her."

The questions erupted in his head like a volcano and molten fury spread throughout his body until Maeve squeezed his hand and a soft exchange of turquoise energy passed between them. He wondered if Rosemary and Garrett, as attuned to the spiritual world as they were, could see his aura leaking out in mustard waves.

"Protecting her from what?"

"Your father."

That was it. His brain incinerated and he closed his eyes, trying to sort through all his emotions. His mother had been close by all this time? She'd allowed him to suffer through foster home after foster home until he'd finally ended up here? Near her, but not knowing her? And these people—his parents, for God's sake—had kept it from him?

Betrayal ate a hole into his gut like a canker sore. He felt his face growing hot and red and his hands formed fists, crushing Maeve's. She didn't pull back. She held on. God bless her, but she held onto him as he tried to process what his mother was saying.

"Please explain."

"Your father was an angel."

And there it was again. Angels. *Nephilim.* He hadn't wanted to believe Rashnu, but the evidence was beginning to pile up.

"What? Wait, backup. If this is true, then why are *you* telling me this? Take me to my birth mother. I want to hear it from her."

Rosemary looked at Garrett, but he shook his head. "I'll take you to her," Rosemary said, "but you'll still have to get your answers from us."

"And why is that?"

"Because she doesn't have a soul."

And this shit just kept getting better.

Rising from the table, Nate paced the room, trying to put yet another puzzle piece into place. For once, it would be nice to see the whole design without any holes.

"How long has she been here?"

"Twenty-seven years."

"Since I was born? Was I born on coven grounds?"

"Nearby."

It took a great effort for Nate not to yell at his mother.

"Let me get this straight. You know where I was born, where my mother still exists. Yet, I was given away to strangers time and again before being adopted back into the coven. Does that sound about right?"

Rosemary worried her wedding ring around her finger. "Yes. That's true. You—and your twin sister—were given away."

Nate blinked.

Sister? Oh, hell no.

He gripped the edge of the sink, his knuckles turning white as he struggled to compose himself. Staring out the kitchen window at the frosted landscape, he wondered how things could have gone so wrong so quickly.

"And where is my sister?"

"She was also adopted. Nate, we gave you away because we had to. To protect you and give you a normal life. We were forced to separate you from your mother because she couldn't care for you. Your sister was adopted first, but we requested that you wouldn't be adopted together. Together, there was the risk that you might draw the attention of...dangerous entities."

"My father?"

"Yes, among others."

Garrett shifted in his chair and Nate turned to look him. "Nate, this was a Coven Board decision that was made to protect us all. Your mother—Rosemary—did everything in her power and beyond, including black magic, to heal your biological mother. Physically she has survived, but mentally, spiritually, psychologically—in every way that matters she is gone."

Rosemary continued. "We followed you both into the foster system and kept tabs on you over the years. When you began to have repeated problems and bounce from family to family, we knew we had to step in. We didn't want your...*talents* to be manipulated in the wrong way. Your Wiccan knowledge, your sigils, the coven's circle of protection all helped to mask your inherent gifts once they manifested. But then you grew up and moved away to your own life. We hoped...We prayed you would be safe. Yet, the darkness we sought to save you from has found you all the same."

"And my sister?"

"We kept track of her. Nothing unusual manifested in her childhood as far as we could tell, and we allowed her to live her life. It's only recently that we've lost track of her. The less contact she had with us the better. For both sides."

"Take me to my mother."

"We can do that, but you should know she hasn't aged. She looks the same as she did the day she arrived. The day *you* arrived."

Fresh anxiety filled Nate. "Is she a reaper?"

"From what you've told me—" Rosemary squeezed Garrett's hand. "—we think she might be."

Chapter Twenty-Five

Ruth was at wit's end. Exhausted from too little activity and too much sleep, she could not escape the worrisome feeling that something was wrong. Very wrong. While the baby and her pregnancy seemed fine, some hunch told her that the other shoe was just waiting to drop. Bocephus, who was whining softly in his sleep at the side of her bed, seemed to feel the same way. That dog missed Nate something terrible. And right now? The big galoot seemed to be in some sort of physical pain, rising, circling and readjusting before lying back down again, trying to find a comfortable position.

She could relate. Deacon and the other members of the Authority had been home sporadically for meals since Nate and Maeve left, but most of her days and nights had been spent alone. Temperance's company didn't count. Olivia wasn't even around all that much, spending more and more time at the food shelter she'd set up downtown. They'd all been catching rest where they could and making real progress on the demon cleanup while Camael continued to hide beneath the radar.

They were "making hay while the sun shined," as Raguel had said earlier. He'd cast aside his southern Italian colloquialisms and adopted the local sayings way too quickly. But given how charming he was, it was pure entertainment for the rest of them.

Man, she'd give anything to be off reservation for a few hours, but with Temperance holding up the east wall of the trailer, an escape seemed very unlikely. She was still plotting her imagined departure when Deacon appeared at the foot of her bed, startling a scream from her.

Temperance sprang to action, her wings spreading and filling the room, followed by a bright shimmering red iridescent cloud that made it impossible to focus on what was happening. The glint of a sword stopped Ruth's heart for one long terrifying moment before recognition kicked in.

"Shit!" Ruth skittered off the bed.

Deacon had pulled out his scythe as soon as he recognized Temperance's intent to attack, and the two of them filled the small room with menace. Bo growled, low and threateningly, his head touching Ruth's shoulder as he stood his ground, protecting her. The angel shot a look of disdain at Deacon and folded her wings back until all that showed were the two top arches, mere millimeters below her ears. She leaned back against the wall, as nonchalant as was possible for the angel.

"Maybe use the front door next time. Someone's a little edgy," Ruth said.

"At least she's on task, unlike I have been this afternoon."

"What do you mean?"

"I checked out your lead for you," he said with a smile.

"And? Did you find her? Or…her house anyway?"

"I found 337 Birch Street. It wasn't her home. It was a cemetery, outside of Bolton."

"Oh."

"I also found an Elaina Carter, or at least her grave and headstone. She was twenty-nine the day she died."

"And when was that?"

"Your birthday."

***

Camael finally settled on a host. It was time to stop lamenting things that couldn't be changed and start getting back into the game at hand. His head seemed to be clearing and the latest reports from his demon minions were enough to snap him out of his sentimental reverie. The reapers had been busy, it seemed, and they were making a serious dent in his incursion. Without a leader, the demons were no more than a bothersome nuisance up top. Like the children they were, they needed constant guidance and supervision. On a bad day, he was a glorified babysitter, on a good day? Well, on a good day, he was Hell incarnate.

Standing tall before his long dressing mirror, he admired the host form he'd settled on. This human was an outstanding physical specimen, heavily muscled and healthy, his tanned head slick and bald—a welcome change from Maeve's high maintenance coif. The full-body tattoos extended along both arms and across his chest and back. Only his legs were free of markings. The ink boasted numerous symbols that were well known in Camael's adopted neighborhood. The swastika gracing his pectoral muscle was one of his personal favorites. How many souls had fallen with that emblazoned upon their skin in the past century? It was inspiring what a little branded marketing could accomplish. It had gone from being a symbol of life, luck and strength for three thousand years to one of total domination and evil in fifty. Amazing.

The true power of any symbol lay in the eye and heart of the beholder.

His chosen host was a one-owner model. One who had foolishly summoned a demon. He was a human who *desired* to be possessed. A fact that had allowed Camael's demons to lead him right up to the gates of Hell and walk him straight to Camael's door, new and never previously possessed. If there were possession CARFAX, this one's record would be clean as a whistle.

Camael dismissed the attending demons. Enough of this nonsense. He stretched inside his new skin. Yes, this one would do for now. Maybe he would even last a week inside one so strong.

And wouldn't that be a miracle? It would give him just enough time to complete his mission.

Just once, Camael wished Lucifer could experience the frustration of his limitations up top. Lucifer had been the first to fall and in his all-consuming wrath, God had bound him to Hell as a condition of his betrayal. Lucifer wouldn't be able to leave until the last soul was freed from Hell, but he'd still retained all of his powers, not to mention his wings. It came in handy that the Big Guy hadn't been clear on the condition the souls needed to be in when they were freed. A loophole Lucifer fully intended to exploit. The last souls would indeed be free of Hell very, very soon…just not in the form anyone had expected.

Camael, on the other hand, had fallen in the last quarter century, countless millennia since Lucifer, and he'd slid into Hell, and out of reach of God's wrath, in the nick of time. His punishment was the loss of his angel body outside of Hell, which—along with his traitorous heart—was what had caused the entire chain of events leading to his fall. So he'd been left to languish in Hell or ride a host, just like the demons. He'd spent the last quarter century reliving his last few days, hours and minutes on Earth.

Having been alive for nearly as long as Lucifer, these past twenty-seven years—the blink of an eye in his life, really—had been by far the longest. He'd been in Hell in every sense of the word before finally pulling out of his stupor and beginning to plot his revenge.

Opening the final portal for Lucifer would be a sweet victory. God had taken everything Camael loved from him. And now Camael could return the favor.

There was one place Camael would visit again before heading back to Meridian to find the location for the final portal. His sacrifice wasn't ready yet, but after some self-reflection over the past few days, he had come up with a new plan that he was confident would work.

Even a half-baked plan was better than nothing, and after this latest setback, he was ready to accelerate things or die trying. He would experience one last indulgence before drawing out his prey and completing his mission.

He flashed out of Hell and headed to Bolton.

***

Nate followed Rosemary and Garrett back to the hub where the Yule fire had burned down to a still smoldering pile on the cold, late December morning. Crossing the hub, they continued in silence onto Mabon Street, moving past several Arts & Crafts style homes. Tension coiled in his gut as Rosemary came to a stop in front of a dusty blue home accented with white trim. A two-foot tall, gray, fieldstone fence lined the front and left side of the yard, broken only by the narrow driveway, which led to the attached carport. A wooden sign hung from the front door announcing, "The Witch Is In."

Nate's heartbeat quickened. A few more steps and she would be there. His mother. How many times through the years had he walked past this very house, not knowing who was inside? Hundreds. His chest ached.

Climbing the wooden stairs to the tidy front porch, Rosemary reached for the cast iron doorknocker. The gentle tapping on the solid cedar and pine wood front door filled Nate's chest with a slow burn of unease.

He heard the latch click open and then a wiry but elderly woman emerged in the doorway, her eyes crinkling at the corners with her smile.

"Rosemary, so glad to see—" She stopped when she looked past Rosemary and took in the sight of the crowd gathered on her porch. "Oh."

"Fiona, we've come to see her."

Fiona looked past Rosemary to Nate, who recognized her as the coven's librarian. While Nate hadn't been a frequent visitor to the library, he'd always known her to be kind and patient, even with the rowdier kids.

"Oh, dear. Are you sure?"

"Yes. It's time."

Sadness crossed her face and she backed away from the doorway. "Very well then. Come on in." They walked into the cozy living area. "There won't be room for all of you at once, of course."

"I'll go in with Nate for now." Rosemary reached back for his hand, but he couldn't bring himself to give it to her. She nodded and led him down a narrow hallway toward the back of the house. Garrett and Maeve stayed in the living room with Fiona.

Sunlight streamed through high, stained glass transom windows as they passed a small bedroom, an office and a personal library. They stopped at the back of the house before an open archway leading to a converted sunroom. Windows lined the southern wall of the room and the remaining three walls were painted a painfully cheerful color of purple. To the left of the doorway was a queen-sized bed that filled most of the narrow, rectangular room. Lying upon it was a woman.

Rosemary crossed the room and stood in the narrow space between the edge of the bed and the wall of windows. Nate remained in the doorway, reluctant to make the last three steps to her side.

"Nate, meet your birth mother, Elaina Carter."

Nate's world imploded. Ruth's *birth mother* was named Elaina Carter. His mind raced as he tried to make sense of the new knowledge that overtook him. A hard lump formed in his throat and he was reduced to his five year-old self, cold, afraid and alone in a cemetery in the middle of the night. For the first time he remembered the details of the headstone he'd landed against when he flashed there twenty-two years ago. The stone had read *Elaina Carter.*

Yet here she was. Elaina Carter. Alive if not well.

No, not well at all.

And Ruth was his sister.

As the pieces rearranged, one last puzzle piece clicked into place. If his father was an angel, and he and Ruth were indeed nephilim, then there was only one fallen angel they held in common.

Camael. Could it be? But his mind couldn't wrap itself around that, couldn't even process the truth about Ruth while he stood here in the same room as his birth mother.

He closed the space between them and looked down at Elaina in wonder. The first thing he noticed was her lack of an aura. Her long, dark hair fanned out beneath her head and she reminded him of Sleeping Beauty. Her hands were folded across her stomach on top of the quilted blanket covering her.

Even through her thinness, the sickly paleness of her lips and the translucent quality of her skin—every vein and artery seemingly apparent in her visible flesh—he could still see evidence of the beauty she'd been. Almost as beautiful as Maeve. But her thin arms now consisted of mostly bone, and her clavicles protruded through her thin gown just above the edge of the blanket. Even beneath the coverings, it was clear her hipbones projected through the quilt in two pronounced points, leaving him with little doubt about how skeletal the rest of her body was.

"We've tried a variety of treatments through the years, from feeding tubes to black magic, but nothing has helped. We've tried to keep her comfortable, nourish her body as well as we can, but she continues to deteriorate, albeit slowly. She's never spoken since we found her moments after you were born."

"Where was she?"

"In a cemetery a few minutes from the coven. In a town called Bolton. We had no idea how she got there or why she was there, but you and your sister were wrapped in the same T-shirt. You were still in her arms when I found you."

"Why were you in the cemetery?"

"I was on my way home for the summer solstice celebration. The cemetery is on a hill, visible from the main highway, but about a half mile off the road. I sensed a great discharge of magic from that direction as I drove by, and I couldn't ignore it. When I went to investigate, I found the three of you, and…"

"What?"

"Another body. A man. He was decapitated. I left him there."

"And you didn't call an ambulance? Or the police?"

"Nate, it wasn't the first time we had seen her. She came to us alone a few days earlier for help, drawn in by the power of our magic, I'm sure. She told us an impossible story about who and what was pursuing her. She was almost nine months pregnant. Of course, we were going to help her. And from the things she told us, we were the only ones who could. She stayed with me and Garrett at the healing center so I could help her with her pregnancy. How or why she left the coven that night and ended up in that cemetery, we still don't know. But if I hadn't been driving by…"

Nate leaned across the woman and gently lifted her top eyelid with his thumb to examine her. Silver-gray eyes stared back at him, unseeing.

She was soulless, all right.

Taking her hand in his, he forced a shot of Reiki light into her. Her long-starved body latched onto the offered nourishment, but he watched as it leaked back out through her damaged chakras as it passed through her. He placed his fingers along the pulse in her neck and waited. And waited. And waited. Nearly three minutes later, he felt one labored throb of her heart. Another three minutes passed before he counted another beat.

No doctor would have waited so long before pronouncing her deceased.

This is what a true and complete reaper coma looked like: defenseless, depleted and as good as dead.

"Can you tell? Is she—like Maeve? Like, you? A reaper?"

"Yes."

Rosemary was silent for several long moments as Nate considered the possibilities. He had an idea about why she might have been in that cemetery. Elaina was obviously a reaper, so she had probably been trying to access the consecrated subway. He knew from his experience with Ruth that using that means of transportation was a last resort for a pregnant reaper.

So what had forced her to take the chance?

"Did you know my father, too?"

Rosemary shook her head adamantly. "No. She only told us that he was an angel. Of course, we didn't believe her at first, but she was so sincere and so afraid that we eventually accepted it. Someone or *something* was after her, and she was terrified."

"My father?"

"No, but she was hiding from him, as well. She said that if he knew where she was, he'd be in danger, too. We hid her with magic...until she left the coven. Then we couldn't protect her any longer."

"Then who was after her?"

"Supernatural bounty hunters. She said they were after her unborn children."

"My father, did she tell you his name?"

"She wouldn't. She said he could be invoked if we knew his name, and she never wanted that to happen. She feared for us as well, but we assured her that we could protect her from anything supernatural. And we have."

Nephilim.

Rashnu had been trying to tell him. Hell, the entire universe had been trying to tell him. He just hadn't wanted to believe it. He and Ruth were some sort of bastardized version of the nephilim. And Camael was their father.

"But she had a grave?"

"Yes. We did that. She had been trying to live a normal life. She had a home and everything until *something* scared her away. We sold her property and 'buried' her in Bolton, hoping it would put an end to things."

And now what?

He'd found his mother, but his sister? And his father? It was too much to process. Impossible. Still, the sick feeling in his gut prodded him with the truth, even though he couldn't let his mind take that trip yet.

For now, Elaina was as safe as was possible, but how much longer would she hang on in this state of suspended animation? He shuddered to think that he'd been willing to allow Maeve to persist in this same indefinite state. Of course, he had known all along where Maeve's soul was. Where was Elaina's? If she'd been reaped, then her soul would have been sorted and sent to its Heavenly rest. Yes?

But could her soul even be processed if her body still lived?

Was she something beyond a wanderer?

He had no idea where her soul might be. Deacon could search for her in the realms. Heaven would be easy, but Hell? Deacon had gotten his fill of Hell. They all had. There was one angel who would know unequivocally if she'd been sorted.

Rashnu.

Chapter Twenty-Six

Nate and Maeve landed at the Authority compound just before full dark. He'd wanted to take his biological mother with him, but she was being cared for as well as possible under the circumstances. His parents and the rest of the coven protected her this long. The only way he could help her now was to find her soul, and even then it was likely long too late.

How long could a soul exist on its own, without a body and without being sorted? Forever? Deacon had once referred to such souls as sleepers. Lost on Earth, untethered and unclaimed. There were a few special reapers who actively searched for such souls, but it was like finding a needle in a haystack. Deacon had happened upon just two in his two centuries of life. What happened to the souls that were never recovered?

Deacon had also explained that the souls in Heaven received new bodies and ascended through the various levels of the realm over time. Kara had ascended to the fourth Heaven in the hundred years since her passing. In

Hell, there was no need for a new body. Depending on the level to which they descended, the souls might be reissued their bodies, often just so their previous forms could be perpetually ground away in the Sea of the Dead. A torturous game of a bored Lucifer.

Nate had witnessed it first-hand from the viewing platform on the ground level of Hell's Palace when he'd helped rescue Deacon. The thought of his mother's soul being tossed into that pit filled him with a rage that pushed him beyond rational thought.

Maeve squeezed his hand. "Hey. We'll find her soul."

Nate was still trying to piece together the ridiculous scenario that was his life. At least now he knew which side his reaper genes came from and why he was so supernaturally fucked up. He'd felt like a freak all of his life for good reason.

He was one.

They stood outside the communal area door, Nate desperate to get his shit together and trying to decide how much he was willing to share with the Authority. The right answer, of course, was *everything* because how could they help if they didn't have as much information as he did. His instinct, however, was to clam up and continue with his Lone Ranger tactics.

And Maeve? He didn't know what the hell was going to happen with Maeve. She seemed solid. A blessing, when at the moment, he was anything but.

He felt like he was digging a hole in the sand that was his past. The deeper he scooped for answers, the more sand slithered down the edges to fill his hole back up.

"You ready?" Maeve asked.

"No."

"Me either. Let's do this."

He twisted the door handle a half-turn to the right and was immediately tackled to the floor by two-hundred-and-fifty pounds of muscle, fur and drool. Bo licked his face and neck so enthusiastically, Nate felt like a layer of his skin was being sloughed off with the beast's abrasive tongue.

"Okay, already. I missed you, too. Jesus, Bo. Off."

Bo backed to the side and sat by the wall, wagging his tail so aggressively against the sheetrock that an indentation appeared.

"Bo, heel."

The dog returned to his side a bit less aggressively and sat, leaning into his hip and shoulder.

"Now that was a greeting." Maeve didn't even try to hide the smirk on her face.

"Nate! Maeve!" Ruth yelled from the living area.

Nate sighed, his heart heavy as he crossed the room. Apparently Ruth and Temperance were the only ones in the compound right now. He made his way to the couch, searching Ruth's face as he approached, comparing it to his memory of Elaina. Any further proof he might have needed was right here before him. Certain of his own features were there in Ruth's face, a fact that was heartbreakingly clear to him with his new perspective and knowledge. Why hadn't he seen it before?

Anticipation nearly bested him as he seated himself beside her. Putting what he'd learned into words seemed an impossible task. Having Ruth as his sister was a gift he'd never expected. Having Camael as their father was a curse he didn't know if he—or she—could endure.

Temperance stood watch nearby, her back pressed against the wall behind Ruth. Her wings arched upward a few inches behind her back, a sign that she sensed his uncertainty. He tried to calm his drumming heart as he wondered over the machinations of fate that had brought him and his sister together in this way.

"Ruth, how are you feeling?" Nate took her hand in his and searched her face.

"Forget about me. I'm old news. How are you, Maeve? You look amazing!" Ruth all but bounced off the couch.

Maeve stuffed her hands into the front pockets of her jeans and rocked back onto her heels. "Better."

"Like a hundred percent better? Do you remember everything? Olivia said you were having trouble with that when you left."

"Maybe ninety-five percent better." She shot a quick look at Nate.

"Ooookay. Well, Nate, just so you know, Deacon was pretty dang hot about you leaving and not taking your phone. I think I've calmed him down, but be warned. He may not greet you as warmly as Bo did." Ruth laughed.

"Where are all of the others? Have they gone out already?"

"More like haven't come home. They've been working ridiculous hours since you left. Camael is still underground. They haven't encountered him in the field since you rescued Maeve. We don't know if he's injured or just reconnoitering. Either way, the reapers have been decimating the demon population. With you and Maeve back in the game, you might have them all by the end of the week!"

"I can't hunt demons right now, Ruth. I have something more important to do."

"What could possibly be more important than saving mankind from demons?"

"Saving my biological mother."

Ruth's eyes went wide and large. "Your mother? What happened while you were gone?"

Nate relayed the entire story to her as it had been revealed to him while Maeve stood beside him. Ruth listened in quiet awe, barely containing her questions until he finally stopped talking.

"She's a reaper? And your father was an angel? And she's alive!"

"*Alive* is a generous assessment."

"This is amazing! Oh, Nate! We're both so close to knowing where we come from. Deacon tracked down a lead for me, too, this week. You know, the one thing I remembered from the adoption binder was my birth mother's name. I've traced hundreds of leads by phone and online over the past few weeks, but one was very close!"

"How close?"

"Less than an hour away. In a little town called Bolton. I'm still not sure if she's the right one, but the timing is perfect."

Nate's mouth went dry and every ounce of his blood drained from his head.

"Ruth, there's one more thing…"

"What, Nate? What's wrong? You look ill." Ruth pressed her hand to his forehead.

"My mother's name. I know it."

"Yes? What is it? Maybe I can find out more about her, too."

"You already have. Her name is Elaina Carter."

Chapter Twenty-Seven

Camael stood before the headstone. It had been years since he'd even allowed himself to think of this place, let alone return. Humans liked to pay their respects to the dead, but there was no body in this grave. Only the marker. And the knowledge that this was the last place that he'd seen his beloved.

Everything had happened so fast that night; he'd only reacted. He'd known with sickening certainty that he wouldn't be able to save them all. As it turned out, he hadn't been able to save any of them. For one fleeting moment they were a family, and the next...nothing.

Why was he even here now?

Because somewhere inside him was the slightest weakness that needed to be squashed once and for all. He wanted to remind himself of why he needed his revenge. Of how ruthlessly the bounty hunters who had been sent by Heaven destroyed his family.

The hunters had chased Elaina through the consecrated subway like she was prey. Then after she'd gone into premature labor and gave birth to the twins, her body had failed…which was when the hunters tracked her down. After he'd found her and the reaper bounty hunters, he'd unleashed his full angel fury upon them, killing one by tearing his head from his shoulders with his bare hands. The other had managed to escape, vanishing back into the consecrated subway like the cowardly vermin he was.

After Camael had beheaded the reaper, Elaina's soul had streamed out of the reaper's shell and hovered over her fallen body. He'd appropriated an urn from the nearby crypt and captured it. After wrapping both of the bloody and squirming infants in his shirt, he'd clutched the urn and scooped them and Elaina's body into his arms before trying to flash to a safer location. He'd landed alone and empty-handed, save for the urn. By the time he'd returned, just moments later, Elaina's body and the infants were already gone.

He had no idea how they'd vanished so quickly, but he could smell the residue of magic in the air. The reaper's body remained. He'd grasped ahold of the head and body and carried them straight to the gate of Heaven, leaving them there as a portent.

After that, he'd searched every square inch within a hundred miles of the cemetery for any trace of Elaina or the children.

Nothing.

He petitioned Grim for the names of the hunters who'd been sent for him, demanding justice from the remaining reaper, but his requests were denied. There would be no help from Heaven. God had destroyed the Nephilim once with the great flood. Even though Camael hadn't technically had relations with a human, Elaina was a reaper and cross contamination of genes was still forbidden.

But the heart wanted what the heart wanted.

And now his heart wanted something new.... Vengeance.

He would start with the reapers.

***

Nate's hold on reality was tenuous at best. Ironically, it was Maeve who grounded him and unhinged him all at once. "You're Nate's sister, Ruth."

"That's not possible."

"Nate's mother's name is Elaina Carter. Your mother's name is Elaina Carter. She's a reaper. Nate had a twin."

Now it was Ruth's turn to look stricken. Temperance moved forward, unsure of the threat, but sensing that her charge was overwhelmed.

"No. It can't be." Ruth's face turned pale and her hands trembled in her lap as she twisted them.

Nate sat down next to her, sinking heavily in the leather couch. "Ruth, she's right. Look at the evidence. We should have put this together sooner. We were both adopted, and we have the same birthday for God's sake! We both had strange abilities we didn't understand as children? And now...you're looking for a woman named Elaina Carter whom I just met in the flesh. My mother—Rosemary—said there were two infants. Twins. They separated us on purpose to try to protect us and themselves from Elaina's pursuers."

Ruth shook her head, trying to dislodge what she must already know to be true.

"And our father?"

"An angel. I think our father is Camael."

"No. That's not possible. There are other angels. Our father could have been any of them."

"Only one has fallen since our birth, Ruth. Are you really going to write that off as a coincidence?"

"I can't even think about that possibility right now. It's just too much. Take me to her, Nate. I have to see her."

"You can't travel through the consecrated subway, Ruth. You know that."

"No. But you can drive me." Ruth gave Temperance a hard look. "Don't even think about keeping me from my mother, Temperance. Come along if you must, but I *will* see her. You'd better help me if you don't want me to do something drastic."

"Ruth, we can go there, but I need to find Deacon first," Nate said. "Elaina is safe for now, but her soul is missing. If we can find it, maybe she can still be saved. Like Maeve."

"You think you can reinsoul her?" Ruth gaped at him in awe.

"It may be too late. But we have to try if it's possible. Right?"

"Yes. But I'm not waiting any longer to see her. I'm going. Alone if I have to."

"Ruth, she won't even know you're there. Not yet. Besides, you don't know where to begin looking for her. The coven is hidden." Even as he said the words, he knew the same excuses wouldn't have stopped him from looking for his mother.

"I know where to start! Bolton cemetery."

Maeve shook her head in disgust. "No. She can't go off on her own. You take her, Nate. Once you're inside the coven's circle of protection, you'll be safe. It will take longer by car, but with Temperance, you can make it. I'll find Deacon and bring him to you. I'd take Ruth instead, but—"

"She can't drive," Ruth said. "You really need to work on that."

REAP & REVEAL: BOOK III OF THE REAPER SERIES

"Ruth, it's too dangerous right now." Nate knew he was losing. The women had made a decision. Right or wrong, they were stuck with it.

"I'm not waiting, Nate. I've waited twenty-seven years."

"No!" He was losing his ever-loving mind. This was the worst plan ever.

Temperance's wings began to unfold as an orange glow enveloped her. "You will remain here. I command it."

A spear appeared in her hand and her red hair radiated tendrils of flame, licking the air around her head like a blazing sun.

"You are not the boss of me, Temperance!"

"Dammit, Ruth! Temperance! Both of you stop. No one is leaving this compound except for me. You too, Maeve. You're going to stay here to protect Ruth and yourself. Got it? Or have you already forgotten what happened to you at the hospital, Ruth?"

Ruth jerked back from him as if she'd been slapped. He'd never spoken to her so roughly, but she was about to engage in a suicide mission. Deacon would have his head if he allowed her to do this. Sister or no. She was not leaving this compound.

Maeve moved to his side and held out her hand to him, pulling the bracelet taut. "You're going to have to remove this if you want me to stay here with Ruth."

Nate took her hand in his and searched her eyes. With the binding spell, she would have to remain by his side or in the trailer where he could protect her. Without it, she was just as vulnerable as the rest of them....

Kneeling before her, he focused on the knots, chose one and began to unravel it. If he didn't trust her now, she'd never trust him in the future. She wasn't a pet, and she'd never be happy being caged no matter how much it terrified him to release her back into the world.

Love sucked.

His sigils tightened across his biceps at the thought and magic coiled around the symbols. He pulled the rope strands apart and it was done.

Maeve was free.

God help them both.

"Thank you." Maeve bent down and pulled him into a kiss, his arms wrapping around her waist.

Ruth laughed. "I *knew* it!"

"Your weapons are in my trailer, Maeve. Go get them and do not let this one—" He pointed to Ruth. "—leave under any circumstances."

"I know what I'm doing. This isn't my first rodeo. Besides, *Firestarter* over there will blow a fuse if she tries anything."

"If I lose you…"

"You won't."

***

Nate retrieved his phone from his trailer while Maeve saw to her weapons. He tried to call Deacon. When he didn't answer, Nate employed the GPS tracker.

Activating the tracking program, he pinpointed the location of the Authority reapers, as well as the two replacement reapers responsible for maintaining the normal flow of souls to Purgatory. The Authority members were spread across the city, some clearly not even working in teams anymore. Effective, but dangerous.

The other two reapers, whose names he couldn't even remember, were near Oakland Hospital on the edge of the city while Deacon was moving briskly along Richmond Street in the downtown area. He would flash to Deacon's location first so that he could tell him about Maeve's memories and what he'd learned about his relationship to Ruth. Then he would return to Rashnu to demand information about where Elaina's soul had been sent.

He checked the phone display again, making sure of Deacon's location, when he saw the two replacement reapers walking along Starnes Street disappear off the mapped grid. There were plenty of reasons that could happen. Their phones could have been damaged, their signals interrupted, but for it to happen to both of them? In the middle of the street? Nowhere near consecrated ground? They were vanilla reapers. They couldn't flash from anywhere like the members of the Authority. The dread that flooded through his chest in a surge of adrenaline told him the problem was something else.

They were in trouble.

The chance that any of the members of the Authority had noticed them vanish was slim. They were concentrating on the demons, not other reapers.

He turned to Maeve and grabbed her arm. "Maeve. Change in plans. There's trouble. I'm going to the replacement reapers first. You go to Deacon. Tell him to check my tracking and find us. Something bad is going down, and Deacon needs to know about Camael."

"Ruth?"

"Temperance won't let anything bad happen to her." He slid their spare phone into her front pocket and pulled her to him, planting a quick kiss onto the top of her head. "I don't have time to recast the circle. Ruth can release you as soon as you're ready. Hurry."

The pull of the consecrated subway drew him away from Maeve and toward Starnes Street.

He knew in his gut it was already too late.

Chapter Twenty-Eight

Camael was dismayed.

Not at the two decapitated reapers before him, lying on the cemetery grounds, but at the blood and overflow of bodily fluids currently defiling his clothes and body. Smiting was so much cleaner. What he wouldn't give for his angel firepower. Sure, his bare hands—or, rather, his host's bare hands—along with his residual strength had given him more than enough potency to rip their heads from their shoulders, but smiting...now *that* was enjoyable.

Arranging the bodies in front of the crypt in Maple Park Cemetery, he went for something artful and abstract. The moonlight glistened off the blood still pooling on the concrete base beside corpse number one. Satisfied, he stepped back to admire his display. Yes, this would send the appropriate message.

He *could* just wait for the members of the Authority to come for him, but where was the sport in that? These two would be found before the night was through. He was sure of it. The reapers swept the city each night, including all the cemeteries. Leaving the bodies in town risked the police finding them first, and they wouldn't appreciate the irony the way the Authority would. Still, it was worth it.

His new plan for securing the sacrifice should have occurred to him before, but he'd been—intoxicated—by Maeve's reaper mojo. It was the only explanation. Something about the bitch was defective and the longer he was out of her shell, the clearer he felt. His new human ride wouldn't last as long as he'd hoped under the strain of his revamped vigor, but there were a thousand more to take his place. As a matter of fact, there was an entire prison full of them. Literally.

He'd instructed his demons to go to the State Penitentiary to collect the best potential hosts, those who were most similar to his current model. That place was like a demon candy store. One way in, one way out, and once the ball started rolling, it would be all downhill. Camael could make up his losses tonight in one fell swoop.

As soon as his post-Maeve fog began to lift, it had all seemed so obvious.

While the Authority reapers might pose a bit more of a challenge than these two, he was tired of toying with them. Three steps forward, two steps back wasn't getting the job done.

He was ready to bring to bear the full force of his diminished legion. Prancing around the city in Maeve's body had been foolish in retrospect. His hubris and subsequent sulking had cost him half of his new recruits. He was a freaking Duke of Hell, for Lucifer's sake. It was time he started acting like one.

Nothing upped the stakes like a few heads on pikes. Or in this case, laps.

It was time to get this party started.

Reinvigorated on the heels of such a stellar success with the two vanilla reapers, he flashed to find some more.

Success.

And reapers.

***

Ruth was not taking 'No' or for an answer. This was bullshit. She felt fine. She'd experienced no cramping or bleeding in the four months since her return from the hospital, not so much as a hangnail. And not even a squirrel had touched the circle of protection since Nate's work reinforcing it. Now that she knew her mother was alive, the knowledge was consuming her. There was no way was she sitting here and waiting it out.

Determined to catch Nate before he left, Ruth kicked off the fleece blanket covering her legs and slid off the communal couch, heading for the doorway. Temperance, of course, flashed in front of her exit before she'd taken three steps.

No matter. If the angel wanted her to stay, she'd have to bodily detain her and so far she hadn't touched her with anything more than a hard glare. That whole spread-her-wings-and-glow-fire thing was a little intimidating, yes, but Ruth doubted Temperance had the clearance or the balls to turn her angel mojo against her.

Temperance was, after all, supposed to be protecting her. Toasting Ruth like a reaper marshmallow would surely be frowned upon. A slight twinge of guilt gave her pause, but it was quickly replaced by righteous resolve. Her mother was out there and she was going to find her. If Nate's magic could protect her here in the compound, she was certain that the magic of the entire coven could keep her even safer while she visited her mother. She just had to get there.

"I command you to move your ass, Temperance!"

Temperance crossed her arms across her chest and snarled like a pissed off punk rocker.

"I demand you allow me to pass!"

Nada. Nothing. All red-haired defiance.

"By my free will, I disavow your help and refuse your aid. Temperance, I reject you!"

Temperance's body began to shimmer, cutting in and out like a stormy satellite signal. The air sizzled with electricity as the angel's barely contained power leaked out in an orange glow. A light bulb popped behind her and Ruth flinched, turning in time to watch the glass fall to the floor. Another bulb shattered, then a third as the air hummed with power.

Ruth's fear built in intensity along with the power until every bulb shattered, leaving the radioactive glow of Temperance's energy the only light in the room.

The hair along Ruth's arms stood at attention and ice cold dread climbed up the back of her neck. What had she done?

The angel tried to hold her ground, her hands curled into fists, blood dripping from them as her nails bit through her palms. The muscles of her thin neck corded and strained with her effort to undo Ruth's words, but it was too late. Temperance's body blinked again, and she vanished into the consecrated subway, leaving a void of dark silence behind her.

"Shit."

Ruth reached for the doorknob and pushed out and into the yard.

"Shit, shit, shit, shit." She chanted as she crossed the frozen lawn in her gown and fuzzy slipper socks to Nate's trailer. So much for planning ahead.

Maeve opened the door, scythe drawn. She likely felt the shift in power before Ruth even arrived at the trailer.

"What happened? Are we under attack?"

"Not exactly."

"Are you injured? Is it the baby? Did Temperance hurt you?" Maeve searched the yard left then right. "Where is Temperance?"

"I—um—sent her away."

"You what?"

"Nate! Come out, please!" Ruth grasped the handrail and began to hoist herself up the trailer steps and past Maeve.

"He's already gone. He thinks the replacement reapers are in trouble. He left to help them. I've got to leave right now. I need to let Deacon know what's going on so he can bring backup."

"Dane and Carlos? How does he know?"

"He checked that phone app thing, and they dropped off of it while he was watching it."

"What do you mean they dropped off of it?"

"Hey, I'm not Steve Jobs here, but he said it was highly unlikely that they would both lose their phones at the exact same time."

"Maybe they flashed into the consecrated subway."

"They weren't anywhere near consecrated ground."

"Right."

"You'd better get back to your trailer. I'll help you." Maeve stepped down the stairs and waited to escort Ruth back.

"No. I'm going to go find my mother."

"Nate told you to stay here, Ruth. We don't have time for your drama. You're putting yourself in danger. You're not thinking clearly. I know I've been out of commission for a few months, but I still know that you're supposed to be on bed rest. If you think I'm going to incur the wrath of Nate and Deacon to let you do something this crazy, you are nuts. Now go to bed." Maeve took Ruth's elbow in her hand and tugged her toward the trailer.

Ruth jerked free of her hold. "I can go without you."

"You could. But where are you even going to go? Nate and I took the consecrated subway. You don't even know where to aim. And you *can't* use the subway."

"I'll go to the Bolton cemetery and...and..."

"Are you listening to yourself? Seriously, which one of us is mentally damaged here? You're talking crazy! No, no, no. Stay. Nate will take you as soon as things settle down. I'm sure of it. For the love of God, stay!"

Ruth looked down at her hands and dropped her shoulders in defeat. Maeve was right, of course. So was Nate. She'd just have to stay here and wait. More.

"I hate leaving you here alone now. You shouldn't have sent Temperance away."

"Bo is still here. I locked him in the communal room. I'll take him with me to my trailer." She turned to walk back.

"One more thing before you go."

"What?" Ruth asked, hope flaring in her eyes.

"I need you to walk me out of the circle."

"Oh."

Ruth escorted Maeve to the edge of the lawn and reached for her hand before crossing outside of the circle of protection. Maeve passed into the tall grass where she would be able to flash.

"Thanks."

"Sure." Ruth turned and made her way silently back to her trailer.

The slump of Ruth's defeated shoulders tugged at Maeve's heart and she called out to her. "Don't worry. We'll all be back soon. The circle is strong."

"Right."

Chapter Twenty-Nine

The best thing about the prison plan was that detained criminals were very compliant when the carrot of freedom was dangled before them. At least in the short-term. Without even knowing what they were signing up for, the prisoners had filed onto a bus headed his way. Of course, the alternative—staying in the prison—must have appeared less than attractive since they had watched their cellmates and guards lose their souls to demon attackers. After that, getting on a bus had to seem like a lesser evil.

Neither Camael nor his hellish minions could penetrate the reaper compound because of the magical shield created by their witch. There was nothing Camael hated more than magic. Okay, maybe reapers. Magic was certainly a close second.

But magic could only keep out the supernatural.

Not humans. Even their witch couldn't conjure that defense.

His display in the cemetery would soon draw all of the Authority reapers to investigate. He had no doubt. In the meantime, he would collect his missing piece while the Authority was otherwise engaged, and on Christmas Eve he would open the final portal. With the sacrifice, the portal could be kept open permanently and all of Hell's demons would be unleashed to reap his—their—harvest.

No more dicking around.

He waited and watched from his concealed position near the compound. Luckily, there was very little activity, which indicated that the distractions he'd set up in town had funneled the Authority resources there, just as he'd hoped. Movement caught his eye and he gasped when Maeve stepped out of one of the traveling tin-cans-on-wheels to talk to Ruth, who stood unprotected on its steps.

Clearly, he had been remiss in not confirming her demise, but he'd pulled her soul free on his way out. He'd felt it, seen it. That alone should have been enough to render her useless. He'd taken no care in shielding his thoughts from her while he occupied her body because he had planned to destroy her once she was no longer beneficial to him.

And now she was not only alive, but lucid and dressed for combat?

Frustration mounted inside him. This was one more in a long list of disappointments.

At this point, Maeve was a distraction he couldn't afford to pursue. Whatever the Authority might have gleaned from her was of no concern to him now. The wheels had been set into motion and no amount of interference would stop the momentum of what was about to happen. In a few more hours, his work would be done.

Relief filled him when Maeve flashed, leaving Ruth alone at the compound. He'd thought about capturing them both the moment Ruth stepped out of the circle of protection, but he needed to keep his own vessel intact and a physical method of transportation to get Ruth to the final portal. He couldn't afford any damage to his vessel to achieve his goals. He had a plan. He just needed to work it. The one question that he still pondered as he waited for his reinforcements to arrive was whether to kill the rest of the reapers before or after opening the final portal.

It would be so much sweeter to wait, forcing them to witness the full glory of their failure. Then again, killing them first would be equally satisfying. After all, the reason he had signed up for this mission in the first place was to revenge himself on reapers....

Well, they would die either way. He just needed to choose whether it would be quickly or slowly.

Decisions. Decisions.

Perhaps he'd flip a coin to decide.

As soon as he had what he needed safe and secure, he'd make his choice.

For now, he was content to watch the reaper compound from the edge of the circle of protection, careful not to get near enough to set off any alarms. It would take at least another half an hour before the demons brought his human minions by prison bus. Mechanical transportation was a pathetic, albeit necessary, limitation of being human.

Camael could smell the hellhound inside from where he stood, but he didn't see it on the grounds. Surely they hadn't made a pet of the thing and allowed it inside.

Savages.

Killing it would almost be more enjoyable than dispatching those two reapers tonight. He hoped he would get the opportunity. Even with the circle of protection, he could sense four souls inside the structures: the great betraying beast, Ruth and his quarry, and someone else. The fourth seemed somehow familiar, but who…or what could it be?

It wouldn't be much longer now.

***

Nate landed at the last known location of the replacement reapers and found a whole lot of nothing except for two crushed phones. The reapers had definitely been abducted. Sweeping his eyes over the street, he looked for any possible clues as to where they might have been taken. Nothing stood out. He was no detective. And without Bo, he had no idea how to start tracking them. Why hadn't he brought the dog along?

He wasn't thinking clearly. With everything that had been happening, he was beyond fried. This was just the sort of bullshit cowboy stuff that got a guy killed. The shitty thing was that he knew it. Would have kicked his friends' asses for it. And here he was doing the same damned thing. His emotions had made him weak.

And this reaper and angel and demon nonsense? What happened to the good old days when he'd thought all the bad guys were humans? Drunk drivers and serial killers.

He really wished he could forget the shit he'd learned over this past year. And after the latest revelations, that list of wishful unknowing was getting longer by the hour. Maeve might not be so lucky to have her memory back after all.

He needed to get to Deacon. So much was going down that he was completely unaware of, and now this diversion.

He checked his phone again. Deacon was less than four blocks away. The remaining reapers were scattered across neighboring streets. As Nate watched the screen, Maeve appeared on the radar, too, popping up in Maple Park Cemetery, probably out of sheer force of habit. The Authority reapers were still getting used to the fact that they no longer needed to use consecrated ground for flashing. She would be heading toward Deacon next. Nate slid back into the consecrated subway, relieved that he would be with both of them soon.

It was as good a place to start as any.

**

Bo growled beside the bed as Ruth beat her pillow into submission. She couldn't believe she was finally alone and she couldn't even enjoy it. Guilt racked her. Temperance had only been trying to help. Deep down she realized it, but dang it! She'd finally broken free of her self-imposed chains only to be imprisoned by new ones. Even if they were *for her own good*, it didn't make it any more palatable.

Bitter medicine was bitter medicine no matter how much bubblegum flavoring you poured into it.

While it had surprised her that she'd actually managed to send Temperance away, for the first time in a long time she was afraid. Ruth had no doubt that the circle of protection would hold, but something felt off. A flutter brought her hand to her rounded belly. It was way too early to feel a kick, but something was definitely going on in there. A wave of fear flooded through her. What if in all her hysterics she had hurt the baby after all? She was so stupid. Selfish. Stubborn.

Maybe she was genetically inclined to put her child in danger. If what Nate said was true and her mother Elaina had traveled the consecrated subway while nine months pregnant? Maybe the apple really didn't fall far from the tree.

Another twinge amped up her panic as the skin across her stomach grew tight for a few seconds then relaxed.

False labor? No, way too early for that.

She should never have read that stupid *What to Expect When You're Expecting* book.

Still, she knew something was agitating her unborn baby...and Bo.

She refused to act like a B-movie victim and go searching for trouble in the dark. She would, however, happily hold the sawed-off shotgun across her lap, aiming it at the trailer door. Deacon had given her quite an education on the gun. With the plug removed, it now held six shells. While he hadn't actually let her fire it, it seemed like a very effective weapon that required little finesse.

Pump. Shoot. Pump. Shoot. Repeat.

It was the next best thing to a hellhound...and a guardian angel.

As she grabbed the gun and rested the barrel across her stomach, she almost let herself believe that.

***

When Nate reached Deacon, his friend was busy dispatching yet another demon. He watched as the reaper surrounded the demon in an orange glow of energy before drawing it into his body. Deacon was the last stop for demons. The Authority reapers had taken to dropping the hosts in various secluded locations downtown, then clearing them in groups. It wasn't ideal, but it saved them dozens of trips to Purgatory every night to dispose of the bodies that would otherwise be littering the streets.

The non-Authority replacement reapers, the ones he searched for now, didn't have the special powers of the others, so the fact they'd vanished into thin air didn't bode well at all. Deacon could probably find them with his enhanced Powers sensitivities, but given all the craziness that was going down, he'd been a little busy.

Nate felt a twinge of guilt. It had been selfish of him to do nothing but search for and then take care of Maeve, but he'd been consumed.

Deacon noticed him as he approached and the relief on the dude's face was visible. Nate wouldn't let him down again.

"Thank God. You ever pull that disappearing shit on me again, I'm going to kick your ass six ways to Sunday. How's Maeve?"

"She's good. She'll be here any minute. We have a problem."

"Well of course we do. What now? Other than the obvious?"

Nate filled him in on the status of the replacement reapers, and then hit the highlights of his trip to the coven with Maeve. There wasn't time to get into the nitty-gritty, but the bombshell about Elaina Carter and Ruth possibly being his sister would be enough to throw Deacon off balance. Not to mention the incendiary fact that Maeve knew how Camael could be defeated.

"Finally we catch a break. Unbelievable. I can't wait to hear more. We need to shut this shit down...and now we can. He's going to try to accelerate his plan." He nodded at Nate. "Here comes your girl."

Nate cringed. He doubted Maeve would appreciate being referred to that way and he doubly doubted she was anywhere close to being his girl, despite their night together. Things had seemed much clearer while they were cocooned together in his basement room. Now he had no idea where they stood.

Maeve looked shaken as she walked toward them, her jet-black hair swaying between her shoulders.

"What is it?" Nate asked, concerned by the vacant look in her eyes.

"I found your reapers."

"That's great. Where are they?" Deacon asked, searching the street behind her.

"Dead. In Maple Park Cemetery."

"What the hell?" Deacon exploded in a fit of rage.

Nate took hold of her shoulders, forcing her to look at him. "Are you sure?"

"They're holding their heads in their laps. So, yeah, I'm sure. There's more." She looked back at Deacon. "Ruth sent Temperance away. She's pissed off and home alone. I didn't want to leave her, but Olivia wasn't back from the food kitchen yet and I knew I needed to find you, Deacon. She was talking crazy before I left. I think I talked her down, but…"

"Crazy how?"

"Like she-might-leave-the-compound-to-find-her-mom crazy. She wanted Nate to take her, and then she asked me when she realized he was already gone. I told her there was no way I was going to take her."

"Deacon!" Dardariel called as he and Ouriel emerged from a nearby alley.

"For the love of God, what now?"

"Something's going on at the prison. The place is coming apart at the seams. At first we thought it was a riot, but it's demons. The place is three-quarters empty. The only humans who are left are dead."

"Any more good news for me?"

"Raguel is missing."

***

Camael was pleased to see the bus pull down the long driveway after what had seemed like an eternity. The prisoners' arrival was a good omen. By now, the prison would be empty and the city would be full of wanderers and criminals. That should keep the Authority busy for long enough for him to collect what he needed and get everything into place.

His remaining demons would be busy ferrying the prisoners' souls to Hell. Soon the final portal would be open and they would all be free to play.

The bus came to a stop outside the circle of protection and Camael skirted the edge of the woods toward the vehicle. The door folded open and the first of twenty-four men walked down the steps and gathered in a group before him, several of them clearly evaluating all possible escape routes.

When one rather scrawny specimen started running toward the woods, Camael flashed over to him and tore his head off with a flourish. The man's body crumbled to the ground. Camael lifted up the head by the hair, careful not to get any more schmutz on his host than necessary, and walked back to his troops. There were no more runners after that.

Heads roll and people start paying attention.

An unusually tall, well-muscled human stepped forward. "What is this place?"

"Your name?"

"Little Stevie."

"Well, Little Stevie, this is the boonies, and if you can manage to accomplish a very simple task, *this* will be your ticket to freedom."

"If it's so simple, why don't you do it yourself?" A few prisoners grunted their approval from behind him.

Camael tossed the head at Little Stevie's feet. "Do not worry your pretty little head, dearest Stevie. I will be doing more than my fair share in tonight's activities.

Now, are you in? Will you claim your freedom by fulfilling this one small task or will you join the friend whose head is currently resting at your feet?"

"He's not my friend."

"Choose."

Little Stevie gave the head a sturdy kick, punting it away from him like a soccer ball. "What do you want us to do?"

Camael pointed toward the trailer where Ruth was holed up. "See that trailer? The one with a light on? All you have to do is go over there and bring the woman who's inside it here...to me. Nothing else."

"Why can't you do it?"

"Again with the questions? If you bothered to ask this many questions in your previous life, you would most likely not have been incarcerated in the first place. Do it or do not. It's your choice, but you will join your non-friend if your choice is no."

Little Stevie turned to the men behind him, evaluating his odds. "Let's do it."

Camael smiled as they crossed through the circle of protection without so much as a hiccup. So easy.

They walked toward the trailer, some using cover as they could. Two others traipsed right up to the front door and one turned the handle. The hellhound was through the door before the second man's foot touched the bottom step.

Their throats torn out, they didn't stumble far before dying in a gurgling pile in front of the door. Several of the other men stepped back, reevaluating their resolve.

"If you come back empty handed, *I* will tear your throats out. I suggest you proceed."

Little Stevie split the prisoners into two groups, one to deal with the dog and the other to make another attempt on the trailer. The first blast blew through the doorway as the next man breached the trailer. The dog swept through the distraction crew while five more shots blasted through the trailer door. When the shooting stopped, Little Stevie lunged through the doorway, reappearing a moment later with his hand around Ruth's throat and a blade pressed to her stomach.

The dog hunkered down and watched him as he brought her down the steps.

Little Stevie eased them back through the yard and toward Camael, using Ruth as a shield. A few more feet and Camael would be free to inflict some pain if need be.

"Camael, I assume," Ruth said.

"Yes, dear. It's wonderful to see you again."

"You have got to be batshit crazy to kidnap a pregnant woman."

"Oh, you are much more than that. Where is the other soul?"

"What are you talking about?"

"Another soul is near. Who and where?"

"What you see is what you get, Camael. There are no others."

She did not appear to be lying, but Camael could still feel the fourth soul nearby. "Put her on the bus." The demons grabbed hold of her and walked her up the stairs of the bus.

Bo charged toward the circle of protection after the straggling prisoners as they made their retreat. The great beast pinned the last man to the ground.

Camael watched with amusement as the man screamed for help, then summoned his demons to return to him. Before they could, Little Stevie walked up to the hound and sliced its soft underbelly with the blade he'd held to Ruth's stomach seconds before. The dog wailed and retreated, hunkering against the frozen ground, apparently helpless to leave the circle of protection without Ruth. Panting, the beast whimpered softly as blood pooled around its sides.

Killing the hound had been easier than he'd imagined. Camael laughed in admiration. "You are perhaps more helpful than I anticipated, Little Stevie."

Camael turned and walked back toward the bus when a glow behind him brought his attention back to the dog. The beast was radiating an aura.

What the hell?

As the glow grew more intense, the hound's panting increased as well. A bright explosion of light flashed, temporarily rendering Camael blind. When his vision cleared, the angel Rashnu crouched naked beside the hellhound. The fourth soul.

"Now things are getting interesting. Everyone onto the bus, you know where to go. Do not stop for anything. I'll be along shortly."

The bus cranked to life, turned in the yard and disappeared down the long driveway.

Camael stared at the angel as he found his bearings and stood.

"Naked as a newborn. So you've been hiding in the hellhound all this time?"

"Not hiding. Observing." Rashnu rose to his full height and stretched. First one wing then the other unfolded behind him, his aura glowing bright pink around him.

"You can't take Ruth, Camael."

"I already have. Or are you blind as well as stupid?"

"She's not the one you want."

"You're right about that. It's the soul inside her. Her child is the one I want."

"No. You've miscalculated. I've seen both possible paths, Camael. You won't win."

"I already have. Your premonitions are useless as always. You're just too dense to know when to give up."

"She's still alive, Camael."

Camael stilled, the words pinning him to the ground as sure as shackles.

He knew to whom Rashnu was referring, of course, but it was a trick. The angel would say anything to stall him until help arrived. He was trapped within the circle of protection and couldn't do anything until he was freed.

Camael turned to leave, refusing to acknowledge the statement.

"And the child is your grandchild."

"Liar."

"Have I ever lied to you, Camael?"

"You've done worse than lie to me, brother."

"You brought all of this upon yourself. None of us wanted for this to happen. The moment you lay with the reaper woman, you sealed your fate."

"As have you. Stay on Earth a while. You can watch the show."

"It doesn't have to end this way. You can still change course. You can be redeemed. Maybe even…reinstated."

Camael laughed, his chest aching with the effort. "*Reinstated?* Is that your best offer? I seriously doubt you have enough authority to make that happen. Besides, as I mentioned before, I know you to be a liar."

Camael turned away and walked toward the driveway. He was finished with Rashnu and his ridiculous claims. Grandchild, indeed. The mere thought of it was preposterous, but it was a button Rashnu would know to push.

These were tactics used by his new boss, too. Tricks he'd used himself.

Still, the angel's words had their intended effect and burned a torturous hole through his gut all the way back to the cemetery.

Liars.

Chapter Thirty

Ruth sat in a middle seat of the bus as it pulled onto the highway. The pitching and bouncing along the long gravel road left her nauseous. Her thin nightgown wasn't enough relief against the cold. Curling her legs and feet up underneath her body, she wrapped her arms around herself, shivering from the temperature as much as the unknown.

One of the men noticed her and removed his prison issued sweatshirt, offering it to her. She took it.

"Thank you."

"Sure."

"Where are we going?"

"Ma'am, you know as much as I do. An hour ago I was behind bars doing time. Now I'm here. Ain't that a deal?"

"Are you a demon?"

"I've been called a lotta things, but never no demon. Nah. Is that what he is? That dude back there?"

"He's an angel."

"Damn. I thought they was the good guys."

"Shut up." Little Stevie made his way to them and motioned for the friendly man to move to the front of the bus. Once he was gone, Little Stevie took his seat.

He stared straight ahead, ignoring her. She took notice of her surroundings. The padded bus seats and tiny half windows didn't offer much in the way of potential weapons or escape routes. Allowing one's self to be moved to a secondary location during a kidnapping was the worst possible scenario. Few people survived the abduction from that point onward.

And she had the hours and hours of true crime television she'd watched in the past few months to thank for that nugget of info.

She didn't even have decent shoes for God's sake. Leaning against the side of the bus, she rearranged herself so her arms were wrapped around her knees and her feet were angled against the seat. If the best weapon she had was kicking, she'd use it if need be. So far everyone was keeping their distance.

A few of the men were recounting their victory in the front of the bus. The men in the rear seemed more subdued. Ruth got the feeling that none of them knew what they were in for, herself included.

She prayed. Hard.

How she wished that she'd never sent Temperance away. She regretted taking her protection for granted, but she was determined to survive. Whatever Camael planned, she knew that the full force of the Authority was about to come down on his ass. And sitting helpless inside the bus while Rashnu appeared next to Bo? She didn't even know what to think of that.

A tear leaked from her eye.

Poor Bo. Such a good hellhound.

Nate would be heartbroken. Ruth reached up, surreptitiously wiping away the tear. No way was she crying in front of these assholes. The only thought that consoled her was that most of these men weren't possessed.

Yet.

***

The city was in chaos.

There were so many wanders and escapees running the streets that the citizens quickly fell into vigilante or victim mode. The State Penitentiary had held fifteen hundred prisoners at capacity, and now it was empty of life. Sirens wailed across the city and alarms pierced the night.

Even now, from Maple Park Cemetery, Nate could hear storefront glass breaking as looters took advantage of the bedlam. Maeve stood beside him and he resisted the urge to take her hand. Her presence was a comfort even if her demeanor was fierce. Maeve was pissed. She'd passed from mildly shell-shocked to full-on attack mode the second they got back to the cemetery, and now she was rocking on her heels in agitation, waiting to spring into action. Clearly there were still some unresolved emotional issues she needed to work through because she was a ticking time bomb when she was like this. That sort of all-consuming anger distorted a person's judgment.

Like he was one to talk.

Judge not others lest you be judged? Wasn't that the verse in the Bible?

Of course, it was easy to see fault in others.

He took her hand and let her pull his light into her. When she turned to him, the fire in her eyes lessened to a slow burn. It pleased him that he could ease her mind, if only slightly.

And that she didn't pull away.

Lost in the feel of Maeve's hand in his, he was surprised when his protection sigils began to twitch and dance in warning. Something was happening at the reaper compound. The boundaries were being tested. Repeatedly.

Deacon walked around the bodies, examining them as best he could while the Authority reapers arrived one by one through the consecrated subway. The reaper's souls had been reaped already or, more likely, stolen.

"Ouriel, take their bodies to Purgatory. There's nothing we can do for them." He faced his team. "Samkiel, when did you last see Ragu? Where was he working?"

"I talked to him three hours ago, and he was on the east side. Near the abandoned hospital. Do you think that freakin' angel got him, too?"

"Deacon," Nate interrupted. "Something's challenging the boundaries of the circle of protection at the compound."

"Of course, it is. Nate and Maeve, go home. Make sure everything is okay and stay with Ruth. Kylen, make sure Olivia stays at the homeless kitchen tonight. It would be better for her not to walk into whatever may or may not be going on at home. We're going to need everyone to try to settle things down. Dare, Oreo, Zak, Leo, Sam…we'll start at the prison and clear everything block by block until things are under control. Hopefully, we'll find Ragu kicking some ass along the way. We'll stay in visible range of one another, and we'll regroup in Purgatory if things go south. Nate, call me as soon as you get home and tell me everything is all right. Got it?"

"And if we don't find Ragu?" Samkiel asked.

"Not an option. Let's go."

Nate held Maeve's hand in his and concentrated on home.

***

Ruth's heart rate kicked into high gear as the bus pulled into a cemetery. Not only because it was a cemetery, but because the iron arch above the gate read *Bolton Cemetery*.

Her mind reeled.

The one place she wanted to go more than anywhere an hour ago and now she was here.

Be careful what you ask for was the sentiment of unusual wisdom.

The bus parked outside the gates, but Ruth stayed put. Despite her raging curiosity, the bus was the safest place for her for the time being. If they wanted her to leave it, they'd have to carry her off, kicking and screaming.

She looked out the window into the darkness. Traffic cruised by at regular intervals along the highway that ran through the narrow valley below the cemetery. With the slope and curve of the highway and the elevation of the cemetery, the car lights never angled up to the hillside enough to illuminate what was happening there. No one would see them on this outer road, sitting outside a rural cemetery in the middle of the night even though they were in a big, white prison bus.

Rashnu and Bo had been the only witnesses to her abduction, and she was fairly sure at least one of them was dead by now. She'd been praying incessantly for Temperance's return, but either she hadn't yet hit on the magical combination of words or no one was listening. What she wouldn't give to see those wings spread on her behalf again.

Stupid girl.

She couldn't even imagine what would come next.

217

Unfortunately, she wasn't going to have to wait much longer.

Chapter Thirty-One

Nate and Maeve landed in the yard of the Authority compound. They headed to Ruth's trailer but were sidetracked by the sound of Bo whining. Drawing his short sword, Nate eased between the trailers toward the sound, Maeve on his heels. Bo's pitiful cries were interrupted by soothing words delivered in a familiar voice.

Passing Ruth's trailer, Nate saw Bo lying on his side in a pool of fresh blood. A naked Rashnu had his palms pressed to the dog. They were bathed in a green glow and Rashnu's wings were wrapped around them both.

Nate's brain tried to process what his eyes were seeing, but couldn't make sense of it. Bo moaned again and Nate kicked into gear.

"What are you doing to my dog?"

"Healing him. And you will address me with respect," Rashnu said, his voice booming through the darkness.

Nate gripped the stainless steel handle of the short sword and did a quick mental walkthrough of the most obvious reasons why he shouldn't slice the angel's head from his shoulders. The list was short. He'd had more than enough nonsense from this bastard.

Bo lifted his giant head and cried out in discomfort. Nate kneeled beside the dog and placed his own hands on him, winding his fingers through his thick fur and stroking him in long passes.

"Bo." The dog relaxed and began to pull Nate's energy into his body, as well.

"What happened to him? Is Ruth okay?" For the first time, Nate noticed the yard was littered with bodies. Most of them torn to shreds. "What the hell happened here? Maeve, go check on Ruth, now!"

"Don't bother." Rashnu rocked back on his heels and rose to his feet. "She's gone. I couldn't escape your supernatural prison to save her. Bo was injured protecting her."

Nate staggered. "Gone? As in…"

"No. Not dead. Not yet anyway. Taken." Rashnu continued to stare at the hellhound, watching the dog's wounds knit together before their eyes.

"You just let her go?"

"Of course not."

"It was Camael, wasn't it?"

"Yes."

"Goddammit, if you can't—"

Rashnu spread his wings to their full expanse and lit up like a Yule bonfire. His green eyes shone with white light. "You will *not* take the Lord's name in vain."

Nate stepped back, and Bo rose to his feet and growled at the angel.

"Ungrateful wretch." With effort, Rashnu toned down his display and returned his wings to their folded position behind his back. Once his aura had faded, the wings disappeared completely. "I require clothing."

"Where did Camael take her? And how did he get past the circle of protection when you can't even leave it? In fact, how did you get here in the first place?"

"While I'm more than happy to recount the night's activities, it is rather cold, however, and I'm underdressed."

"I noticed," Maeve said with a smirk, retreating to Nate's trailer for clothing.

"Talk, angel. Where's Ruth?"

"Camael sent in humans to take Ruth and drag her through the circle. From there, they took her on a bus. Camael left on foot."

"Where would he take her? On a bus of all things?"

"He has reason to know that she can't travel through the consecrated subway in her condition. He mustn't be taking her far away, but I don't know where they're going."

Maeve returned with a bundle of clothing and boots, tossing them at Rashnu's feet for him to retrieve.

Rashnu nodded at her. "You're too kind."

"Tell us more, Rashnu. I'm at the end of my rope here," Nate said.

"Careful, reaper. My powers in this realm are not as limited as you may think." Rashnu pulled on the jeans Maeve brought him, then slipped on the shirt. He picked up the light jacket, slid it on and zipped it shut.

"I'm not a reaper."

"As unceremonious as this announcement is...yes, you are quite obviously now a reaper. Although, it's also apparent that you are much, much more than that. Which, I think, you already know."

Nate ignored his comments. Two could play this game. "How did you get here? And who's minding Purgatory?"

Rashnu looked to the sky as if for answers or perhaps patience, which he was clearly lacking. "I've resided in the hound for some time, trying to keep an eye on the progress down here. When you didn't take Bo with you outside the circle when you left, I became trapped inside him. I couldn't depart until he left the circle of protection or, as it happened, nearly died. And now you know as much as I do."

"Oh, I doubt that very much. Why won't you just tell me what the hell is going on so I can stop it?" Nate asked.

"This is your battle to win or lose, Nate, but I can occasionally point you in the right direction."

"Now would be a fine time for some of that pointing."

Rashnu looked from Maeve to Nate, then back again. "You'll find your answers, Nate. But they may not be what you expect."

"For the love of all that's holy in—" Nate balled his fists in frustration and began to advance on Rashnu. He was fed up with this asshole and his puzzles.

"Nate, stop!" Maeve stepped between him and the angel, pushing him back with one hand. "As annoying as Rashnu is, he's not our enemy. We need to tell Deacon what happened, and we need to find her. Now."

Energy flickered between them where Maeve's hand was pressed against his chest and he immediately calmed down. "Better?" she asked.

Nate lowered his fists. "Yes." Bo protested beside him. "And you? Are you all right?" He bent to examine him.

"He's fine. Better than new. He would have healed on his own in a few hours even without my help," Rashnu said. "There's only one way to kill a hellhound and disembowelment isn't it."

"And that would be?"

"Well, I can't tell you all of the secrets of the universe, now can I?"

The vein along Nate's temple pulsed. "Angel, you're coming with us. If you have any worthwhile mojo up here, now's the time to use it."

Rashnu's brows rose, but Maeve didn't give him time to argue. She grabbed his hand and Nate's, and the four of them flashed to the east side of Meridian.

Chapter Thirty-Two

Ruth was ashamed of her weakness, but the cold had taken most of the fight out of her. That, along with the crushing fatigue that weighed down on her, was more worrisome than the men on the bus who ignored her, carrying on with their own rowdy banter. All but Little Stevie. He'd cast more than a few questioning glances her way, his mouth set in a grim line.

A flutter rolled through her belly again, almost as if her unborn child were as frightened as she was. She couldn't let that happen. She needed to control her emotions. Now.

Trying to conjure a calming aura, she closed her eyes and drew in a deep breath, just like the Lamaze breaths she'd been practicing with the help of YouTube videos.

"What are you doing?" Little Stevie's eyes grew large and she could see his fear.

"Trying to relax. Is it bothering you?"

"You're…glowing."

How could he possibly see her manufactured aura? Humans often pretended to see them, but it was almost always a ruse. There was no way he could know what she was doing, let alone see it. She stopped immediately.

"Bring her out. Carefully." Camael's voice boomed from outside the bus.

Little Stevie stood and reached for her, then pulled his hand back. "We can do this the hard way or the easy way. Your choice."

Ruth could tell he didn't want to touch her after her aura display, which was just fine with her. She didn't want him to. Her plan to start kicking and screaming was quickly falling to the wayside in favor of self-preservation. If Camael wanted her off this bus, any one of these men would be capable of achieving that goal. She wasn't much of a match for them without her weapons and full reaper faculties.

Rising from the seat, she tugged the sweatshirt down over her stomach and hips as low as it would go, and then shuffled into the aisle. The prisoners filed out before her and she couldn't help but feel she was marching to her death.

Still, Ruth shuffled down the stairs and onto the frozen grass, where the moisture from the ground soaked through her thin sleep socks. She tried to see the layout of the cemetery, but the sliver moon didn't cast enough light for her to make much out.

Bolton Cemetery.

Even under the circumstances, the thought rose unbidden: *My mother was here!*

She was so close to finding her. Actually meeting her. And if Nate could reinsoul Elaina like he'd done with Maeve? She might even get some of the answers she'd always wanted. It was too much to wish for...but she did.

Ruth tried to make out the names on the grave markers. While she knew her mother's body wasn't really here, she still wanted to see the grave. She wanted to reach down into the earth and check for herself. But Camael hadn't brought her here to sightsee.

"Come." Camael walked toward the back of the cemetery, expecting her to follow. She was surprised when her feet began to do just that.

What was she doing? She could flash now. Leave them all behind. The ground was still consecrated, but it was failing quickly. She could feel it. But what would be the consequences? Would the baby die? Would she?

It was an impossible choice and one she wouldn't make. Whatever happened to her would happen to them both. She would die protecting her if need be.

Her?

It.

Her.

Suddenly she knew she was carrying a girl. Maybe she would name her Elaina.

Elaina Grace.

"Why are you smiling?"

Without realizing it, she'd stopped walking and Camael had turned to glare at her.

Emboldened, she shared her news, hoping it would make him rethink his plan, whatever it was. "I'm carrying a girl. I'm going to name her Elaina Grace."

Camael staggered backward, nearly falling onto the headstones behind him. His reaction was baffling, but satisfying. Maybe he'd let her go and abandon his foolishness. There had to be some good inside him still. Wasn't there? He had been an angel once.

"Rashnu told you to say that."

Ruth narrowed her eyes. "No. I decided just now what I would name her. And I think you know why."

Camael hesitated and gave her a hard stare.

"Let me go. Whatever you have planned, there's still time to stop it. You could do better. You could *be* better. There's still hope."

Camael closed his eyes and shook his head. "That hope is what will get each and every one of your pathetic reapers killed. The sooner the better."

He walked toward an eight-foot by eight-foot concrete crypt and pushed open the door. "Inside."

"It's too cold in there. I'll die."

"Yes, you will die. But not inside this crypt." He reached over and yanked a former prisoner forward. "Take off your clothes and give them to the girl."

The man obeyed, undressing and handing her a stack of clothing. Mercifully, he left on his underwear. She'd seen all the naked men she cared to tonight. An eyeful of Rashnu would haunt her for the rest of her days. Days that seemed to be decreasing in number by the second.

"Go."

Ruth's heart hammered hard in her chest as she played several possible scenarios through her mind. He had to be confident that she wouldn't risk flashing if he were planning to leave her here alone. Another wave of indecision flooded through her. She wanted to scream almost as badly as she wanted to scratch Camael's eyes out. She thought to challenge him further, but feared his wrath. Clearly she had been wrong about the fallen angel, which made the thought that the monster could be their father all the more unbearable.

If he could leave her here, pregnant and alone in a cold crypt, then there was no hope for him.

There was no hope for any of them.

Chapter Thirty-Three

Camael wanted to be alone instead of face-to-face with a dozen of the worst humans he could possibly imagine in the graveyard where his wife had died. Or at least that's how he thought of her. When he allowed himself to think of her.

Despite Rashnu's desperate talk, he knew a man, an angel or any creature, for that matter, would say or do anything under the right circumstances. Admit to anything. Divulge…anything.

Ridiculous. He was just baiting me.

He wouldn't have dwelled on it any more if the whoring reaper hadn't invoked *her* name. How did she even know it?

Impossible.

But now wasn't the time for him to start second-guessing himself. He'd come way too far to do any soul searching and was hours away from achieving his final retribution. With the sacrifice on ice, so to speak, he could rally his troops and open the portal. And how wonderfully perfect that it would happen at the best possible time for a sacrilegious slap in the face of his enemy.

Christmas Eve.

The added irony of using a pregnant reaper to achieve his goal did not escape him. An innocent soul was required to hold the portal open. What could be more innocent than an unborn child?

Originally, he'd thought he would have to wait for the sacrifice to actually be born, but in retrospect...why? Was it not fully formed already? Named in the book of life?

For all intents and purposes, it counted. Killing its mother in the process was a bonus. As soon as he opened the portal and made the sacrifice, the other reapers would descend upon this place and the demons would darken the skies for a hundred mile radius as they fled from Hell until it was empty. Camael wasn't a math genius, but with some quick calculations, he figured the total annihilation of mankind should take around seven days.

Seven days to create.

Seven days to recreate.

With the desecration of the Earth complete, the bonds of Lucifer would be broken and he would be free as well.

After that, Camael didn't care what happened.

He was an angel with nothing left to lose.

While he'd originally intended to open the portal closer to the city, it really didn't matter. Once the demons were free, they would cover the distance quickly. Bolton Cemetery was as good a place as any to open the portal. Besides, his sacrifice was secured on the location now. And the whole execution of his plan had a lovely symmetry to it.

"Boss? Boss? Boss?" One of the pecker-gnat humans called to him.

"What!" Camel snarled.

"Um—erm—what now? You want us to drive you somewhere?"

Again with the urge to smite…en masse.

He searched the group, ignoring the idiot who'd questioned him. Spotting his charge, he smiled. "Little Stevie, please return the bus with our very helpful friends here back to Meridian. Then you are free to go and participate in the merriment. Live as though it's your last day."

Little Steve didn't ask any questions. He turned and mounted the bus steps, commandeered the driver's seat and waited for the bus to fill with the other prisoners.

Smart man. An anomaly for sure.

Camael reveled in the silence filling the empty cemetery, interrupted only by the occasional hum of a car from the highway below and the wind through the trees. He walked to the edge of the cemetery one last time to visit Elaina's grave. He would be back tomorrow night, but there'd be no time for reflection then.

As it was, perhaps he'd allowed himself too much time for reflection.

A strange glow on the far horizon caught his attention. Globe-like, it pulsed like the glimmering of a tremendous forest fire, yet it was more consistent and controlled.

Almost like a circle of protection.

Interesting.

He flashed out of Bolton Cemetery to investigate before making his final preparations.

***

Nate and Maeve landed with Rashnu and Bo within a block of Deacon. Flashing through the consecrated subway wasn't an exact science even on a good day. This was far from a good day. When he hadn't been able to reach Deacon by phone from the reaper compound, Nate had left a text message telling him that Ruth was gone, but he knew Deacon was probably engaged in a skirmish and wouldn't get the communication anytime soon. This was the sort of bad news that was best delivered in person, but he'd been anxious to get through to his friend.

The Authority reapers were traveling eastward according to the phone app, away from the prison. Raguel was still off the map.

Rashnu was wide-eyed and full of wonder as he surveyed the street before them.

"This isn't your first trip topside, right?" Nate asked.

"No. But it has been some time since I've been here in this form." Rashnu walked forward with purpose.

"Where are you going?" Maeve asked, drawing her scythe as Nate drew his weapon.

"Into battle."

Maeve looked at Nate as the angel walked away from them. "Do you think he knows what he's doing up here?"

"Do any of us?" Nate started forward.

The street was empty of visible life, strange even for this late hour. Cars were parked along the commercial street in an orderly manner that suggested nothing untoward had happened, but when they passed a few bars, he noticed that though music blared into the night, no patrons remained, inside or out.

Nate checked his phone. It was 12:03 a.m. Not even last call yet, but officially Christmas Eve.

He wasn't feeling all that festive. An occasional tightening in his gut had him worried. The last time he'd experienced a similar sensation was the night Ruth had nearly lost her baby.

He kept that tidbit to himself as they closed the distance to Deacon.

Bo followed at his side, more subdued than usual. Of course, Nate didn't blame him. Being disemboweled had to put a damper on things. It was comforting to know he couldn't be so easily dispatched, but Rashnu had been less than clear about what actually could kill the hellhound.

Less than clear summed up every communication he'd ever had with the angel. Nate wondered what his physical and metaphysical limitations were outside of Purgatory. He had an idea he was about to find out firsthand.

"Rashnu, I assume you have some sort of plan for finding Ruth? For helping us to clean up this mess?"

"My plan is to return the soulless bodies of God's children to Purgatory."

"And? Camael and his demons can do as they please, but it seems like you can't be bothered to lift a hand? Why did you even crawl up from Purgatory then?"

"Must you question everything?" Rashnu turned to face him. "Have you no faith in the power of good?"

"All I know is that it appears as though the Authority reapers have been hung out to dry. Each disaster is worse than the last. Two dead reapers. Two others missing? You commission us—them—to do a job, then sit idly by and watch as we are beaten into failure when it's obvious you could be doing more to help."

"And what would you have me do, nephilim? Your continued existence is evidence enough of the mercy of God. You and your sister could bring about an end to all that he has created. Or you could save it. Even so, he *chose* to allow you free will instead of destroying you as he once did all who went against him. Peace and love is what he desires for you and mankind, yet each of you continues to choose the most selfish path possible, making that future appear impossible. The pattern continues over and over and over."

"Do you have free will?"

"Of course."

"Then use it and save the souls who have been lost tonight."

Rashnu sighed. "If only it were that easy. Every choice has its consequence. The souls that were stolen by demons this night are beyond even my help."

Maeve spoke up. "But isn't there a chance they can be saved? Why else have we been taking the wanderers to the Purgatory holding area?"

"Once the soul passes into Hell without its body to protect it, there's no reinsouling. Period."

"They why did you keep all the wanderers we sent to you?" Maeve asked.

"We didn't. As soon as the location of their souls was determined, we destroyed their physical bodies. Ashes to ashes, dust to dust. You know the drill."

"All of them?" Nate asked, appalled.

"Then what about me? How was Nate able to save…me?"

"Yes. All were destroyed. It was the only remaining option. Maeve's soul was never brought to Hell. That was the only saving grace that made your act possible, Nate. That and your heritage."

"Because I'm nephilim."

"Yes."

"If you were able to determine the whereabouts of the wanderers' souls, then tell me where my mother's soul is, Rashnu."

The angels hesitated, visibly weighing his response. "There are some questions you may not want answered."

"Bullshit. Tell me and I'll decide for myself. No more puzzles or half-truths. Where is she?" Nate advanced toward Rashnu, his anger building.

"Her soul was ferried to Hell."

Nate's stomach clenched, cold and hollow. He'd expected as much, but to hear it aloud was somehow worse. "So she's dead then. Just like the rest of these poor bastards. No hope at all."

"Not exactly."

Nate closed the distance between him and the angel, and pushed him back and against the brick wall of an abandoned pub, a mustard colored aura seeping from him in waves.

"For once. Say it clearly. What do you mean by 'not exactly'?"

The angel drew in a long, harsh breath then exhaled, looking as though he'd enjoy nothing more than to smite Nate into smoke. Nate wondered why it hadn't already happened. Rashnu wasn't known for his patience. "It means that her soul is in Hell, but it hasn't been released. It's still entrapped, and as of this moment, it has been untainted by Hell. Her soul is still pure."

Nate eased his grip and allowed the angel to collect himself. "Pure enough to be reinsouled?"

Rashnu shook his head. "No. It's been too long. Her body will have failed beyond healing after this long. If she even has a body any longer."

"So you don't know where she is?"

"Her soul? Yes, it is as I told you. We've known for years."

"Her body."

"We are in the business of tracking souls, not their shells. Do not build up false hope, Nate. Even with your unnatural skills, you won't be able to reinsoul your mother."

"Maybe not, but her soul could be sorted to Heaven if it were recovered now?"

Rashnu tugged at the hem of his shirt, straightening his rumpled clothing. "If that is its intended location...yes. In its current condition... it would be *possible*."

The first sounds of real conflict echoed down the alley from one street over. Bo barked and raced toward the action.

"We're not finished here, angel."

"I've no doubt."

Chapter Thirty-Four

Maeve's head pounded as they reached the action on Starnes Street. Ouriel walked down the center of the street, exuding an orange aura that was ensnaring a group of shambling wanders in its metaphysical web, then vanished into Purgatory. Dead bodies littered the street and sirens wailed in the distance. The human officers were spread thin across the vast city as chaos reigned everywhere.

Deacon followed behind him, vacuuming up demons as they streamed forth from the fallen bodies.

Maeve's head had been killing her since they left the Authority compound and now nausea began to roll up from her stomach, lodging in her throat and forming a hard lump there. The streetlights melted in her vision from crisp light to muted halos, and her hands tingled from her wrists to the tips of her fingers. She gripped her scythe tighter.

She didn't have time for this shit.

She counted back the hours since she'd last eaten. Eighteen? Breakfast with Nate's family?

Had that really only happened yesterday morning?

She continued forward, moving one foot in front of the other, but couldn't concentrate on anything but the strange feeling in her body. Coming to a stop, she shut her eyes. A surge of energy coursed through her body and an aura began to manifest around her against her will. She could feel it begin, but was helpless to control its progress and inevitable release. White light exploded behind her eyelids and she squeezed her eyes more tightly shut.

Fear charged inside her. She knew this feeling. The white light. The pain.

This was the energy that had killed her brother.

Terrified that she might not be able to contain it, she fell to her knees behind Nate, her scythe clattering to the pavement as she struggled to hold herself together and tamp down the growing storm inside her.

Something had triggered this reaction. Too bad she wasn't sure what.

Forcing her eyes opened, she watched in a pain-blurred haze as Samkiel continued to gather the wanderers for transport. Unexpectedly, grey streams began to rise from the fallen bodies still on the street and others rounded the end of the alley and streamed toward them.

Uncollected souls?

She clutched at her head, desperate to slow the surge of power. To flash. To get away from here.

Away from Nate.

Her poisonous energy consumed her as she rocked herself on the pavement.

"Maeve!" Nate knelt by her side and reached for her.

She scrambled away. "No! Don't touch me!"

"Maeve, what's wrong! What's happening?"

Her skin was on fire as energy crept beneath its surface, barely contained within her body.

"Rashnu, help her! What's happening to her?"

Rashnu looked down at her, his right eyebrow rising in surprise before he looked back at Nate. "She's actuating into a Valkyrie."

Maeve heard his words, but couldn't comprehend them. Another of Rashnu's riddles?

Valkyrie? No. Impossible.

She'd been assured during her reaper training that her energy disability would prohibit such a thing from ever happening. She was defective.

The souls continued to stream from the bodies, several dozen of them now. They swirled down the street in a solid storm of activity. Certain she was about to pass out, Maeve pressed the heels of her hands to the sides of her forehead, trying to relieve the excruciating pressure building there.

The storm of souls stopped spinning, recalibrated and swarmed toward Maeve at an impossible speed. Striking her in the heart chakra with the full force of a blow, she fell back, her head cracking against the pavement as they streamed into her, filling her body.

This was the end.

As the souls penetrated her body, jockeying for position inside her, she said her mental goodbyes and made peace with her life. Accepted the end.

Maeve's body shook with seizures as the souls continued their relentless swirling. There were too many, far too many. She reached for something solid to hold onto, both physically and mentally, afraid they would tear her to bits here in the street.

How many souls were there? Two—three—dozen?

Maeve's hand made contact with something warm and familiar. Nate's hand closed around hers, gripping it tightly. She tried to jerk away, but as he pushed his turquoise energy into her, filling her with his light, the souls began to settle down inside her.

The pain in her head subsided to a dull thud along her right temple, uncomfortable but tolerable. Nate whispered words of encouragement, but they were drowned out by the thunderous drubbing of her heart, which echoed in her ears.

She needed relief.

She needed the souls gone.

***

"What's happening to her, Rashnu?" Nate held onto her hand, encouraging her to stay conscious and fight whatever was threatening her.

"She needs to ferry the souls to Purgatory."

"I'll take her," Nate offered.

Deacon finally reached them. "What the hell are the three of you doing here? And who's with Ruth?"

"Deacon, Ruth is missing."

Deacon grabbed Nate's collar and pushed him against the side of parked van. "What do you mean? She's not in the compound anymore?" he growled.

"No. Camael took her. Rashnu was there, but he couldn't stop him."

"Because of your magical shield, I might interject," Rashnu said.

"He's been hiding inside of Bo. When Bo was injured trying to protect Ruth, Rashnu was flushed out. He's been spying on us. We've got to find her. I can feel her. She's in trouble…like before."

"The baby? Is she having problems with the baby, too?" Deacon's hands tightened and a mustard yellow aura leaked out around him.

"I'm don't know, but I'm fearful for her."

Deacon released Nate and fell on Rashnu with the sort of rage Nate felt percolating in his own heart and soul for the asshole. Deacon's aura surrounded him in a cloud of fury. "Find her, Rashnu. Help us."

"I can't track her from here. If we retire to the reaper lounge, then perhaps I can make some inquiries."

Deacon jabbed a finger into Rashnu's chest punctuating each word. "You. Will. Find. Her. Alive."

"We can hope."

Chapter Thirty-Five

Nate scooped Maeve into his arms and stood, her face pressed into his chest as her body continued to tremble with the weight of too many souls. Everything was spinning out of control: Camael, the demons, Ruth, Elaina, Rashnu, Maeve, not to mention the mass of humanity lost.... It seemed as if the world had already gone to Hell.

He dared to imagine what else could go wrong.

Then it did.

His phone buzzed before they flashed and he managed to fish it out of his pocket. Rosemary's name appeared on his screen in a green bubble with a message that sunk his heart: *The coven is under attack.*

What exactly was he supposed to do? Who could he save? Maeve? His mother? His adoptive parents? His sister?

He wasn't even confident he could save himself at this point.

Rashnu's two paths played out in his mind again, the drawings from his room, Maeve's memories. Which was the right choice? Would the wrong one damn them all?

Nate was being torn apart at the seams.

Bo nudged at his elbow, urging him to flash.

The life in his hands...well, perhaps he could do something about.

He prayed everyone else could hold on a little longer.

They flashed to Purgatory.

***

Camael summoned his imps and demons to the bizarre compound he'd discovered beneath the ethereal glow of a powerful circle of protection. He commanded them to return Little Stevie and his bus-load of prisoners as well. The humans might come in handy yet again.

He'd scoured the countryside for miles after Elaina and the children vanished. How had he missed this place?

From his earlier vantage point on the mountain, he could see that the compound consisted of a small city, hidden by thousands of acres of national forest as well as the magical shield that covered it. Humans would be repelled by the magic if they somehow managed to wander this far into the woods.

The fact that the witches had taken such pains to conceal the place piqued his interest enough to temporarily sidetrack him. Something more than magic radiated from within its walls.

Something...familiar.

Anxiety bubbled up from deep inside him. Here he was...waiting for humans to do his bidding. It was getting ridiculous, this dependence on lesser beings. He hoped Rashnu was enjoying equal amounts of frustration on this plane. Even before Camael fell, his powers had been greatly diminished while on Earth.

He'd let his guard down to the point of stupidity back then. By the time he met Elaina, he was especially vulnerable. He had been searching for a guardian angel, who—it turned out—wasn't lost at all. Earth had become the Florida retirement option of angels who wanted out of the rat race Heaven had become.

After two or three millennium, the repetitive nature of daily life wore on an angel. Camael could understand that well enough—once he realized there could be a different life for him, it became all he could think about.

Elaina had been searching for a similar change.

Humans liked to think such a meeting was fate, a predetermined future planned out by a great and powerful overseer with one's best interests at heart. Complete bullshit, of course. Humans had free will. Sure there may have been an original master plan, but one diversion from the path, one different choice set the whole thing reeling into chaos.

Now he *was* the chaos.

And he had no more idealistic notions about fate, only action and its direct results. He was a creature who made things happen.

The first step was to send in his humans to break down the magical shield. Then he'd work on breaking the consecration of the grounds. An area this large wouldn't take much—he'd simply let his human minions carve a path of destruction leading to the city center. Then he'd be free to investigate as the masses fled.

And they always fled.

This diversion would take time, but he was still near enough to his final staging ground that he could justify it. A chunk of flesh fell from his forearm. His host body was already deteriorating. He'd have to upgrade before tonight's activities.

He had already chosen his next host, and as luck would have it, the bus pulled down the narrow lane just as the thought crossed Camael's mind. Maybe there was such a thing as fate after all.

Camael smirked at his own foolishness.

Little Stevie would make a fine replacement.

The bus lurched toward him down the gravel road, which led to an open field at the edge of the powerful circle of protection. The bus came to a halt in front of him and the doors folded open. His demons began to arrive as the men made their way down the rubberized steps and gathered in the yard.

"Change in plans. Your services are in need once again."

Little Stevie spoke for the group. "What now? What do you want us to do?"

"You, dear Stevie, I want to stay right here. The rest of you will walk straight into the small town before you and do what you do best. Destroy and wreak havoc. Have your way with whom and what you find, but make it quick and make it thorough. My associates and I will follow behind you as soon as you've cleared a path for us."

When there was no movement from within the group, Camael bellowed, "Do you need an incentive? Which among you would like to volunteer to be said incentive? Have you already forgotten our last interaction?"

Reluctantly, they moved forward, unsure of what to do without Little Stevie to lead them.

"Go. Do what he says," Little Stevie said. "We'll be along."

The group passed through the magical barrier and disappeared into the city.

"Now what?" Little Stevie turned to Camael and then took a step back, having finally gotten a good look at him in the moonlight.

"Yes, as you can see, my form is failing. That's why I'll be taking yours."

Camael abandoned his host body, letting it crumple to the ground before he slammed his essence into a very surprised Little Stevie. He filled the man's slightly smaller frame to the max, then stretched inside him, testing his boundaries and liking his new accommodations just fine.

There was nothing better than a fresh host.

The knowledge that this host would be his last made the feeling all the sweeter.

Demons paced the edges of the circle in their host bodies, anxious to please their master, and then his imps arrived, too, bounding out from the inky blackness of the forest and across the grassy field. The entire family was here to play. His remaining minions filled the woods behind him. What a perfect pre-party destroying this compound this would be. A succulent taste of destruction to come.

The screams began to sound like Sunday church bells from within the now breeched circle of protection. But it wasn't the sound that pulled him forward, it was that something else that he'd sensed earlier. He watched as the aura of magic faltered then sputtered out.

So easy.

Maybe too easy?

Camael sent the imps through first to test the barrier. When they met with no resistance, he commanded the demons through next. They fanned across the city as Camael made his way into its heart, pulled by a force much stronger than magic. Stopping in front of a small house, he walked around the stone fence lining its front yard and onto the porch.

Not bothering to knock, he pushed open the door then closed it behind him against the beautiful sounds of terror and mayhem.

"I knew you'd come for her one day."

His head snapped to his left. An elderly woman sat in a rocking chair by the window. She held his gaze, her expression defiant, though he could tell that she trembled inside.

"For whom, old woman? Whom do you keep here?"

"I think you know."

Trepidation curled along his spine. "And do you mean to stop me in my pursuit?"

"What will be, will be."

Camael scoffed. He hated that sort of godly reasoning. Wanted to smite her for mumbling such nonsense, but there wasn't time. Something lay at the end of the hallway, something that was waiting for him...and him alone. This close to the source of the beacon that had drawn him here, he was surprised to find doubt creep into the mix.

The hallway seemed to stretch forever in front of him until at last he stood inside the doorway. One more step and he'd have what he'd been looking for. One more step and...

A gasp escaped him before he could fully process what he saw before him. His heart recognized her before his brain caught up. Even deteriorated and wasted away, he knew her instantly.

Or what was left of her.

Elaina.

Chapter Thirty-Six

Nate set Maeve down on the couch in the opulent reaper lounge in Purgatory. Bo rested his head on her boots. No matter how many times he was here, Nate would never get used to it to this place. He didn't want to be a reaper. Didn't want to be a nephilim.

He wanted the people he loved to be safe, secure and happy. A category which none of them currently fell into. Samkiel and Deacon stalked out of the room through the heavy wooden doors—Samkiel to discharge his cargo of wanderers, which trailed behind him in a long line, to the holding cell and Deacon to dispose of his demons in privacy.

Holding cell.

More like a tomb.

Now that Nate knew the truth about where the wanderers were headed, he was less and less impressed with Rashnu and his kin.

Maeve moaned softly beside him. "How do we purge the souls from her when she's in this condition? How long must she suffer?"

"I can do it." Rashnu reached forward to place his hand on her forehead, a glow of energy preceding his touch. A bright light like a static charge sparked and bit him before he could make contact. He jerked away from her in surprise.

"I guess it will need to come from her. I can't seem to facilitate the change. Which means it will take as long as it takes." Rashnu retreated to the bar. "Unless…"

"Unless what?" Nate shifted and pulled Maeve up and into his lap, cradling her body against his. She drew energy from him even in her compromised state.

"You seem to have no problem sharing energy with her. It would speed things up if you were to push the souls from her."

"How the hell would I do that?"

"The same way you share energy with her now, only with more intent. Fill her with your light until there is no room inside her for any soul but her own. The rest will flee when pressed. Then she will be free to finish her transformation."

"Will it hurt her?"

"It will be uncomfortable this first time, but after her transformation is complete, each reaping will make her stronger. She must continue to stretch her capacity to reach her full potential. The first time is always the most painful."

Maeve moaned and pulled her knees into her stomach. Nate couldn't stand to see her suffer in any way. If he could help, he would. And the sooner, the better. He needed to get to the coven, but he couldn't leave Maeve to suffer if he could ease her pain. He pulled her closer, making as much body contact with her as he could, then bent to kiss her. The light built inside of him until his body trembled with the accumulating power and it could no longer be contained.

His energy poured into Maeve, filling her from stem to stern, lighting her chakras up like a string of Christmas lights. When he pulled away from her, his energy continued to flow from every point of bodily contact, absorbing into her like rain into peaty soil. Maeve's mouth sprang open and her head hinged backward as souls began to stream out of her overtaxed body. White light beamed from her eyes as one soul after another flowed out. Nate watched in amazement and awe.

Soon thirty-six souls were swirling around the exit chimney in the center of Rashnu's chamber and Maeve collapsed into a faint against him.

Nate's light diminished and exhaustion overtook him. He fought for consciousness as he watched Rashnu dismiss the souls with a wave of his hand. They streamed up and vanished through the chimney.

"Where will they go?"

"They will be sorted along with the others."

"Is your alter ego still out there? Sorting?"

"Of course. Death never stops."

Maeve appeared to be unconscious and oblivious to their conversation.

"Well done, reaper."

Barely able to speak, Nate couldn't let the address go unchallenged. "I'm not a reaper."

"We'll have to remedy that soon." Rashnu placed his hand on Nate's shoulder and pushed a warm glow of energy into him. "Now, recharge Maeve and let's get back to the battle. Shall we?"

"You're coming back topside?"

"I wouldn't miss it."

Nate started to pulse energy back into Maeve. "Have I chosen the right path? How are we going to defeat him, Rashnu? Is it even possible?"

"All things are possible."

"Rashnu, if Ruth and I are nephilim and you once sent hunters to kill us…why are we still alive? What changed?"

"Even Heavenly hearts can change. Something that was once misunderstood does not need to be forever feared. Diversity, it turns out, can be a good thing. If you had been captured by our hunters instead of hidden by the coven all these years, the outcome would have been different. You three would have been destroyed as was ordained. But time has a way of either softening or strengthening grudges and fears. When God realized your very existence might be the one thing that could change Camael's course of action, he called off the pursuit."

"So he wanted to use us as bait to draw out Camael?"

"More a secret weapon. The ties of family are what drove Camael to the brink. Perhaps they could also bring him back."

"You think he can be redeemed? After all the lives he's taken?"

"Redeemed? Perhaps. But not in the way you are thinking. He will not go unjudged regardless of what happens above. He will pay for his crimes against humanity."

"What am I supposed to do?"

"Whatever your heart tells you."

Maeve stirred in his arms and when her green eyes opened, relief flooded through Nate's body. She stretched out long and languid like a cat, then smiled up at him.

"What did I miss?"

"The beginning of the end."

Nate stroked her face before turning back to Rashnu. "Deacon is going to be back soon. Please find Ruth."

"Believe it or not, I want to find her just as much as you do." Rashnu walked behind the bar and poured a drink for himself.

"Is that your answer for everything? A drink?"

"Hardly, but it does open oneself up to possibilities." He drank the liquid, then set the glass onto the bar, closing his eyes in concentration.

"And what do you call that particular concoction?"

"Bourbon."

After several minutes passed, Deacon returned before Rashnu delivered any proclamations. Both of them agreed that they'd go after Ruth first. Whatever was happening at the coven would have to wait a little longer. Nate's parents and the coven board had kept their location hidden for years. Surely with more than four hundred active witches in residence, they could hold their ground for a little longer.

They would need to.

Rashnu, who had been drinking throughout their conversation, lost his balance and slapped his palms on the bar for support. His face twisted into a grimace of pain and his eyes squeezed shut as he began to chant. Nate stroked Maeve's hair for comfort. His as much as hers.

His nerves, raw and sensitive, snapped at every stroke through her hair, his palm tingling with the exchange of energy between them, crackling like static.

Rashnu fell into a fit of coughing, which drew him back to attention. "I can't find her."

"Is she...dead?" Deacon asked, his voice barely a whisper.

"I don't know. I've never searched for a nephilim before. We have people who do that."

"You mean bounty hunters."

"Yes. And they are much more adept at such things."

"Then find us a bounty hunter, angel, before I come unhinged," Deacon said.

"You had one, but she was sent away."

"What are you talking about now? For the love of…" Nate said.

"Did we not have this talk already? Watch your words, reaper. Temperance is more than a guardian angel. She's also one of our best hunters. Unfortunately, we've never had to track an angel/reaper offspring before."

"Why was Temperance sent to guard my child in the first place? To kill it when it was born?" Deacon asked, his eyes blazing with rage.

"Hardly. The goal was to keep it alive. That child is the one being that can undo us all."

"How?"

"The child is the sacrifice Camael needs to hold open the portal to Hell."

Nate rose to his feet. "It's about damned time you started talking some sense. Where would he open this portal?"

"He could open it anywhere. Meridian is the center of a great flow of energy, but he can't open the main portal there without taking a chance of shorting it out completely. Lucifer will want to control that flow of energy, not destroy it. The permanent portal will be opened nearby, but not inside the city. Somewhere close that he would still consider holy in his irrational way."

Maeve's clutched at Nate's sleeve. "Bolton Cemetery."

***

Ruth was freezing. She was so cold she was beyond shivering, which she was pretty sure was what happened right before folks who were freezing to death started shedding their clothing and bathing in non-existent sunlight. Her body was so weak that her window of opportunity for flashing had passed even if she were willing to try. She'd never survive the trip.

She knew it.

If she spent much longer in this crypt, she wouldn't have to beat herself up over her indecision any more. She listened hard for any movement in the graveyard outside, wondering if Camael had perhaps left a human or demon guard.

After being locked inside, she'd sat quietly, waiting and listening for the others to leave, then she'd called out for a good half hour, begging, bargaining and threatening just in case anyone was out there to hear her.

She'd gotten no answer and was now convinced she was well and truly alone. Deacon would never find her here. And even if he did, she feared it would be too late. Whatever Camael had in mind for her would most certainly be fatal. As in permanently fatal. He hadn't put her here just to keep her out of the way or as bait. He'd put her into cold storage.

Ruth lost track of the time after a while, since the crypt was pitch black inside, another aspect of this situation that was steadily picking away at her good reason and sanity. Her only consolation was that if she'd been merely human, she'd most likely be dead already.

Lucky her.

Over the past several months, she'd gained a wonderful man, a future child and, only hours ago, a brother and a mother. Now she was on the verge of losing them all. Not to mention the end of humanity.

There was that.

She'd spent her time in captivity trying to piece together all the little bits of evidence they'd gathered regarding her mother. Their mother. The revelation that Nate was her brother explained so many of the feelings she'd formed for him.

Their relationship had always been special, with both of them sharing more with the other than with friends of longer standing. And then there was the time when Nate had sickened because of the complications with her pregnancy.

Now she understood why the bond between them was so strong. They were twins. Ruth had read stories of people experiencing sympathetic responses to their twin during times of stress or even happiness. Strong emotions often conjured strong responses.

That was exactly what had happened with Nate.

And now? Would he feel her stress? Her fear? Her discomfort? Even if he did, could he find her here, hidden inside a crypt miles away from home?

She wouldn't hold her breath.

She worried about Deacon the most. He'd transformed since they first met. Physically and emotionally. With so much on his plate, he'd already managed to give her more life in a few months than she'd experienced in the twenty-seven years before she met him. He was a gift.

Seeing how devastated Kylen had been to lose Kara made her fearful for how Deacon would react to losing her. And their child. In her heart, she prayed his friends and the Authority could hold him together when she and the baby were gone. She prayed he didn't do anything drastic. She loved him. If Kylen could find love again after his terrible ordeal, then Deacon could, too.

He'd just have to open his heart to the possibilities.

Ruth closed her eyes and leaned back against the cold concrete blocks, trying to imagine the crypt as an igloo instead of the tomb it was. She clicked through her mental sticky notes, rearranging all of the leads and facts she'd collected on her mother, and the horrific possibility that Camael might be her father. She could feel her synapses slowing down, and she was desperate to keep awake and alert.

Ironic that she might be dead before Camael even returned to exact his revenge.

And what exactly was the purpose of his madness? It was bad enough fighting against him when she'd thought he was just evil incarnate, but now…Well, it would be nice to know his motive. He had to have one, after all. Was any creature born purely evil? Okay, maybe demons. And imps.

Definitely them.

Slimy bastards.

But Camael had been an angel once. She tried to imagine the circumstances that could have led him to her mother in the first place. And why had he abandoned his family? Or perhaps Elaina had kept the information about the twins from him. If so, why? To protect herself? Only one thing was clear to her: it was unthinkable for an angel to have chosen Hell over Heaven unless something drastic had happened.

Only two emotions could drive a creature of the light to such an extreme: love or hate.

What on Earth could have made him want to fall?

She wondered if he'd lost his soul when he joined ranks with Lucifer. What other explanation could he have for his behavior?

Would it make any difference to him if he knew she and Nate were his children?

Ruth lost consciousness while praying for Temperance to return to protect her. She wasn't even ashamed when the praying turned to begging.

Chapter Thirty-Seven

"What about Bolton Cemetery?" Nate helped Maeve sit upright on the couch, her weakness apparent.

"I think it's where Ruth might be." Maeve wiped her palm across her eye and face, and then looked around the room. "Where are we now?"

"Reaper lounge. Purgatory. Welcome." Rashnu offered from behind the bar.

"Why do you think Ruth is at Bolton Cemetery?" Deacon asked.

"Rashnu said it would have to be somewhere Camael considered holy. He held that cemetery in reverence. I don't know why."

"Ah, yes," Rashnu said. "Well, that could be because someone he once cared about is buried there. Or at least her marker."

The one common link for them all—Ruth, Camael, Nate and the Coven—was the cemetery where Elaina Carter's headstone stood. And as he allowed his memory to replay through his mind, he finally allowed all the details he'd repressed in the past to click into place.

The first place he'd flashed to as a child.

His reaper mother's fake burial place.

The cemetery where Rosemary had discovered them.

Where Ruth might be held captive.

Where Camael could open a permanent Hell portal.

"Say what you mean, Rashnu." Nate's mustard aura boiled forth in anticipation of the answer he already knew.

"Camael is your father."

All of the air exited Nate's body and the room began to swim in waves before him. The angel's confirmation was too much to bear.

"How could it be true?" Nate whispered, his last defense against the truth. Deacon grabbed both of Nate's arms, restraining him before he could act on the rage and disappointment boiling up inside of him. Rashnu got his glow on and stretched his wings out behind him across the back wall, at the ready in case Nate chose to act upon the violent emotions swirling within him.

"Just because you do not want to hear a thing, does not make it untrue. I warned you that you might regret knowing some of the answers you sought. As to the how? You'll have to get those answers from Camael himself."

Maeve's hand on the side of his face brought his attention back to her. "It's true, Nate. Camael's memories make sense to me now. Your drawings? What you told me of Rashnu's two paths? Everything points to the truth that you know here...." Maeve stepped in front of him and pressed her hand flat over his heart chakra, pushing her turquoise light into him.

The warmth of Maeve's energy spread across his chest and along his meridian, filling each chakra before returning to her to complete the circle. Images flashed through his mind—Maeve's memories from her time with Camael and his own recollections, rearranging the pieces until the picture that fell into place was irrefutable.

After all these long years, he'd found his biological father.

And now he had to kill him.

***

Camael gathered Elaina into his arms and carried her from the bed, dragging the quilt as he crossed the room to the bank of windows. Even with the heavy quilt still wrapped around her, pulling her down, she weighed next to nothing. He could feel every bone as he cradled her and stared out into the growing light of dawn.

What he held was her husk.

Even if she could open her eyes and see him, would she know him in his borrowed shell? Without his angel form, would she—could she—recognize his ruined soul? The pain burning through his chest said otherwise. His soul was damaged beyond redemption, beyond recognition.

He hoped she would never find out what he had done.

His mind raced through all the possible options. His plan, so imperative an hour ago, was now diminished and irrelevant. The discovery of Elaina changed everything.

There would be hell to pay for any delay. Everything was set.

All he had to do was open the damned portal, make the sacrifice and watch hell break loose from his front row seat. But what would he do with Elaina if he continued with his course of action?

He couldn't leave her here, at the mercy of the monstrosities he had already unleashed. He wouldn't.

Obviously this was—had been—a safe place for her for all these years. She still lived. Or at least her body did. And if there was any way to reinsoul her, to bring her back to him, he would move Heaven and Hell to do it.

He longed for his wings. What would he give for the chance to wrap his healing light around her?

Everything.

But after she died—or so he'd thought—Camael sacrificed all the good he'd ever had to offer. How was it that her body continued to live even now? What if he'd found her sooner? So many questions ran through his brain. None of which mattered now. He had no hope of a Heavenly intervention on his behalf. He'd burned that bridge long ago.

Without her, he had wanted no part of Heaven's pitiful hope and lavish promises. Heaven was dead to him. He'd begged at the gates once before. Never. Again.

Inside this house, everything fell away. He watched out the window as snow began to fall through the slight moonlight, curling in the wind in hypnotic swirls so surreal his eyes began to burn with the beauty of it. The pendulum wall clock to his right swung back and forth, registering the slightest click with each swipe. The *tick* then *tock* was a physical reminder that his time was running out.

That time was running out for all of them.

Could he put a stop to what had been set into motion? What difference would it make for his Elaina now? And his children? Surely Rashnu was wrong; surely they'd been taken by the bounty hunter. Destroyed.

The slightest flicker began to grow inside him like a cancer. Because that's all hope was—a cancer—a caustic weakness that would eventually kill you regardless of the pretty package in which it arrived. He snuffed it out, refusing to allow it to grow.

He couldn't take her to his quarters in Hell. Not like this. Her soul was still untarnished inside the beautiful prison which held it. He'd used the last of his angel magic to forge the impenetrable hourglass from meteoric diamonds, but her husk would never survive the trip through the portal.

Realizing he had no allies left, no safe place, not even in his own heart, he carried her back to the bed and laid her down on it, arranging her with gentle care into what he hoped was a comfortable position before smoothing the quilt over her. Picking up the brush from the nightstand beside her bed, he sat on the edge of the mattress beside her, then slid his arm beneath her shoulders to bring her into a sitting position so he could brush out her hair.

Careful not to pull at the slight tangles he'd created by moving her, he drew the brush down her raven locks, over and over until it was smooth and silky. He eased her back down, fanning her hair out beside her head with his fingers.

Despite everything, she was still beautiful. His beautiful Elaina.

The sound of breaking glass snapped him from his spell, reminding him of what he had wrought upon this place. Leaning down, Camael pressed his lips against his love's cold forehead, breathing in her scent, recommitting to memory the feel of her flesh.

He rose and made his way back through the hallway to the formal living area to find the old woman waiting for him.

"Did you find what you were looking for?" she asked, maintaining a steady rocking rhythm in the antique chair.

"More than I'd expected."

"And what now? Will you kill me? Kill us all?"

"Have you cared for her this whole time?"

"Yes. Since the day she arrived."

His reply stuck in his throat. "Thank you."

"Action is worth much more than words, don't you agree?"

He walked to the door and pulled it open. Stepping out onto the porch, he surveyed the carnage he'd unleashed. A home down the street went up in flames as its residents fled. A man and a woman with children in their arms ran toward the woods pursued by two imps, who spurred their pray onward by snapping razor teeth at their heels.

Camael had a good idea what awaited them there.

"I would suggest you replace your circle of protection after we leave. You're going to need it."

He walked with purpose down the street he now noticed was named Samhain.

An entire town of witches. Hidden in this forest all along.

Hundreds of them had protected his Elaina all this time. Even now, seeing it with his own eyes, he could barely comprehend it.

Camael spread his arms wide as he continued toward the bus and summoned his minions back to him: demons, imps, men. Plenty of damage had already been done to the town. Well, he couldn't turn back time, but he could cauterize the wound he'd inflicted and stop the hemorrhaging while he decided what he wanted to do.

He still had time. A few hours if he was to open the portal on Christmas as Lucifer had requested—demanded.

Splitting the earth in front of him, he opened a crack through the bedrock, penetrating to the core of Hell. "Demons and imps all, return to Hell and await my call."

Without hesitation, they stepped off into the abyss and vanished.

The remaining humans stood by silent and afraid.

Camael closed the chasm. "You'll return to Bolton Cemetery and await further instructions. Do you understand?"

Several of them nodded, but he could sense their feelings of betrayal. After all, he inhabited Little Stevie's body now. None of them would be at Bolton when he arrived because none would want to be next. As it turned out, he didn't even care. They'd exceeded their usefulness. An hour ago he would have shoved them down the chasm himself, but his heart just wasn't in it anymore.

He needed to think.

And the only place he could do that was in Hell.

Clearly his judgment was clouded here.

He waited until the bus disappeared into the sunrise. The horizon was filled with streaks of pink as the snow continued to drift over him, beginning to accumulate.

Perhaps there would be a white Christmas after all.

Such a human thing to wish for.

Chapter Thirty-Eight

Ruth heard footsteps outside the crypt. She tried to scoot herself up into a sitting position, but her limbs were too cold to cooperate anymore. Instead, she huddled into the sweatshirt, locked in a fetal position around her own fetus.

The sound of rattling at the door snapped her eyes open. Was this it? Was Camael coming for her?

"Hey, you in there?" a man's voice asked.

"Who's there? Help me! Can you get me out of here?"

"I dunno. There's a palawk on it."

Ruth tried to translate in her head. "A padlock?"

"Yeah."

She scrambled. If she had a willing rescuer, surely he could come up with some way to help her to escape. "Can you find a big rock or...a headstone to break the lock?"

"I kin try."

"Please! Hurry!"

Silence filled the crypt again and several long minutes passed. The wait was so long that she was sure he'd lost his nerve and left. A crack echoed through the concrete tomb and she nearly jumped out of her frozen skin. She was surprised she didn't crack into two herself with the unexpected jolt.

After several more strikes, he seemed to find a rhythm. How long would it take? They were so far away from anywhere. No one would hear the noise he was making unless Camael came back before he accomplished his task. Helpless to do anything to advance her own rescue, she offered words of encouragement to her unseen rescuer.

"I know you're close! Keep trying! You can do it!"

"I shoulda come sooner."

"No, no, it's okay. Were you on the bus?"

The pounding stopped.

"Don't stop! It's okay. Just keep going. We can talk when you get me out!"

"I was scared."

"I know. I am, too, but we have to get out of here. What's your name?"

"Carl."

"Carl, I'm Ruth. Please don't stop!"

Rather than answering, Carl continued to pound against the padlock on the door of the crypt. It never took this long in the movies. Just when she was sure it was never going to happen, she heard the steel hit the concrete ledge outside the door. The door pushed open and the first rays of the sunrise blinded her as Carl stood in silhouette, filling the doorway. He was one big man. And she'd never been so happy to see someone in her life.

"You okay?" he asked, folding himself in half to inspect her.

"You gave me your sweatshirt on the bus. I would have never made it this long without it, Carl."

"Weren't nothing. Shoulda come sooner. Kept thinkin' that bad man was comin' back anytime. I slipped away, hid in the woods after we got here. Finally gave up and did the right thing."

He slid an arm around her shoulders and another under her knees, and scooped her up like she was nothing. Ruth pulled his bald head down to her face and kissed the top of it.

"Thank you, Carl."

"Don't thank me yet. Let's get somewhere safe first."

As Carl started walking across the valley, toward the highway, Ruth caught a glimpse of the impossible. Just above the tree line on the mountainside opposite them, hidden in the still dark forest was a glowing dome, like half a snow globe.

It was a circle of protection. And to project an aura like that, it had to be a powerful one. It was not the sort of magic one or even a handful of witches was capable of producing. This sort of magic took a village.

It had to be Nate's coven.

Carl carried her under the Bolton Cemetery sign and out of the cemetery. He stopped at the gravel road and turned right, back the way they'd driven in earlier.

"No, Carl. We have to go straight ahead, then across the highway and through the forest on the other side. We can't take the roads this time. He'll find us."

Carl looked out across to the other mountain. "That a long way, Ruth. I can carry ya, but you're cold. This way they's a town at least."

"No, Carl. Please. I think my people are over there."

"And by you people, you don't mean more of that bad man, right?"

"No. I mean the good guys."

Chapter Thirty-Nine

Camael sat on the end of his bed in his lush suite in Hell with his forehead pressed against the cool surface of the hourglass. Elaina's soul pulsed with gray-blue energy inside. His host body was deteriorating quickly despite having travelled through his personal portal. Bits of flesh were already peeling and falling to the floor from the slightest agitations, which was indicative of his internal frame of mind, as well. His resolve was crumbling along with his body.

He was sick of it. All of it.

Sick of changing forms. Sick of the constant battle. Sick of his pain, both physical and emotional. This urn at once held the key to his freedom and his imprisonment.

Now that he knew Elaina was alive, he also knew why he'd kept her soul hidden for all of these years. Why he'd kept her.

Hope. It had been with him the whole time after all.

Maeve's reappearance plagued him with questions. He'd witnessed her soul detach itself from her body.

There was no return from that. Yet she *lived* and, from all appearances, was back in the battle.

How was it possible?

Reapers had been known to persist indefinitely, some even after being buried alive for years and depleted to the point of a reaper coma, but without a soul? No. If he hadn't seen it with his own eyes, he never would have believed it possible.

Elaina's body had persisted, and her soul remained firmly within his grasp. Was it possible to reanimate her as Maeve had been reanimated? Could she be reinsouled? Even in his misery, Camael knew the chance was miniscule. It was foolish to even entertain the thought.

He'd held Elaina's famished and ruined shell in his very arms. She was too far gone. Not only that, but it was much too late for him to try. Lucifer wouldn't tolerate any delays or setbacks. Not when they were this close.

Camael opened the padded case next to him, seated the urn back into the indentations and sealed the latches. Conflict still warred inside him.

He rose and paced to the full mirror hanging on the wall beside his bed, examining his reflection. How he longed to take his own form and be rid of this ridiculous shell. To be whole again, if only for a moment.

Sensing his master's presence before he even fully manifested, Camael turned to find Lucifer on his balcony, wearing soft denim jeans and a long-sleeved, black dress shirt, starched to perfection. His long, blond hair flowed past his shoulders and the glow from the Sea of the Dead back lit his head, forming a red halo around him. Camael suppressed a sarcastic chuckle. It wouldn't pay to laugh in the Devil's face.

"Tidying up?" Lucifer cast a judicious look around Camael's suite.

"Tying up some loose ends is all." Camael's heart pounded in his chest as he silently willed the fallen angel to leave.

"A few more hours and all our hard work will come to fruition. You've been with me for how long now, Camael? Twenty years?"

"Twenty-seven," Camael corrected, cringing inwardly.

"Time does fly. It seems like only yesterday when you were broken and worthless, flailing about and blind for vengeance. I took you in. Offered you not only a place, but a position of worth. Here you have had the opportunity to achieve everything you wanted as well as the means to do it. You must be just as excited as I am to finally see our project nearing completion." Lucifer made his way around the room, picking up accoutrements and studying them.

"Yes. Thank you."

"Yet..." Lucifer settled onto the end of Camael's bed beside the case and rested his hand upon it, drumming his fingers on the wood as he shook his head from side to side. "And yet, I feel a change in you, Camael. A hesitancy perhaps? I can't quite put my finger on it." Lucifer tapped the case for emphasis. "Where is the fire inside you that burned so brightly just hours ago? What has happened...now, so close to the end of our mission, that has you sulking in Hell instead of shredding open the portal you have prepared for me? *Promised* me?"

Camael felt sweat break out along his host's back and trickle down his spine. "Nothing, my lord. It isn't hesitancy you sense. It's anticipation. I'm only making sure there are no loose ends to trip us up in this final hour."

"You have chosen a location for the portal?"

"I have."

"I can expect it to be opened within the hour then?" Lucifer studied Camael with a scrutiny that burned through him, trying to ferret out his lies.

"Soon."

Lucifer's eyes wrinkled at the corners. "When you were broken, I offered you respite. When you despaired, I offered you retribution. Have I not given you everything that was within my power to offer you?"

"Yes, my lord."

Lucifer jumped up abruptly and clapped his hands together. "I know you will not fail me, Camael. Soon we will both have everything we have ever wanted."

"Yes, my lord."

"I look forward to seeing you topside, very, very *soon*."

"Yes, my lord."

As quickly as he'd appeared, Lucifer vanished. Camael sucked in a long breath and then let it out slowly. He knew what needed to be done.

He took one last look around his suite and added a long fur coat to his refreshed wardrobe. It didn't help the appearance of his host body any, but it helped against the chill that had penetrated his body. If he failed, he wouldn't be returning to this room...at least not in any recognizable or usable form. If he failed, he'd become oil for the machine he'd help build. If he failed...

He wouldn't fail. Couldn't.

Camael picked up the case and tucked it inside the coat.

The case was the one remaining possession in his long and miserable existence that had any meaning to him at all. He flashed out of Hell. There was one stop he needed to make before returning to the coven. He couldn't get through the circle of protection alone, but he had another idea.

There was still time.

He'd make it.

***

"Stop here, Carl."

Ruth studied the circle of protection. It was much brighter up close, a physical shield that pulsed with power far above their heads like an aurora borealis. The shield emitted more power than she'd ever witnessed.

She knew she couldn't cross it without being invited inside. Carl, however, could walk right on in. Sure, there was probably a repelling spell attached to the circle, but if he made it through the worst of it, he'd be perfectly fine. She would have to wait outside the boundary until he brought back someone to let her in.

Assuming they *would* let her in.

Her child's survival depended wholly on the kindness of strangers now. The thought of hanging out here alone in the snow seemed a little worse after being trapped in the crypt for several hours. It had taken much longer than she'd expected for Carl to carry her through the blowing cold to reach the coven. The stormy skies dampened the brightness of the earlier sunrise, and they came to a rest at the metaphysical coven gates under the gloomy grayness that had developed. Carl was exhausted, but so was she. And bone cold. She was a reaper for crying out loud.

Suck it up, buttercup.

Sometimes being supernatural sucked.

She had drained much of her Reiki light in her efforts to keep herself warm, and she needed a boost.

"Put me down, please." Carl lowered her feet to the ground. "Thank you. Carl, you're going to have to follow the road into the town and find someone to come out and get me. I can't go inside by myself."

"Why not? You don't need to be staying out here. You don't even got shoes on."

"I know. You won't be gone long. It may take some convincing for them to lower the barrier so I can come inside, but you have to try. We'll be safe inside. When you get inside, ask for the Blackburns. Tell them…tell them Nate's sister is outside."

"I don't like it. It feels evil out here." Carl cast an anxious look toward the woods on either side of the gravel road leading into the coven.

"It's not evil. It's magic. It's a spell to make you turn away, to try to keep you out, but it won't hurt you. I promise."

"I'm scared."

Ruth took hold of his pylon-sized bicep. "You're brave. And strong. Look how far you carried me. Look how you saved me. Please, Carl. You need to hurry."

"Okay. What's the name again?"

"Blackburn. Nate Blackburn. I'm his sister."

***

Ruth held her breath as Carl gathered his courage and turned toward the town. Taking one hesitant step after another, he disappeared out of sight, leaving her alone with the wind and quickly accumulating snow. She shivered and prayed he would indeed hurry. She'd stripped the shirt Camael's lackey had given in half while in the crypt, wrapping her feet as best she could, but her feet were soaked through all the same and beginning to freeze.

Her best hope was that the coven would stir into action on her behalf when they heard that she was Nate's sister. It was the only card she had to play. If not for Carl, she would have perished out here already. He was a blessing.

Ruth blew lukewarm air into her cupped hands and tried to keep her toes and feet moving to circulate her cooling blood. She was cold to the core and feeling lightheaded. The last thing she wanted to do was sit on the even colder ground. If the rest of her clothes got wet, she was a goner. The snow, which was coming down so thick and fast she couldn't even see the road, had soaked her hair. The wind picked up and howled through the trees, bursting straight through her thin clothes. A chill ran down her spine, but she realized she'd stopped shivering again.

Hurry, Carl!

Hunkering down, she tried to balance on the balls of her feet, but her dizzy head and the driving wind were having none of it. She tumbled onto her side, but when she struggled to right herself, her eyes lost focus and her eyelids slammed shut. No amount of fear or self-preservation could hold them open any longer. She couldn't help but succumb. She'd lost too much energy trying to keep warm.

Camael was the least of her worries as she slid into darkness.

***

Camael flashed into Bolton Cemetery. First he'd gather the sacrifice, and then he'd head to the coven. With Ruth in hand, he could kill two birds with one stone. Not only would he be able to use her to hold the portal open, but she would be the bait that would lure the reaper/witch and Maeve to the coven.

He didn't know how or why Maeve had been successfully reinsouled, but he was confident he could force them to do the same for Elaina so long as he had the right leverage.

But when he reached the crypt, the lock was broken. Ruth was gone.

Well, of course she was.

Only the human minions had known where she was. One of them must have doubled back for her and set his sacrificial lamb free. Without her, not only would he fail to keep the portal open, but he had no leverage with the reaper/witch.

Filled with righteous rage, he flashed to the coven.

Taking care not to be spotted, he stayed just inside the wooded edge. No need to play his hand until he had to. After his last visit, he doubted the witches would send a welcoming committee to greet him if he walked up to knock on the metaphysical door. A lynch mob was more likely. He needed to be subtle. A near impossibility considering his history and current frame of mind, but he couldn't take a chance of losing Elaina's soul in any kind of struggle.

The package under his arm gave him some comfort. He liked having her near, but the thought that she could be easily compromised filled him with dread. He couldn't stand to lose her all over again.

Before he opened the portal, unleashing Hell on Earth, he would make one last attempt to save her. If it worked…well, then he could decide what to do next.

He wove his way toward the witch compound through the driving wind, and just before he reached the edge of the circle of protection, his foot kicked into a brushy stump in the snow. Raising his foot to climb over it, he heard a soft moan beneath him. When the pile shifted ever so slightly, he lasered his attention in on the quickly developing shape beneath the dusting of snow.

Camael squatted beside the pile and brushed away the snow.

He was unable to believe his great luck.

Ruth.

He looked around the clearing, but couldn't see more than a few feet ahead of him in the blowing storm. What were the chances? Briefly he worried it might be a trap of some sort, but when she didn't respond to his prodding, he knew she was alone. Someone had released her from the crypt. She hadn't escaped alone. So where was her rescuer now?

Refusing to examine his good fortune any further, he knelt beside her and brushed the remaining snow from her body. Placing his case over her stomach, he scooped them both up into his arms and carried her right up to the front gate.

Screw subtlety. He had collateral.

Chapter Forty

"The coven's in trouble, Deacon. I need your help." Nate reached out his hand and helped Maeve to her feet as Deacon and Samkiel paced the room.

Come to think of it, if not for the ball of dread eating its way through his own stomach, he had to admit he felt pretty good. Rashnu's shot of angel mojo was a supersized dose of Reiki light, and while he was mostly the conduit for Maeve, its effects on him were lasting. Physically, Maeve didn't look any different, but Rashnu was certain her transformation to valkyrie had been a success. Nate was just happy that she was alive and awake.

The home sigil across his shoulder blade blazed along his skin. The coven was still in serious trouble. And Ruth? At this point there were so many fires to put out he didn't know which one to aim at first. The remaining members of the Authority were shoulder-deep in the chaos that was downtown. The daylight had not deterred the demons from their mission. If anything, they seemed emboldened.

It was Christmas Eve and Nate had no doubt that Camael intended to open the portal before midnight. He didn't know how Ruth played into his plan, but he was certain it wouldn't end well. Camael would likely have put their family history together by now, as well. What that meant for him and Ruth, he wasn't sure. He just knew that he wasn't looking forward to the family reunion.

"Before you go, Nate, we have another piece of business to address. Maeve isn't the only one who has experienced a transformation," Rashnu said, reaching behind the bar.

Nate gave Deacon a questioning look, not sure what was coming next. "What now?"

Rashnu brought forth a soft leather scabbard in his hands and presented it to Nate. "You have proven yourself a reaper, Nate. While you are indeed nephilim, your heritage has allowed you to evolve into a reaper capable of very special talents. Beyond nature, yes, but you are still a child of God. The power of reinsoulment is a near God-like ability and one you must guard judiciously. With the acceptance of this scythe, you officially join the Authority as a reaper with full recognition and benefits. You've already proven your allegiance to protecting the ones you love. Now, go forth and protect the realms, as well."

Nate reached forward for the weapon and took it from Rashnu's hands. He pulled the blade from the sheath and turned it in the light, examining its sleek design, the handle beginning to glow under his touch. Nate looked on in awe as the steel became imbued with the same sigils that marked his own body.

"It is your weapon alone, Nate. No other can empower its magic. You are a breed apart. Use your power wisely," Rashnu said.

Samkiel stepped up beside him to examine the weapon and clapped a hand on his shoulder. "Nice blade."

Nate removed his short sword and slid the new scabbard into the straps. He pushed his arms through the loops and tightened the weapon across his back. Reaper.

It was a title he'd never expected to own.

"We're going to have to split up. I have to find Ruth and you need to get to your coven. We're running out of time," Deacon said. "Samkiel, go with them. I'll call Kylen once I'm topside and ask him to check our compound. I'll go to the cemetery. If Ruth is there, I'll get her to safety. Nate, keep your phone on. I'll track you to the coven and be there as soon as I can. This ends tonight."

Maeve reached for Nate's hand.

"I think we can do this the easy way." Rashnu spread his wings and the room filled with light until they each began to dissipate through the consecrated subway to their destinations.

***

They landed just outside the perimeter of the coven to the most unlikely welcoming committee Nate could have imagined. On one side of the boundary, Garrett, Rosemary, the coven board and a man Nate didn't recognize stood in a line, on the other stood Camael, who held Ruth clutched in his arms.

Nate blinked hard, trying to make the image register. Maeve was in motion before he could stop her and yelling rose up all around him as the members of the coven crossed out of the circle of protection, magic blazing.

"Do not come any closer. I'll flash her from here, and we all know how much danger your dear Ruth will be in if I do that." Camael turned to face Maeve, whose scythe was drawn.

"Let Ruth go, Camael. She needs our help or she's going to die," Nate said, inching forward.

Samkiel edged to their right, ready to act when needed.

"Not just yet." Camael surveyed Maeve. "You are alive and reinsouled. How is this possible?"

"Ruth needs help now. We don't have time for this nonsense," Nate insisted. "Rashnu, do something."

Rashnu walked around Nate and came into the full view of Camael. "Tell him what he wants to know, Nate."

"You call that help?" Maeve growled.

"What's in the case, Camael?" Rashnu asked.

"Nothing of your concern," Camael snarled.

"I think it concerns all of us. Is it Ruth you want most…or is it whatever is in that case? Tell Nate what you hold and then let him decide if he will help you."

Camael's expression faltered and Nate suddenly knew what was in the case.

"Nate, tell him how you reinsouled Maeve," Rashnu pushed.

"I don't know how I reinsouled her. I just did it."

"And she has not been impaired by the experience?" Camael shifted Ruth in his arms and she moaned softly. "Could you do it again?"

"I don't know."

"Would you…try?" Camael locked eyes with Nate and dared him to answer.

"What are you asking? Why the hell would I do anything at your request? Ever? You are insane beyond comprehension."

"Tell him what's in the case, Camael. I can feel it from here," Rashnu said.

"A soul," Camael offered softly.

"Whose?" Nate asked, pressure building inside his head as his heart pounded in his ears.

"Elaina's."

In the ensuing silence, Deacon and Kylen suddenly appeared in the clearing behind the group. Deacon froze, his eyes glued on Ruth. "Holy hell," he said, shifting his gaze to Rashnu. "What the fuck is going on here?"

Nate looked at Rosemary, who began to cry gently, all of the fight drained out of her. He was standing in the middle of a meadow, surrounded by witches, angels and reapers, and his mortal enemy wanted his help. The only thing that could make this all any weirder was...yeah, nothing. He couldn't even make this shit up.

"Camael has our mother's soul," Nate said.

Silence filled the meadow and the world stood still for a few long moments as Nate decided how to proceed. They couldn't trust Camael, but right now they wanted the same thing—to save Elaina or set her free. At this point, the latter seemed more probable. And Ruth? God only knew what Camael had planned for Ruth. The only way to help ensure her safety was to cooperate.

"I'll do it."

"Very well," Camael said.

"I have conditions," Nate said.

"Of course."

Chapter Forty-One

It was nearly dusk when the unlikely alliance filed into the coven librarian's house. Deacon and Samkiel tended to Ruth in the living room, giving her light doses of Reiki and slowly warming her by the fire. The stranger, who had introduced himself as Carl, waited with them like a loyal watchdog. Meanwhile Rosemary and Garrett were huddled with the coven board around the kitchen table, holding hands and uttering protection incantations to bind Camael to the house. They weren't taking any chances that he would escape and proceed with his plan of disaster.

Nate, Maeve, Rashnu and Camael filed into the sunroom where Elaina lay.

"You can't leave this house, Camael. The coven has bound you," Nate said, setting his shiny new scythe on the dresser within arm's reach of the bed. "And if a portal so much as pops a nail in this floor, Deacon and Rashnu will smite you. No jury. No trial. Do you understand?"

"Yes."

"And when this fails, and it will, you will go with Rashnu to face the judgment you deserve. Do you understand?"

"Yes."

"Why don't I believe it's going to be that easy?" Nate asked.

"Open the case, Camael," Rashnu commanded.

Camael hesitated, taking a moment to search Elaina's face, then set the case down on the edge of the bed and unclasped the latches. His host was even more grotesque here in the bright light of the sunroom. Open sores laced across the backs of his hands and disappeared down the neck of his shirt and beneath the long fur coat he wore. He laid open the two sides of the case to reveal an hourglass urn, illuminated from inside with a soft blue-gray glow. As he laid hands on the glass, the stream inside came alive, moving frantically within its glass cage.

"How do you release it?" Nate asked, his hands opening and closing with nervous energy by his sides.

"It must be shattered. I sealed it with my last remaining angel light, so Rashnu will have to break it open." He cradled the urn between his palms and held it up to the angel, who placed his own hand across the glassy curve. He pushed a bolt of light energy across the glass and the urn shattered to dust across Camael's boots. The soul burst into the room and scattered into a thin veil, stretching against its new boundaries before reassembling into a ghost form above Elaina's body and hovering there.

"Now, Nate. Do it now," Rashnu commanded.

Nate drew in a deep breath and reached forward, pushing his hands through the soul, making contact. His aura built and a bright orange glow encompassed him as he willed the soul toward him just as he'd seen Deacon do hundreds of times. Collecting Maeve's soul had taken no effort compared to the intense struggle that raged within him now. His insides seared as the soul slowly slid down his throat and settled inside him.

His mother's soul.

"Don't let any part of it attach to you, Nate. She'll need her soul complete if this is to work." Rashnu summoned Deacon and Samkiel. "Reapers, her body is frail and most likely beyond resurrection, but you should try to fill her with your light as Nate pushes her soul into her—otherwise I fear it will leak right back out. You need to force it to take hold. Then it's up to Elaina."

Camael stood by in silent anticipation, his hands trembling at his sides.

Maeve and the other reapers circled the bed, pushing Camael back and against the wall so that they could lay hands upon Elaina's ruined body. Nate bent to her face, tilted her head back and pressed his mouth to hers. The room exploded in a kaleidoscope of colored light as he pushed her soul into her. Reaper light leaked from her, just as Rashnu had feared, but they continued to fill her with their glow until her body began to absorb it.

He withdrew from her and the reapers did the same. Elaina's body convulsed on the bed, her back arching upward, and then she stilled. No other visible signs of change could be detected. For all intents and purposes, nothing had changed, but the soul remained inside her. One small blessing.

"It's done," Nate said, dropping to his knees beside the bed.

Deacon and Samkiel moved to the doorway.

"Did it work?" Camael asked, taking a step forward before he was stopped by Nate's glare, which pinned him in place.

"Her soul is in there. Unless she wakes, we'll never know," Nate said. "It took Maeve several days."

Maeve stroked Nate's back and Camael turned away, staring out of the wall of windows into the darkness.

"We don't have several days," he said.

"No," Nate agreed.

***

Lucifer paced along the viewing deck in Hell as the sky above him roiled with a tumult of black demons that were waiting for the portal to open. What was taking so long? This was what happened when you were forced to rely upon others. He'd sensed Camael's resolve weakening...but why now? He'd thought about killing him in his chamber, but the small satisfaction that the act would have brought him wasn't worth the chance that he was wrong. He needed a strong representative topside to make his mission a success. He could open portals, but he couldn't *hold* them open. Not without the key. The key Camael possessed.

And without an agent topside to direct the battle, the demons were useless. Their driving motivation was to inhabit hosts and return their bounty to him, which was all well and good, but he had bigger ambitions. Much bigger ambitions. Lucifer wanted to walk in the light again, to be a free angel, and he couldn't do that until the very last soul had been freed from Hell.

As time ticked by, Lucifer became more and more certain that Camael had deceived him.

The demons continued to press against the metaphysical ceiling, straining for freedom. All he needed was a crack and they could push through. The portal wouldn't hold without Camael's assistance, but at least he'd be able to summon Camael to his side. Then he would make his duke wish he hadn't failed. He wanted the demons released tonight. He'd waited long enough. Five millennia. He was done with waiting. It *would* happen tonight or Camael would pay the price.

***

Hours passed and to say the conversation was strained would be an understatement. They had bound Camael, physically and metaphysically, to a chair in the corner of the room. It was satisfying to see him beaten, but Nate was still far from having any closure. He had questions. And so far, the angel hadn't been ponying up any answers.

"Any change?" Ruth asked from the doorway. Deacon stood next to her, a firm, steadying hand on her elbow.

"Not yet." Nate offered a smile he didn't feel.

Ruth cast a weary look at the corner of the room. "And him?"

"Not. Helpful."

Camael raised his eyes to them both. "And what would you have me say?"

"You could start by explaining what you planned to do with Ruth. Your freaking daughter, by the way, who's carrying your grandchild. It's fairly clear you weren't planning on bringing her on a father/daughter date," Nate said.

"I only recently realized you were my…children. That you were alive. That you were *all* alive." Camael looked at Elaina.

"Uh huh, why do I find that difficult to believe?" Nate asked.

"What were you going to do with Ruth, Camael?" Maeve asked.

"The final portal cannot be held open without the sacrifice of a pure soul. I was going to throw her into the portal after I split it open so all of Hell could be released."

"And Lucifer could be unbound," Rashnu added.

"Yes."

"How was Ruth's soul more pure than any other supernaturals'?" Maeve asked. "No offense, Ruth."

"None taken."

"It wasn't Ruth's soul they wanted. It was her child's," Rashnu offered. "That's why we sent Temperance to protect her."

"Temperance. Another Heavenly bounty hunter. Some protection," Camael scoffed.

"Things have changed since your fall, Camael. We don't hunt the nephilim any longer. We seek to protect them," Rashnu said.

"And why now? Why send hunters to exterminate my family but protect others?" Camael spat.

"Your defection and your family's subsequent disappearance caused us to reevaluate our policies. By the time we realized your offspring had not only survived but were...valuable, you were too far off the reservation to be redeemed, Camael. If only you had held on."

"And how—or why—would I do that when all I loved had been taken from me? How could you even expect me to continue to serve the one who had destroyed everything?"

"You're right, redemption is not an option for you any longer. But forgiveness? That could still be yours."

"I doubt that."

"And that is why you fell in the first place. Doubt."

Elaina stirred beneath her coverings and Ruth gasped when her mother's eyes flickered open then shut. Nate and Ruth fell to her side. Camael struggled to rise to his feet for a better look, but was still secured to the chair.

"Mother?" Ruth stroked her hand across Elaina's sunken cheek and light leaked from her palm, drawn in by Elaina's body.

Nate took his mother's skeletal hand into his own and light poured from his body, drawn by the same vacuum. This time, her cheeks pinked with the infusion of their light.

"Nate." Ruth looked up at him.

"I see can it," Nate said.

"What's happening to her?" Camael asked from the corner, straining against his bonds.

Every word spoken to his father was an effort Nate was nearly incapable of making. "Our light is taking root in her now."

Nate's hatred for the fallen angel was only tempered by the fact the asshole had somehow managed to retain Elaina's soul and return it to them. It didn't atone—and never would—for all of the lives he'd taken, the hundreds of souls stolen from Meridian, the wanderers who had been destroyed. Didn't make up for the two dead reapers in Maple Park Cemetery. Didn't make up for his possession of Maeve or his willingness to destroy Ruth and her child.

How could a man's—an angel's—love for another have gone so terribly wrong?

"Please, can I see her?"

The look on Ruth's face broke Nate's heart in two. She had sympathy for the monster. Even after all Camael had done to her—had intended to do to her.

"Bring him, Rashnu," Nate said. "Then take him away."

Rashnu loosened Camael's bindings and led him to Elaina's bedside. Bits of Camael's host stayed behind on the chair and left a trail of putrescence as he crossed to the bed.

"Not like this, Rashnu. Please, let me appear to her for one last time in my angel form before you bring me to meet my doom. She'll never recognize me this way, and in my angel form, I could be of some assistance to her. I do not deserve it, but I beg you all the same." Camael bowed his host's head in deference.

"You have got to be kidding me. Why would we allow you to take your form? Even if it were possible?" Nate asked.

"He's right, Nate. In his angel form, he might be able to help revive her. If there is anything left inside of her to save, her soul might recognize his. But like this?" Rashnu said.

"And you can grant this favor to him?" Ruth asked.

"I can."

Chapter Forty-Two

It was ten minutes to midnight when Rashnu laid his hands upon Camael and restored his angel form to him. The light of his transformation engulfed the room. Fuzzy black spots filled Nate's vision until he blinked them away and stared into the face—the true face—of his father.

The resemblance to Ruth and himself was undeniable. The angel's black hair draped across his shoulders and his green eyes shone bright with renewed energy. His previous clothing stretched even tighter across his new form and began to tear and shred as his true body filled out.

Nate's heart leaped when wings unexpectedly tore through the back of Camael's coat and rose above his shoulder blades. The coat fell to the floor in tatters, while the rest of his attire hung around him in shreds. As much as he hated to admit it, the angel was magnificent, barring the whole nearly naked thing.

Camael stretched his wings, struggling to unfold them in the close confines of the room and tilted his head to the ceiling, eyes closed. "Thank you."

"It's temporary. Don't make me regret it," Rashnu replied.

A rumble shook the ground beneath them. "What are you doing, Camael?"

"It's not me. Lucifer grows impatient."

"Can he open the portal without you?" Deacon asked.

"Yes. But without the sacrifice, it won't hold," Camael said, cutting an apologetic glance toward Ruth.

"Why would he open it here?" Nate asked.

"He's tracked me to this place. I had planned to open it in Bolton Cemetery. I don't think he will wait for that any longer."

"Say your goodbyes, Camael. The sooner you're gone, the better off we'll be," Nate said.

***

Camael nodded and leaned over the bed, nearly overcome by a flood of emotion. It was all too much to believe. His Elaina lay before him. His now grown children stood beside him.

His children.

Those babes he'd held for a few fleeting moments many years ago would now be his final undoing...and perhaps, Elaina's salvation.

Never, in all these long years, had he once believed that his children might have survived. He'd been so confident that the reaper bounty hunter had returned to claim his prize that he had helped launch an apocalypse.

His one consolation was that his children were clearly better than he had ever been. Strong. Powerful. Fiercely loyal. He didn't expect or deserve forgiveness in any form. But now that his angel body had been restored, albeit temporarily, he gloried in these first and last moments with his family, however warped the reunion was.

How different would the past quarter-plus century have been if he'd only known they still lived? How many lives had he taken because he'd let grief twist him into a monster? Regret formed a steady beat inside him. He'd nearly destroyed the only good he'd ever brought to this world.

His children.

He had no illusions about the future that lay before him once he left this realm. There would be no redemption for him. He'd be stripped of his essence, decommissioned and then scattered to the winds in retribution for his many sins. The angel equivalent of death. The Lord would employ his full-scale, old-testament wrath against him.

It was nothing less than what he deserved.

But his brief respite, this last chance to say goodbye, made his impending death worth the price. Nothing Lucifer had offered him could compare.

Camael placed one hand over Elaina's forehead and the other over her heart and closed his eyes. Spreading his wings as best he could, he summoned all his energy and pushed it outward and through his wings. He curled the tips of his wings around her fragile body and engulfed her in his angelic embrace, sending the last of his healing essence into her. If this didn't reignite the spark within her, he feared nothing would.

In his selfish quest for vengeance, he'd forgotten what it meant to love another. His heart had become so twisted with hatred and constant proximity to evil that the emotions he was experiencing now felt foreign and strange.

Her body was still too ruined to produce her own light right now, and the light that animated her came from her children and Camael. The light of loved ones could only maintain her for so long. To live—truly live—she would need to begin generating her own light once again.

Maybe that had been the secret to success for Maeve's reinsoulment. Her own light hadn't yet been extinguished.

The floor below him cracked and a board splintered under his foot as Lucifer pressed from below, goading him to finish his original task.

"Camael," Nate warned.

"It's not me," Camael snarled, not wanting to waste any of his precious energy on anything other than healing Elaina.

As he continued to pour energy into her, her body arched off the bed. She pulled in a gasping breath and her eyes sprang open and locked with his. Recognition filled her face.

"Elaina." Camael covered her completely with his wings and pulled her into an embrace. Protected from the prying eyes of the others in the room, if only for a moment, he kissed her mouth and she sobbed into his kiss.

There was so much to say to her, but their time was up. Boards began to pop beneath the bed. Camael withdrew from Elaina's embrace and looked out the window to see the ground sinking into a depression that was slowly making its way toward the house and the room where he stood. Lucifer would have his way. He would open the portal where Camael stood and demand his sacrifice.

And Camael was more than happy to make it happen.

***

Activity flurried around Camael as he stepped back from the bed and toward the window.

"It's time, Camael," Rashnu said, standing beside him.

"Yes. It is," he confirmed.

Camael spread his wings and the glass windows before him shattered. Ice cold wind raced into the room and the ground split before him, the portal tearing open before him across the frozen ground. As the consecration broke, so did his binding. He leaped through the broken window and stalked into the yard, standing on the edge of the quickly opening portal.

"No!" Nate yelled, as Deacon and the others raced after him. Camael turned to face them and spread his wings to their full expanse, light radiating from them upward as he drew power from down below. He was a creature of both the light and the dark now, and could draw energy from both forces. He allowed the mixed energy to build inside him until it leaked from the tips of his feathered wings, singeing the ends until smoke roiled around him and his wings ignited.

"Rashnu, now would be the time to stop him!" Deacon called through the cacophony as the first demons rose from the depths.

Camael took a step away from the abyss and sent his senses into the night, calling his demons to him. Now that the circle of protection had been so catastrophically breached, they were free to answer his summons. Abandoning their hosts, they streamed in through the forest in what seemed a never-ending wave of darkness stretching across the night sky all the way from Meridian.

The disembodied demons circled over Camael and the expanding portal like a reverse whirlpool of evil.

"Rashnu!" Deacon demanded again.

As Camael turned to nod at Rashnu, Nate raced out of the room and drew his scythe behind his back, swinging the blade through Camael's neck in a great arc. The angel's body tumbled into the abyss, and fire exploded from the fissure like a great molten volcano that had suddenly been awakened. Flames rose hundreds of feet into the night sky from the pit, and sulfurous gas seeped from the crevasse. Camael had summoned the demons to him, commanding them to follow him one last time, so they plunged after him as he fell to his complete and final death in the pit of Hell.

Chapter Forty-Three

Deacon and Rashnu sealed the portal behind Camael after the last of the freed demons followed in his final and complete fall. Camael had managed to prevent any new spawn of Satan from escaping. Days later, Nate was still in shock. Elaina had been moved to the upstairs bedroom in Rosemary's Healing Center, and he stood there beside her bed now. She had not yet offered any real conversation, but she'd uttered Camael's name in her sleep and spoken a few words, which gave them all hope that she was on the road to recovery.

Nate and the other reapers took turns feeding her light infusions, just as they'd done with Maeve, and her physical body was improving rapidly.

Nate was exhausted. Each of the members of the Authority had been working to locate and reap the souls that had been left unattached and scattered when the demons fled to Camael. Reclaiming the lost souls was the priority now.

Many wanderers had remained behind as well as free-floating souls. Nate had reinsouled those he could, but some of the humans' bodies had been destroyed in the assault and other souls had simply been detached too long to survive the process. Human bodies weren't as resilient as reaper ones. Still, he'd had a few successes and that was some small comfort to him. Maeve had collected hundreds of souls and ferried them to Purgatory in her new capacity as valkyrie. He was proud of her, but her new position would demand her services on battlefields and disasters across the globe. She would be drawn to death much more powerfully than when she was only a reaper. Nate hoped he could accompany her on her travels when things settled down at the coven and the reaper compound, but he wasn't going to hold his breath. There was still much to do to atone for the sins of his father.

When Camael broke free of the coven's binding and escaped from Elaina's room, Nate had thought the bastard meant to open the portal and free the waiting demons. Instead, Camael had sacrificed himself so he could drag them all back to Hell. Nate's beheading him had helped to seal the deal.

It was too early to tell, but it seemed as though all of the loose demons had followed him through the portal.

Unfortunately, Raguel was still missing.

The Authority had spent every hour since the portal was sealed cleaning up the carnage of Meridian and searching for their comrade. His soul had not been reaped nor had his body been discovered. Rashnu assured them that his soul still existed on the Earthly plane, but couldn't tell them where. He was out there…somewhere. And they would find him no matter how long it took.

Nate looked out the window and watched as the coven board, along with every living board member past and present, circled the burned ground where the portal had opened, casting one final spell. They had reconsecrated the ground and recast the circle of protection immediately after Deacon and Rashnu closed the portal, but they wanted reassurance that no future portals could be opened on the grounds.

Rashnu assured them that Camael had perished as a result of his last act. His soul dissipated into the ether, never to reinhabit another body. Destroyed in his angel form, he was now well and truly dead. He had expended the last of his angel essence in summoning the demons and pulling them to his death. Not even an angel could survive that. Or beheading. Nate's act had spared his father an eternity of torture in Hell.

Nate's feelings for Camael were mixed at best. He still carried an intense hatred in his heart for the chaos his father had wreaked on Meridian, but without his final sacrifice, today would have been day seven of Hell on Earth.

Ruth sat asleep in a nearby chair with Bo curled around her feet like a living bear rug. Most of the Authority reapers had returned to sleeping, when they could, at the reaper compound, but Deacon had insisted that Ruth stay with the Blackburns after they extended an invitation. Deacon spent every available moment with her, but his free time had been sparse lately as the Authority continued to clean up the mess that was Meridian.

The city remained on lockdown even though the disappearances had stopped. Bodies had littered the streets after the last major attack of the demons. There was no whitewashing a problem so large. Civilians had watched it happen, and while they didn't truly understand what they'd witnessed, the news coverage had incurred rampant speculation, from stories about alien attacks to the onset of the apocalypse. Neither of which were far from the truth.

City officials, state police, FBI—none knew if or when their troubles might resume. The Authority couldn't exactly hold a town hall meeting to proclaim that their enemy had been vanquished. Nate took comfort in the knowledge that was indeed true. For now. Camael wouldn't be back, but Lucifier was not likely to give up so easily. Or at all.

Nothing made Rosemary happier than tending to her family, and she had already adopted Ruth and now Deacon into that category. Temperance, returned and reinstalled with Ruth's blessing as the guardian to her unborn baby, Elaina Grace, stood by the doorway as the clock chimed 12:00 a.m. on New Year's Day.

The coven had constructed an arched altar to Janus above the site of the portal. Janus presided over the beginning and end of conflicts, over war and peace, and was the sentry of doorways, gates and arches. It seemed appropriate.

The demons were gone. Ruth was safe. The baby was safe. And Camael was gone. Forever. The father he'd never really known was possibly the worst creature he'd ever encountered, but at least he'd managed to die in an act of unselfish redemption.

It didn't make things any easier to process. In fact, his mind was a jumble and his heart was brimming with so many confused emotions that he felt at sea. Maeve put a hand on his back and he turned to face her, pulling her in close.

"We almost lost everything." Nate pressed his face into Maeve's hair, breathing her in.

"But we didn't. As awful as Camael was, he did manage to stop Lucifer's plan."

"For now."

"Sometimes the present is all we have, Nate." She cradled his face in her hands and pressed her forehead to his. "Come downstairs. You need rest."

"I'm sorry my family has gotten so out of control."

"You're lucky to have your family, Nate. All of it. The good." Maeve kissed his neck. "The bad." She kissed his ear. "And the ugly." She smiled then kissed his mouth.

"I don't think rest is what I need."

"Then come downstairs and take what you need."

***

Maeve led Nate to his basement bedroom. She didn't understand everything that had happened, but she did understand one thing. Her feelings for Nate had crystalized. She had been transformed over the past few weeks, both physically and emotionally. If the portal had opened, this next hour would have been spent in the fight of their lives. Instead Maeve ran her hands up and under Nate's shirt, across his warm, hard chest.

She had survived not just Camael's possession, but her transformation into a valkyrie. Life was much more precious to her now, and she didn't want to waste a minute of it.

Peeling Nate's shirt up his torso, she kissed the line of invisible energy chakras from his bellybutton to his throat, then pulled the shirt over his head. She unbuckled his scabbard and let his scythe drop to the floor behind him.

"Let's hope you won't be needing this again for a while."

Nate closed his eyes as she unbuttoned his jeans and slid them and his underwear down his thighs. He stepped out of them and she kneeled before him, cupping his balls in one hand and his butt in the other. She urged his erection into her mouth.

His hands threaded through her hair as he pushed into her with a moan. His balls tightened in her hand as she stroked his shaft with her mouth. He needed release and Maeve needed this connection with him. When she sensed that he was close, she slowed her pace and backed away, shimmying out of her own clothes. Groaning, Nate cupped her breasts in his hands and slid his thumbs across her pearled nipples. A shiver of energy skittered down her spine as she drew in his light.

She'd never tire of the freedom of sharing energy with him.

Maeve backed the few steps toward the bed, pulling him to her and down onto the mattress. His chest brushed against her breasts and his knee parted her legs as he eased over her. Hot breath kissed along her neck and she arched up against him, her hungry body eager for his. A crackle of blue light sparked between them along the entire length of their joined bodies, evidence of their perfect connection.

Nate's hand slid beneath the small of her back, bringing their bodies together as closely as possible. She wrapped her arms around him, up his back and over his shoulder blades and gripped him to her as their energy intertwined. When his erection pushed between her legs and against her core, she opened for him. The anticipation of penetration almost undid her.

"Nate," she begged.

"I love you, Maeve." Nate cradled her face in his hands and drew his thumbs across her cheekbones. A tear escaped the outside corner of her eye and rolled down the side of her face. He kissed it away.

"I love you, too, Nate."

Nate pushed into Maeve and bright lights exploded behind her closed eyelids as he filled her. Her body stretched around him and the exquisite tightness brought more tears of joy to her eyes as he rocked in and out of her.

"God, Maeve."

He maintained the agonizingly slow rhythm as their energy built and Maeve cried out as her release came first and she tightened around him. Nate's body tensed as he hovered over her, barely able to hold his weight off her as his entire body constricted with the power of his building release. Maeve clenched around him and he relented, exploding his light and release into her.

Nate collapsed beside her and Maeve pulled the blanket over them both.

For now, they were safe and together.

She couldn't think of anything better than that. Nate's family was upstairs—alive if not yet wholly well—and the worst of the danger had passed.

Maeve didn't believe in happily ever after, but she was beginning to think she could believe in happy for now.

Because she was.

She traced the new tattoo across his chest, directly over his heart. It was her sigil. Nate had created it to bind them together. She now had the same mark tattooed over her own heart, but to represent Nate. She felt its power surge through her fingertips as she mapped its outline.

"What are you, Nate Blackburn?"

"Yours."

THE END

About the Author

Lisa adores beasties of all sorts, fictional as well as real, and has a farm full of them in her Southwest Missouri home, including: one child, one husband, two dogs, two cats, a dozen hens, thousands of Italian bees and a guinea pig.

She may or may not keep a complete zombie apocalypse bug-out bag in her trunk at all times, including a machete. Just. In. Case.

Keep in touch here:

Website: http://lisa-medley.com/books/
Facebook: /lisamedleyauthor
Twitter: @lisamedley
Google+: +lisamedley
Pinterest: medley3
Amazon: http://amzn.to/1axwex7

Don't miss a thing! Sign up for my New Release Newsletter http://eepurl.com/9Zhcz

Other Books by Lisa Medley

Haunt My Heart
A Civil War ghost gets a second chance at love in the 21st century. - Out now!

Reap & Repent
(Book I of The Reaper Series) – Available Now!

Reap & Redeem

(Book II of The Reaper Series) – Available Now!

Reap & Reveal
(Book III of The Reaper Series) – Available Now!

Space Cowboys & Indians
A sci-fi romance Coming in 2015

Reap & Reckon
(Book IV of The Reaper Series) - Coming in 2016

THE REAPER SERIES:

The only thing worse than having nothing to live for…is having everything to live for.

A small group of reapers and supernatural beings in Meridian, Arkansas are all that stands between humanity and the apocalypse when a fallen angel stages a demonic invasion. In their battle to save the world, each will meet his or her match, discovering the power of love…and the importance of risking everything to protect it.

www.ingramcontent.com/pod-product-compliance
Lightning Source LLC
Chambersburg PA
CBHW071249170626
46809CB00001B/145